Soulshadow

CRAIG PHOENIX

First published in 2007

ISBN: 978-0-9557503-0-4

Printed and Bound in Great Britain by Biddles Ltd, King's Lynn
Typeset by Lisa Simmonds

www.craigphoenix.co.uk

Cover artwork by Trudi Couldridge

Acknowledgements

This page is dedicated to all those people who helped me get this book to where it is today enabling me to achieve one of my many dreams.

A special thanks to Leslie who has been my rock through all my writing efforts. He is one of my closest friends and without whom this book would never have been what it is. I owe him more than he can possibly imagine and for that I dedicate this book to him. Thank you.

Tina - her friendship, support, and words of encouragement through this process.

Lynne Simmonds & Lisa Simmonds for their help, advice and expertise in setting this book out and getting it ready for printing.

Trudi Couldridge you have come up trumps and it is really appreciated.

A big thank you to Robertson Family for allowing me to use the New Empire Theatre as a base for my idea. Visit this website for a list of great shows to see *www.newempiretheatre.co.uk*

For all those who read this book before it was published and encouraged me to carry on especially Jean Brown. Thank you.

Finally a special thank you to my mum who has always had faith in me whatever I do, been there when I fell, listened without prejudice to my ideas, was a shoulder to cry on, and a friend. Love you mum XX

1

"Great another bloody rainy, wet, miserable Sunday evening" I said under my breath as I locked the front door to my first and second floor maisonette. The communal lobby shrouded in darkness just emphasized the miserable night outside. Exiting the main front door the bleak cold air hit me, like opening the door to my freezer. I opened an old golfing umbrella I owned in the hope that this would at least protect me from the worst of the rain.

A typical 'English' winter's day for Southend-on-Sea. I was not looking forward to the 20 minute walk to the theatre for rehearsals, pelted by the rain, buffeted by the stiff breeze that usually associated with it. Normally in these conditions I'd take my car but my dad was servicing it for me, he'd hit a few snags so would not be able to return it until the morning. Thankfully I'd wrapped up warm in the leather jacket bought on a trip to Tunisia the previous year, happy memories. I pulled it tight around me, doing the zip up to the very tip of the collar, thrusting my hands deep into the warm pockets, tightly holding the umbrella, letting it rest on my shoulder. I let my mind wander to the sun, sea, and good company of Tunisia.

I've walked this route many times. Through the back streets which lead from my road, William Street.

Typical of many roads in the area, William Street consists of lots of terraced houses, in blocks of about seven or eight, alleyways running in between, weaving intricate paths around the back gardens sometimes allowing access to unwanted guests. People often attempted to fill entrances of these alleyways with debris and rubbish to help keep out these visitors, but there was always one who wanted access and would spend their days clearing the strategically placed obstacles.

Not particularly an affluent part of town, many of the houses had been converted into flats, tiny little pokey places barely room enough to swing a cat. Two front doors now occupy the same space that was originally designed as an ornate entrance hall for one. Refurbishment is what a lot of them need, no one cares though. The gardens give the characters of the residents, rubbish scattered about them, piled high in some cases, smashed TV sets, fridges, cookers, settees – over the course of time all had become part of the ornamentation. Given long enough they eventually fade from view, covered by weeds sprawling their way over the hills like arteries in an arm, and smothered by leaves that have fallen from the few trees that co-exist in this concrete jungle.

Most who live there can barely afford to pay the rents, the owners live nowhere near, choosing to ignore them as long as they still receive their money, they don't care. The few that have mortgages have little or no spare cash for the luxury of 'tarting' up their dwellings and they leave them to decay year in, year out, praying that they won't have to face a heavy repair bill in the future. Knowing full well that that won't be the case but still hoping that life will deal a different deck of cards with a brighter future where they will be able sell up and move to a nicer area.

I'm one of the lucky ones I own my flat, two bedrooms (one on each floor), living room, kitchen diner, bathroom, and direct access to the forest which is my garden. The bank strictly own it, at the moment, if everything goes to plan I'll take possession of it in about 22 years from now.

I've been in the street about three years. Don't talk to many neighbours, I like to keep myself to myself. You get to recognise faces though; the same ones appear day after day at similar times. My face has appeared in advertising for various shows over the last couple of years, so to some who take an interest in local theatre, it is probably one of the better known ones, for the right reasons. I don't know if that does me any favours or not.

It can take me an eternity to get to the theatre if I'm in browsing mood when I hit the High Street. This particular night I wasn't, wet and cold it was not a time for standing like a statue in front of closed shop grills, spending the imaginary millions that I would like to have, I just wanted to get under cover and in the warm as soon as possible.

Though, I always had time for one shop. 'SoundZZZ'. This was my favourite, having one of the best collections of musical instruments in the area. Over the years, since I left school at 16, 10 years now, I have managed to spend the majority of my earnings as a carpenter, on guitars and saxophones. A hobby. Another dream of mine to be a rock star or some kind of musician.

I think that's what led me to the theatre. I'd seen an add in the paper, open auditions to anyone interested in doing West Side Story at the newly re-opened New Empire Theatre, just off the main high street. I had nothing to lose. Went along, not knowing what to expect, as nervous as hell. Before I knew it I was busy in rehearsals, I got the part of Action, not a main role but a very prominent supporting one.

An interesting experience, met loads of new friends, was taught to dance, some feat for someone like me with two left feet. I had such a good time, I stayed to do the next show. Then again, maybe that had a little to do with the after show parties, every night.

I was now in rehearsals for my fifth show with them, The New Empire Theatre Players or just The Empire Players for short.

The theatre is an interesting building, over 135 years old and steeped in history. It's had many roles to play over its life time, Movie house, Dance hall, Night club back to Cinema, and then sadly it closed down remaining empty for nearly 16 years.

A decaying monument of history, ignored by passers by, including myself. Choosing to walk past, without even raising an eyebrow to glance at the marvellous detail, hidden by years of vandalism, eaten away by the weather beating against it; a crying shame. This building had become just another empty skeleton joining the ranks of the other empty facades that were starting to litter the high street and the many side streets.

About five years ago the doors suddenly flung open again, without announcement, a vacuum filling with air, life pulsated through it's old rotting timbers and crumbling plaster work, lights blinked dimly beneath years of dust as the electric currant trickled through the ancient wiring, every now and then a bulb blinked just before it spluttered it's last particles of light, dissipating out of existence.

It was incredible how this side street, Great Street, suddenly came to life, like the street had never existed before, almost a grand unveiling amid a fanfare of jubilant trumpets.

Shops had always struggled to get their audiences down this lost valley in the high street. Now the colours seemed to come alive as if a magic brush had just put a new coat of polish on them.

I rarely visited this part of town, not much of anything had caught my interest. I wasn't going to explore the far reaches of my universe unnecessarily. I deemed it therefore a waste of my time. The high street had more than enough of what I wanted.

A gust of wind caught me as I approached Claret Street; reminding me how cold I was, the alley I usually took was down this street, it leads its way along the side the theatre.

I knew I would soon be in the warmth of the theatre, well

at least out of the cold. The truth was that this was an old building and the Copperstone family who now owned, and ran it, could only afford to do essential repairs. The heating system, although ancient, still worked albeit inefficiently, and there was a large area to heat so didn't always do a great job. Especially on cold days like today.

The glass double fronted doors stood towering in front of me. Audiences had for years transcended through these into the theatre for their night of entertainment. A sign had been hung on the inside of the door saying 'use STAGE DOOR'. This often happened if you were late and I was five minutes late. The stage door was near the entrance of the alley that I'd come down already.

There was always an insistence on punctuality, one thing I wasn't good at, I seem to have this 'I'll get there eventually' type attitude, therefore, not endearing myself to the directors and choreographers of the group. Come opening night though, I'd always know my lines and moves, this is how I justified it, and I tended to think that that bought me a little leniency. Truth probably was, they were very often short of young men in my age range. Either way, I was there and they allowed me to stay.

Facing the stage door I gripped and turned the handle, the big heavy steel plated door inched its way towards me. Only the sound of the fire handle banging against the inside would give me away.

I walked through, the sound of music, dance steps, and singing reached my ears, the opening number. If I sneaked on from the wings maybe they wouldn't notice that I was late, I thought to myself. Wouldn't work, they're so eagle eyed I'd be spotted straight away. I put my jacket and umbrella down on the nearest chair, deciding not to conceal my entrance and strolled out onto the stage to join my dance partner, Michelle. She was early twenties, taller than I, dance figure, gorgeous to look at, and she had a great personality. We got on well. We'd been partnered a couple times, she didn't seem to mind, except when I stood on her foot, or if I didn't quite lift her correctly. Michelle would get me back though. Probably Saturday afternoon, the matinee show. The time when cast members would play little jokes on each other, almost anything was allowed, on the proviso that it didn't detract from the show, ruining it for the audience.

Immediately I was spotted "Daniel."

'Shit' I thought "Sorry Matthew just lost track of…"

"Can you give the other men a hand upstairs?"

"OK" taken aback.

I hadn't observed that just the girls were on stage. The boys were out numbered three to one, we could easily be lost in the sea of female dancers.

I walked down the steps at the front of the stage and hastened my exit to the back of the auditorium, through the double doors into the foyer, up the elaborate staircase that wound it's way up to the theatre upstairs, which used to be the 'Gods' when the theatre was originally built and before it was made into two cinema screens. Each new adventure had gripped the building changing the layout to suit the new escapade. Walls taken down, floors put in, staircases removed, new doorways made, old ones blocked up, corridors sealed up lost in the mists of time.

I bumped into Adrian as I reached the halfway landing, exiting a door on the left "Wooh, what's occurring?" surprised by the figure appearing in front of me.

"If you go in there, Mark wants these seats taken into the upstairs theatre."

"Where abouts in there?" he was carrying seats similar to those in the downstairs theatre.

"Just follow the corridor they're on the left, you can't miss 'em, they're about half way up."

"No problem."

I walked through the door; it slowly closed behind me.

Barely enough light shone from the naked lights bulbs strung along one wall.

I made my way up the passage and took the chance to take in the full extent of this corridor, wondering on the use of this passage way 135 years ago.

Other cast members had had the chance to explore the theatre fully, all the hidden chambers, dead end corridors, disused basements. I hadn't been around at those particular times, but had heard the recaptured stories. I found it fascinating, to think that some of this had not been touched for over a century. This particular area, I was led to believe, had rarely been used for any other purpose than storage throughout its entire history. It had not been decorated to any degree of grandness like the rest of the theatre had been at the inception.

The door I had entered by was only discovered about two years ago, hidden behind a breeze block façade then hidden under plasterboard. There seemed no logical reason why it had, so surreptitiously been locked away out of sight for so long.

Access was available in the youth of the theatre judging by the graffiti on the walls. I thought that was just a late twentieth century invention, but no, our ancestors seemed to enjoy defacing property as well. I started to read some of it, finding it hard to comprehend, the time and effort made to place a mark on the surface of the plaster. Why bother, simply to put 'Albert Lancaster 1905', 'Harry Smith 1923'? Further along, the inscriptions read like hieroglyphics, more care being taken like a dare set to see who could align these walls with the most intricate of incisions without being caught. The deeper and farther you got into the passageway, the darker it got, out of sight, obviously made it easier to spend longer periods making the marks. They started to make the walls look like someone's jotter, full of doodles. Some poems, a good forty lines long, cartoon caricatures, stick men, and love hearts.

Reading a couple, I was losing track of how long I'd actually been in there. This was so fascinating. A particular one caught my eye, drawing me to it, like a child to chocolate. I started to read out loud…

Here in death I lye
Never fearful of the final goodbye
Time will see
Me rise and return to thee

Ever so sweet
Revenge will be neat
Make the ends mine
Blood runeth like wine

My shadow will rise
To the sound of human cries
Ash from the ground
I will scourge this town

Rid it of all ill
O' such a sweet pill
Be the cure
Death thee endure

Carry me from night
'Til the time be right
Steal the breath of life
Cold steel, the knife

Rise I say and breathe
Be flesh and bones that are strong
Rise I say and take your place
Once again setting right and wrong

Hadien contien nadya fortrey
Kootra dietra feil hoodray

There was a carved symbol below hidden by years of dust. I brushed it carefully with my fingers and let my eyes wonder over the words again, I started to recite them following their patter. As the dust fell away I noticed a red blotch below, I looked closely caressing it with the tips of my fingers, tracing the edges trying to decipher the mark before deciding it was probably just a blotch of paint or something.

Just as I read aloud the last two lines of the inscription the air around me turned cold, sending shivers down my spine, goose pimples on my arm, every hair on my arms standing to attention. The little light there was spluttered as if about to go out, a breeze came from nowhere sweeping round me like a mini tornado twisting and turning, brushing my ankles first, my clothes rippled, my ears became like radars, picking up any little noise, sound, movement, my hair flurried then all was still.

Was this my imagination? Was I making a situation exist, that didn't really. I couldn't tell reality from my kaleidoscope of thoughts.

Then nothing!

Stillness soothed my imagination. Warmth returned. The hairs on my arm laid down, going to sleep after the excitement. I looked again at the inscription, there was a signature below H Hi.....

A suffocating tightness gripped my body. My breathing became intense, restricted, a cramp contorting my throat. I wanted to fall to the ground, I couldn't. Fingers and toes started to feel like stalactites on my hands and feet, stiff and hard. The sense of sight seemed to fade briefly as tears formed in my eyes.

Every organ became lead, heavy, solid but pliable. Everything I tried was an effort like nothing I'd ever experienced. I felt alive, yet immobile, for what seemed an eternity, could only have been seconds. My skin seemed to come alive, tightening, dancing over the flesh underneath.

Nerve endings twitching, so many at the same time my brain was overloaded with electrical signals. Pounding against my skull, a hammer on rock. Any second now it would breakout into the freedom of the world beyond, ready to explore by itself.

A force penetrated my body like a hand entering into a semi-solidified substance, oozing around it, filling every empty space that had been created, sucking out the life.

I couldn't tell if I was screaming in pain or not. I felt as though I should be. The intensity was too great to make any sense of the sounds I believed I was hearing. Were they internal sounds? Sounds you hear when you put your fingers in your ears, joints moving, and bones creaking against each other.

My heart felt a cold grip, two hands round a ball squeezing, half expecting it to be squashed into oblivion. Instead I felt it being pulled in two directions. My lungs, ready to give up, making one last valiant effort to take in oxygen. No use, the central muscle had been extricated.

With the force of a bullet being shot from a gun, I was thrown against the wall behind me, feet leaving the ground. I know I hit it before slumping down to the ground and falling face up on the floor. A crumpled mess barely conscious, the light fading out.

I saw something looking in my direction. Studying me. Making sure. It wasn't clear.

Trying to move, I failed. I was going. Images fading. I twitched once more then fell motionless where I lay.

2

When I came round there was complete darkness, absolute, I felt I'd lost my sense of sight. Trying desperately to re-orient on my surroundings, I used a trick taught to me in drama; close your eyes after a blackout, count to two and then re-open, this normally allowed your eyes to adjust to the sudden lack of light, making moving round stage easier, especially when exiting into the wings.

Two attempts, still no success. I laid there motionless, not sure what to make of my situation; Was it a strange dream? A nightmare where I just needed to wake up to end it.

Slowly I sat up extending my arms hoping my hands would find something solid, anything. Reaching, feeling in the blackness that seemed like a massive void where I was just an infinitesimal spec of dust. I couldn't find a solid surface to identify. A familiar material, anything. Nothing.

Panic threw its blanket over me, my breathing became laboured and heavy. I knew I had to keep calm, yet it was all too overwhelming, consuming. I was fighting a losing battle my strength scattering. I had to refocus, control it. I closed my eyes, not even sure they were open, I felt confused. I thought about my breathing, talking to it, reassuring it, slow, deep, meticulous breaths. My heart's pounding subsided, returning to a regular constant beat.

I contemplated my surroundings, thinking back to when I entered the corridor. Recalling what I had seen before this event had unfolded. I concentrated hard, imagining my fingers were now my eyes, willing them to find something. Moving my hands slowly around in a big arc either side of me. I caught a glance of an object. There it was again. It was large. The more I believed the larger it became, a wall, I sighed with relief, placing both hands on it reassuringly. I relaxed further.

It didn't feel cold, or rough as I was expecting but it was there, and that's all that mattered. I'd lost all sense of normality, reasoning didn't seem to matter, I didn't fully understand what was happening but explanations would have to wait 'til later.

Putting one hand against that wall and the other against the floor, which also felt strange, solid but not solid, I hauled myself to a standing position. I was slow and cumbersome, more through caution than injury. I didn't feel in anyway concussed or drowsy, nothing ached, and I could sense no bruising.

Sight was the only sense that I was really deprived of, lost in the coal like blackness. Smell, well, I never really had a strong sense of smell. It was now even blander probably the force with which I hit the wall nullifying it further. Hearing seemed fine, although there were no sounds to listen to, an eerie silence that at the same time felt calm and soothing.

Turning on the spot I tried to decide which way I should go. With visibility out of the equation, I was left with only touch to guide me, and I lacked the suredness which I was used to, but it was my only choice. 'My fingers are my eyes' I repeated to myself.

Using the wall as a guide I headed in the direction I was facing, gingerly taking each step cautiously sliding one foot in front of the other at anytime expecting to kick a solid object, or stub my fingers on a protruding obstacle. I didn't hear the sound of my shuffling feet and that seemed eerie.

An eternity passed in this space-less environment, inching forward, feeling the wall. My mind becoming more focussed utilizing the sense of touch in this void. Gradually things started to feel more real, more solid. I could feel the roughness, the indentations of the plaster, some of the graffiti carvings from years before.

At the end of the corridor, there was no door. 'Damn' I thought. I turned through 90 degrees in one direction, hands out, feeling, searching, back through 180 degrees, still no door just walls. The door had to be at the opposite end.

Rotating my body carefully I tried to physically mark how far I'd turned but was unable to fix on a certain point. Making it almost impossible ascertain when I was completely opposing the direction I had come. I had to use guess work.

More confidently I made my way back to where I believed the doorway was, assured this was the right direction. I picked up my pace a little, every step gaining a little more confidence. After already walking this way and finding no obstacles, my mind drifted to the unanswered questions that filled my mind.

Why had no one come and looked for me? Surely they would have missed me? They knew I was here. After all they had directed me in here, I was meant to be helping carry some seats out. Also... the lights had been on. Maybe there'd been a power cut.

In the back of my mind something seemed wrong, nothing was obvious though. An uneasy feeling took hold of me. I pushed my way forward through the black blanket. Urgency gripped my furtive imagination. My pace quickened, not caring whether I hit anything solid, I wanted out of here, and fast. Panic was starting to take a hold.

'I must be near the door', I thought to myself.

Scrabbling around, fumbling in the darkness, this way and that as though my life depended on it. Maybe it did?

Panic was turning to fear despite trying to maintain a sense of logic and with everything I could muster I focussed my mind on my fingers 'these were my eyes' checking out any slight deviation or crevice that could be a door frame, hinge or handle.

Found it.

Then it was gone.

One second in my grasp, then it was not. Reaching into the approximate area, I made another play for the handle, found it. I pushed with all my weight, as if trying to open a thick six foot diameter steel safe door.

I was through, back on the landing halfway up the stairs.

To my disbelief this was also in darkness, although a little light filtered up from the lobby and the outside lights beyond. I'd hoped to find myself back in the artificial light of the stairwell amongst a throng of people milling about. Silence and darkness are all that greeted me. I questioned my sanity. Am I dreaming? Did I really go to rehearsals tonight? Today? What day is it?

Standing very still I listened. Listened to the theatre breathing; expecting to hear some sort of noise, people chatting. If there had been a power cut people would still be here, somewhere! Surely?

Maybe I had touched a live wire. Knowing how old this building is, and with so many places unexplored properly, I could have simply caught an exposed live wire. This would explain why I was flung across the passage against the wall, why darkness had taken over the entire place. But... it didn't explain the quiet and stillness with which I was surrounded.

There would still be voices, lost in the confusion of looking for the problem, making sure everyone was alright, locating the nearest torch, candle, or lighter as there were so many smokers in the group.

Mark knows this place like the back of his hands. It wouldn't take him long to find his way round, not even this blackness could fool him, he was far too clever for that. What of the voices? Or lack of voices.

Should I proceed up the stairs to the theatre or down to the foyer? The foyer would provide most light, as the front doors were glazed enabling the street light to penetrate into the marbled floor area, glistening on it like the sea caught by the moonlight.

That was my best choice.

Step by step, I descended the stairs, feeling more and more relaxed with each step. Closer and closer. Turning left at the bottom of the stairs would put me directly opposite the sweet kiosk. Familiar faces was what I was expecting to see, people sitting around, on the only bench that occupied the area, or on coats upon the floor.

Nothing!

I stood transfixed, surveying the scene. I began to convince myself that I was in one of those nightmares, where just before you wake up you realise that you are the only surviving person at a party, everyone else has been murdered or disappeared and the host's body has vanished. They were the first to die, however, it was all a set up and now with suspicion off of them they are free to kill, and you are the last one left alive, and it's up to you to beat them at their own game.

Disbelief. Incoherence. What was going on? Why had everybody left? I took deliberate, hesitant steps and examined the front doors more closely, the wire grills that protected the glass when the theatre was closed for the night, they were firmly in place, padlocked, signed and sealed, from the outside.

Thoughts circulated round my head so fast I thought it was going to explode. So fast they came into focus then spiralled away in a myriad of other ideas. Not one remained in focus long enough to fathom an answer. Then one thought shone like a bright light in the fog 'I was stuck here for the night'.

I looked at the clock which had hung upon the wall for nearly a century; one of the original features left, demonstrating the craftsmanship with which time pieces were once made, to still be working 97 years after it was constructed and put in place. It read 3.35am.

I didn't understand; Why hadn't someone looked for me?

Surely they must have noticed I hadn't made it to the upstairs theatre and then back down to the main auditorium for the remainder of the rehearsal. I'd seen so many people. Wouldn't it seem weird to turn up and not be seen again? Am I in some sort of parallel universe?

Rational thought was rapidly making a hasty exit. I didn't understand what was going on, and I wasn't sure that I ever would. I decided to find someway to leave this place, despite it being like a second home, it was becoming uncomfortable. I walked to the auditorium doors, if I went that way I could leave through a fire exit. So the alarm would go off, but hey, they locked me in here.

The grand double doors that opened up to allow you to take the journey into the auditorium and the evenings entertainment were locked. A massive chain secured them.

Now what was I supposed to do?

Turning on my heels and throwing my arms up in exasperation I caught sight of the box office. 'Yes' it has a phone, I could ring one of the Copperstone family, Mark or Fiona, I knew their mobile numbers by heart. They insisted on people having to ring them if you couldn't make rehearsals.

The foyer was almost L shaped, the sweet kiosk at one end waiting to serve the clientele, box office at right angles to this. To the left and a little away from the box office, opposing the street entrance were the auditorium doors. The stairs I had come down earlier were segregated by a wall, with a large double width bland archway cutting through the stonework.

Entry to the box office was by way of a door between the kiosk and serving hatch of the box office. Proceeding with urgency I thrust my hand towards the handle, fingers at the ready to make contact and pull the door towards me with force, not because I was angry, merely filled with unease that I wanted to dispel as soon as possible. I expected to make contact with the solid metal handle, yet was taken a back when my hand seemed to pass through it, as a stone passes through a piece of tissue paper, as if it were just a figment of my imagination.

I froze, blinked a few times, as if trying to get a piece of grit out of my eye; not sure whether to believe what I'd witnessed. With some trepidation I tried again. This time slowly reaching for it and closing my grip.

Again it passed right through. I staggered backwards, studying my hand, unable to equate what I'd seen. Again, and again, and again I tried, believing this was someone's sick joke and that they were laughing at me as I played right into it. One hand! Then the other! Both hands! Still, I remained there, not being able to grab a hold of this supposedly solid object.

Panicking I examined the things protruding from the sleeves of my sweatshirt, deciphering, contemplating, like a scientist might study a new life form that had just been discovered. Were they still there? Had they been cut off in some horrendous accident that I'd forgotten about, and my imagination made them seem real to my eyes.

This is a nightmare, it has to be... my vision started to blur.

Outside. I could see the pavement glistening from the rain. I could see the warm breath exhaled, like on a winter's day.

My view changed, slowing panning left, this felt like an out of body experience, the sort you only participate in, in a dream, although I've known people who have had them, described in great detail what it was like. This must be what it feels like.

Where was I? The place looked familiar. I wanted to look around but couldn't. Only viewing it from the direction I appeared to be looking, straight ahead. My peripheral vision seemed to be limited, as if I was wearing blinkers.

The cold night air didn't seem to be affecting me. I didn't feel it. I tried to look towards the ground, but couldn't. I could see the arm of a jacket outstretched in front of me, in the nearby street lamp it looked similar in colour, texture and design to the one I had been wearing earlier. I was standing in the shadows somewhere. It was a garden, a public garden. I couldn't make out much more detail in the poor night light and limited to this viewpoint.

My vision changed direction sharply, there was young girl walking...

...Back in the foyer. Looking round in every direction, questions rushing round my head like bees round a honey pot. Too many to answer! I lost my footing, my legs turned to jelly, they couldn't support my weight any longer, I slumped to the ground, weary and fatigued.

3

Putting my head in my hands, I tried to rub my eyes, clarify the bemusement. There was no contact. I couldn't feel my face. Nothing. Then, like watching a speeded up eclipse, a realization of the evening's events replayed in my mind. Every little snapshot. Arriving at the theatre, entering the passageway, reading the graffiti, the suffocating pain, being thrown against the wall, then coming round in the darkness. The haze that shrouded me was beginning to clear.

Reality was close. I examined the evidence in my head, the door on the landing. The one I'd gone through, not remembering seeing it close behind me. Not really feeling the weight of it as I pushed it open. I was anxious at the time; my mind must have played a trick on me, made me believe I had felt its presence, that I had met some resistance during my exuberant exit. At that time there was no reason to believe it was any other way.

But what now? Was I dead? Questions rattled round my head making me feel sick, sick to the core, but with no substance. I hoped I would be sick. I wanted to feel that uncomfortable feeling, it would make me feel real. Was I dead?! It was more a statement than a question flashing like bold neon light, flashing away in the darkness, illuminating the surrounding area for everyone to see.

The more I thought, the less I could get my head to come to terms with it. It didn't seem right. This was a bad B-Movie, I was the star, I didn't have a script, I didn't know the plot, or how it was going to end. Would I be saved by some miracle?

Or, was I not the star? Just some movie extra, playing the first character to leave the set.

None of this seemed wrong. Rational thought had left long ago. I was caught up in my furtive imagination writing the script as I went along. A ghost. Maybe that was it? Still with some mission to fulfil, before I could finally depart this world, and rest for all eternity.

Had I died? This question appeared like a spike of lightning in the sky. Up in that dark side corridor had I left this planet without realizing? Not wanting to go.

I rotated on my heels and faced the street doors. I was lost. I didn't know what to do next. Where to go?

I must have stared at the doors for an endless moment my whole life cascading before me. A bus passing the theatre broke my concentration. Yet I couldn't remember a damn thing that I'd been thinking about, a trance, a frozen second. The time was lost. Gone. Just like my life.

My life – gone! Just like that.

I became gripped by the notion that I was still able to think clearly which seemed to contradict everything I ever thought about ghosts and their continued role to replay situations, again and again, without comprehension or thought to change the act. A sudden strength and sobering rationale took a hold of me and with an iron hand that was not going to let go, a determination to do something and not just let my time be wasted. What though? I had no clear idea, but something, there had to be a purpose.

Leaving the theatre was the first step and judging by earlier events, if I was thinking clearly and all was true I should be able to pass through these doors without a problem. I wasn't going to go gingerly. I was going to charge at it, a raging bull to a red rag, either successfully exiting the building, or spectacularly failing. "Here goes" I said aloud. Taking a deep breath, for all the good that did, but it felt natural, gave me the strength I needed.

Screwing my hands into little fists, normally if I did this I'd feel the tension of every muscle in my arms and hands, nails digging into my palms. Nothing. I could see them clenched yet not feel the tension. I took one last look at the doors, rocked on my heels and pushed forward with the thrust of a big cat making a strike at its prey.

Bam.

Less than a split second later I was out in the early morning air, studying the familiar surroundings with a new interest. Expecting to feel the cold remembering how it had been when I arrived for rehearsals. I couldn't feel it. In a strange way, I was relieved as I'd left my coat at the side of the stage.

Although I'd seen the bus go past, everywhere now was quiet, totally at rest. Street lights brightly lit this side street.

I pondered, which way to go? Should I go home? Should I go to a friends house?

Truth was, I didn't know what to do. Being dead, if I was, left me with no purpose.

Work? What about work? My family? What were they going to say? This will kill them!

So much to consider. So much to take in. I couldn't change anything. My heart sank again and I began to feel alone and helpless.

Wearily, thoughtlessly, I wandered towards the high street. I'd lost the dogged determination I had gained only minutes before. No reason. There just didn't seem any point in heading anywhere. I was completely dumfounded.

At the junction of Great Street and the High Street I turned in the direction I would if going home, out of habit rather than reason.

Time neither went fast, nor slow. I mulled around lost, looking in shop windows, as I had done many times this time not registering what I saw. Nothing held my interest anymore, Why should it? My eyes followed the ground, trying to find some magic line that was going to lead me somewhere! Anywhere...

This whole situation was perplexing me. I was dead. I was really starting to believe it. Yet, I didn't want to. Something didn't feel right, a strange sense of foreboding. I had a sort of consciousness that belied that. I'd seen many programs on the paranormal, none of them ever explained what I was experiencing now. Is this what death was really like? Contrary to all my beliefs'. There is a consciousness afterwards. No purpose though. A living hell! An inexplicable existence, an eternal view of the world with no participation allowed, watching from the sidelines.

Without realizing it I found myself standing outside 'SoundZZZ'. This was my church. A place that encapsulated everything I was, my hearts desire, a place where nothing else mattered, I could go and forget my troubles. I went to hold the silver plectrum that hung around my neck, a gift from my parents on my 16th birthday, it had become something of a lucky charm and security blanket, I never took it off. It represented everything I held dear to me, my parents and music, I couldn't feel it or see it, my heart sunk and I just stared in through the window at the array of musical instruments inside.

A sense of intrigue enthralled me and this helped me forget. There was nothing to stop me entering the shop out of hours, not any more. A chance to explore without the following, questioning eyes of the assistant wondering if I was going to buy anything.

Out of habit I looked around, the coast was clear, not that anyone would be able to see me anyway. Or could they? Slowly I approached the chain-mail type shutter, with its many links crafted by machine. I braced myself, unsure whether my presence would set off the alarms, cringing with anticipation.

Nothing! No sound and I felt nothing.

Inside I was a kid in a sweet shop with endless amounts of pocket money to spend. Floodlit by the street light the sight was awe inspiring, light reflecting off the shiny instruments that hung so perfectly on their stands. Even if I couldn't touch, there was nothing stopping me from gently caressing the instruments which I adored, normally from afar. Imagining what they felt like in my hands, the Fender Telecaster I always promised one day I'd buy. Beautiful. This was heaven, yet it was also torture.

Wandering round, I took in every detail of the finely crafted guitars. If only I could play them all.

Hours must have passed without realizing. The noise of the shutters woke me from my revelry. They slowly rose, allowing access to the front doors of the shop. My church.

I had to get out of there. What if I was seen? Still not sure if I could be seen.

A shop assistant brushed past me, through me. Now I knew I wasn't real anymore and somehow that made me feel scared. Before it had been supposition, now I knew. Although the events from earlier should have compounded this anyway. I needed reassuring that this was really happening.

I exited the now open doorway, giving way to a person in the opposite direction, habit and I wasn't ready to experience another person passing through me if I could avoid it, it seemed too weird to comprehend.

I heeled my way home for want of a better place to go.

Fascinated by ghosts; I always believed they weren't able to go just anywhere, tied to the spot where that person had actually died. 'The Dead Spot' held by some invisible chain destined to replay the final scene of their life, until the Earth dissipated in a spectacle of explosions. If that were the case was I an exception to the rule? There has to be exceptions. Rules are made to be broken. I firmly believed that. Then what was I?

Heading up the High Street I avoided making physical contact with anyone, preferring to make for the big open spaces, as if I had some contagious disease. A couple of close calls, but at the last second I managed to evade it, much to my relief.

Closer to home I started to wonder. Why? Why was I bothering? My pace slowed, there was nothing there that could help me, I was sure of that. I didn't know what els...

Where was I? I recognised this place. It's my flat. I'm inside my flat. But I was still on my way home, here, How? What?... No, this isn't me. No this is someone else. This is what happened last night. Vision restricted by the fact I was relying on the person to look in the direction I wanted to look, which was not going to happen.

They were exploring each room. My rooms. Trying to uncover... my life, I guess who I was. But why?

Up in the bedroom on the second floor they opened the window seat, lifting out blankets one at a time, putting them neatly down on the floor beside themself. They seemed to be searching for something, with purpose, not a random exploration, they knew where and what to look for. I didn't have any notion what it was they were trying to find. I tried to think what I would have placed where they were looking, what was so important that I'd hide it away.

Removing the bottom of the window seat and then lifting out a box from under a loose floorboard. Opening the box slowly...

Back out in the street again.

Whoah!

What was going on? One minute I'm out here, next I'm in there. Why was I seeing these things? What did it mean?

I was beginning to feel even more disorientated than I did the night before.

Nearly home though, just a couple more streets and I'd be there.

What did I keep in that box? This should have been obvious. Try as I might I couldn't remember. What was in the box? I repeated the question hoping the answer would show itself. This started to bug me. "What was in that damn box?" I said aloud to myself. No, it just wouldn't come and I continued my journey puzzling over it.

I stood on the opposite side of the road looking at my flat, the building towering upwards, not sure what my next move was.

"What was in the box?" I said aloud again trying, believing the more times I asked myself this question the more likely I would get an answer.

"Hello" came a voice that broke me out of my thoughts.

Glancing round I could only see one person, a girl with a dog. A guide dog judging by the special harness the girl was holding onto.

"Hello" she repeated. The dog had sat down looking at her.

She couldn't be talking to me. No one else around though, unless she speaks to her dog. She was brunette about 5' 7" with an encapsulating smile that I found hard to retract my gaze from. She wore trendy designer sunglasses despite that it was not sunny, her dog sat patiently and obediently by her side, it was a Labrador, sandy coloured, just like one we used to have at home when I was a child.

"Hellooo" she re-iterated elongating the 'o' sound as if try-ing to make a point that I was being rude, which I wasn't, inten-tionally.

"Hi" I retorted, not expecting to get a reply.

"Are you lost?"

"Sorry" this was more a question than an apology.

"Are you lost? You seem to be lost, I can't help but sense you feel lost."

"Mmmm... No... I... don't...", this was perplexing. No one had paid any attention to me in the shop or on my way home, no eye contact, smiles, anything or had I just not noticed. Now suddenly I'm having a conversation with a complete stranger, who seemed to know I was there.

"Why are you just standing there then? Don't you have

somewhere to go?" she said with a voice as sweet and soft as I had never heard before.

"Are you a ghost?" my next question was the only possible explanation that came to mind, why else could she know I was there.

"No. I'm blind. I'm Ann-Marie, this is my dog Mojo, he knows you are there too, he can sense you" she stated so matter-of-factly.

"How? Why are you talking to me?" This sounded rude to me but was not meant to be.

"You felt lost, as though in an abyss."

"Yes. No..mmm..I... suppose, I am. But that doesn't explain how you can know I'm here. I was in a shop this morning and no one gave me a second glance, or even a first glance. I didn't think anyone could see me."

"I can't, I'm blind" she said sighing heavily "but I can feel you, or rather I can sense your presence Mojo can too. I can talk with the dead. It used to be scary, but now" She shrugged her shoulders and frowned. "I've had some really good talks with spirits, they don't judge me."

I was amazed, this all seemed bizarre "Oh   true....I   suppose" forming articulate speech was difficult. I was still unsure what to make of the whole situation.

"You seem too solid" she stated matter of factly.

"What?" I had no idea what she meant.

"I mean. Ghosts that I've spoken to normally don't have any sort of substance, but, you do."

I became even more perplexed, yet in a strange way it compounded my own thoughts.

"I'm not sure I understand."

The door slammed and I could see a girl across the road from my flat, out with her dog. Ann-Marie and Mojo, no one else with her. But I was just talking to her.

Turning to face down the road I walked away from Ann-Marie, a

*hundred yards, or so down the road, stopping in front of a blue car.
It was my car! I was seeing everything and was there. Yet there was
nothing I could do. I had no power, no control.*

*Maybe I would catch a glimpse of the reflection of the person who's
life I was viewing in the glass of the car. The angles were all wrong.
Sitting in the car, the person was familiar with everything, krooklock
off, ignition on, into first gear, grating sound of clashing cogs followed by a thud as the gear found it's footing, foot firmly on the gas,
turning the wheel sharply left, pulling away, glancing the bumper of
the car in front, not caring just hurtling off up the road. Every gear
change worse than the one before. The car careered faster and faster. I
took a quick glance at the girl with the dog.*

I was watching the car disappear up the road standing with
Ann-Marie again.

"Hello. Are you alright?" I heard her say, but it took a while
to register.

"You were gone. Now your back. You alright?. What's going
on?" said the friendly inquisitive voice.

"I don't know" I said still not sure what to make of the
situation.

"What happened?"

I looked at Ann-Marie questioning reality "I'm not sure" I
paused, composing my thoughts "I get these visions. Well, they
are not exactly visions, I don't know how to describe them really. It's strange, one minute I was standing here, then I could
see you from over the road, but through someone else's eyes" I
paused realizing how absurd this all sounded.

"What do you mean?"

This stranger stood there talking to me as if I was some old
friend she known for years and was just going through a tricky
spell. I continued "I came out of that door, my front door" I
animated my speech with hand motion, not for her benefit she
was blind but it clarified everything to me. "Not me, them, I
think, I looked over here, then went down to my car" this was

beginning too sound even more bizarre, I continued anyway "got in and drove away. Like a maniac. Then I found myself here again, with you". I half expected Ann-Marie to turn and walk away at this point, I would have done if it were me.

She stood thoughtful digesting all the information "I'm getting cold. Why don't you come back to my place and tell me more. I don't think I can help but I might be able to explain."

I was stunned by the fact that she thought she could explain my predicament in some way she seemed nice and in the short time I'd been in this state I had tasted loneliness. Her company gave me a warm feeling. I walked with Ann-Marie and Mojo up the road.

I hadn't thought about it being cold. The day had brightened up but all relevance was gone for me, the temperature didn't affect me. This was how I could be sometimes when I was real, selfish. If it didn't affect me then it was not important, although now I suppose I had plenty on my mind.

Ann-Marie seemed the opposite; warm and caring. She had a way. A patience about her a curiosity that wasn't over powering, she genuinely wanted to help. I found myself wanting her to. What could she do?

"Thank you" I said somewhat lamely.

We walked in silence for the most part, then she asked me to tell her what had happened, so I started relaying the events of the last 24 hours.

All the time I was talking, I watched her. Fascinated by the way her dog became her eyes. I wouldn't have believed she was blind if I couldn't see the dog, intuitively they acted together, pausing at the edge of a road until Mojo gave the all clear, so natural, a perfect partnership of trust. Occasionally this fascination of mine would break the flow of the story, just a split second then I would continue.

She appeared to have an awareness of her surroundings that most sighted people take for granted, after a while I realised that she would wait until she felt we were not within earshot of anyone before asking me any questions.

Ann-Marie didn't live that far away from me, Clock Street, a ten minute walk for me on my own, so named because there used to be three clock makers in the road at the beginning of the century. One of them, Browen and Sons, had made the clock that hung in the foyer at the theatre. He started to make it before his death in 1883, whereupon his eldest son finished it and presented it as a gift to the theatre, a way of saying thank you for the good times his father had enjoyed there. Gradually the clock makers disappeared one by one; after years of the factories being empty they were bombed out during the World War II, then a row of terraced houses were built.

Ann-Marie's house was typical of these houses, various modernisations over the years had transformed it to its current state, a small porch now adorned the front door where there used to be none. Double glazing had changed the overall look of the place, the standard sash windows now gone replaced with modern openers. It went back a long away, had three good sized bedrooms, immaculately decorated, very warm and inviting – it felt like a home, if somewhat a little busy with patterns.

4

After removing Mojo's harness we went into the kitchen; Ann-Marie made tea for Mojo and herself, placing his bowl on the floor. Ann-Marie and I made our way into the lounge, leaving Mojo gleefully lapping up his tea.

Mojo padded his way into the lounge a few minutes later, curling up by Ann-Marie's feet, resting his head on his tail and closing his eyes. Ann-Marie bent over and stroked him, a sign of her appreciation that he was always there for her, a genuine appreciation that is not seen nearly enough these days even by two close friends, but here it was so natural. Mojo lifted his head briefly, licked her hand and settled down again.

I reflected back to that morning, coming round in the dark corridor, alone. That didn't bother me so much as the fact that no one had even missed me. I'd seen nearly 20 people that evening when I walked into the theatre, friends, yet I had not been missed. This thought kept punctuating itself, like a knife in the heart, stabbing repeatedly, making sure I knew it was there.

I snapped out the semi-reflective state and refocused on the here and now, the real concern. I watched Ann-Marie.

She did everything so effortlessly. I thought she must have built up a good pictorial map in her mind because she made everything she did look so easy. She knew the layout of the room in relation to the door, when she entered she went straight to the armchair placing the cup on the coffee table next to it, feeling for the coaster to rest it on, sitting down without having to establish where the chair was.

"You're watching me?"

"Sorry. Yes!" I was startled by her remark, although she could not see, she had a great perception of the goings on around her.

"Why?"

This was such an innocent question. Yet I found myself feeling guilty, guilty for watching, being curious about her world, of what I didn't know, just guilty "I... I... mm... just amazed at how... easy you find your way around. I..."

"It's alright" she said trying to ease my obvious nervousness "I have been blind quite a while. Kinda get to familiarize yourself with your surroundings" she picked up the mug, with assuredness, no hesitation. I could hardly believe she was blind. She took a sip then replaced the cup where it had once stood.

Finding my voice again "I just find it hard to believe that you're blind, you seem to move around so easily, I've seen seeing people be more clumsy".

She smirked.

"I was thirteen when I lost my sight. I've never seen this house so I've had to build up a picture of it in my head, a map. We moved here when I was fourteen, I think there were too many memories in Staffordshire. That's where my dad died, I was twelve at the time..."

I was out in the open, a wooded area, I didn't recognise it. I wasn't alone. Yet I couldn't hear anyone else. Somebody was there.

There was blood on my hands, the hands I was seeing. I felt my heart pumping, palpitating, adrenalin rushing through my the body, energising every muscle. This all felt so real. I had no control, a puppet being controlled by the hands of its maker. I didn't understand. Looking around, checking the scene. Something had occurred. But what?

I gathered some branches. There was a knife, I'd seen it before, I couldn't place it.

Why did I recognise it? This question reciprocated in my thoughts.

Now running slowly, I could hear heavy breathing, the slurping of the ground under foot. Occasionally my feet would slip in the mud, this way and that, throwing me off balance; throwing my arms outwards I steadied myself. A dirt trail stretched out in front, a faint path, between the wild nettles covering the ground like a blanket; trees spearing the material reaching for the sky, some small, some tall, ivy winding its way up the trunks trying to reach the canopy that loomed up above.

Stationary again; rotating on the spot, fauna reached out in all directions. There was nothing to see except woodland. If it had been any other time I would have enjoyed the outing. I didn't know what was going on. Where was I?

There are many woods in the local area and to the untrained eye, mine, I couldn't tell one from the other.

On the move walking fast, this time, through bracken, undergrowth, grabbing handfuls of leaves and wiping the blood from my hands. I wanted to look to see if I could find a cut, so much blood, there must be a cut somewhere.

There was a couple in the distance, out walking hand in hand, they had dog with them, off it's lead and poking its nose into anything and everything; I looked at them, they saw me but didn't seem to register me. I quickened my pace towards the junction of paths ahead.

Looking all ways, there was a gate in the distance to my right. I walked towards it, slowing my pace, pretending I was on Sunday stroll, enjoying the...

"...Daniel... Daniel..."

With a start "What?... sorry..." I was back in Ann-Marie's lounge.

"You'd gone again, I mean you were here, your soul was,

but your spirit seemed distracted".

"I don't understand what's happening". Agitated I got up and walked to the window, as if expecting to find the answers to all my questions staring back at me. I stood there, looking through the glass into the street but not really seeing the scene outside. I turned to face Ann-Marie, she was looking at me, it didn't matter where I seemed to go, she always knew where to look.

Silence filled the room. I didn't know what to say for fear of scaring her off. I wondered if this was the only person I'd ever be able to talk to again.

Ann-Marie got up. Immediately she moved Mojo was alert and ready by her side. She rested her hand on his back "Ann-Marie's room, Mojo" grabbing her tea they exited the room, leaving me standing perplexed, like some naughty child who was in disgrace.

I watched them walk through the doorway.

"Daniel, you coming?!" I was in a sort of trance. I caught what she said, but it took a while to sink in. Silently I followed her.

I caught her up at the bottom of the stairs. She had slowed while going up the stairs, still very efficient, Mojo to her right guiding her, her left hand resting on the banister, just in case she should slip or lose her footing. She didn't. I expected her to I followed in muted curiosity.

We turned left at the top of the stairs, so we were in theory walking back on ourselves, towards to the front of the house. The walls were littered with family photos. I recognised her in some of them, one in particular caught my eye.

A picture taken on a canal boat, a bright sunny day, she could only have been eight or nine, the man in the photo I took as being her father. He looked young, mid to late thirties, slightly greying hair, a good physique judging by the arms protruding from the sleeveless t-shirt that he wore.

Ann-Marie was laughing. You could almost imagine yourself there, listening to father and daughter playing happily together, they looked so close.

I smiled to myself and this brought back thoughts of my own parents. Up to now I had only spared a brief second to think of them, it hadn't really sunk in, the full consequence of the night before, so caught up in my own dilemma.

My parents lived relatively close to me. I could walk it in 45 minutes. They had a nice small bungalow, downsizing after I moved out, a bit of a hint that they didn't want me to move back. I didn't mind, I didn't want to move back, happy in my flat. I tried to see them at least once every couple of weeks calling in on my way home from work. Sometimes though, I found myself too busy, wrapped up in my own world. Now, although I can see them, will they ever see me? I felt a chill go through me like an ice cube making its way down my back.

I walked solemnly into Ann-Marie's room. A large room, sparsely furnished for the size.

She was sitting on the edge of her double bed, reaching over to her bedside table to find the remote control for the stereo which sat on the chest of draws to the right side of the bay window, Robbie Williams 'Angels' was playing.

This is irony I thought.

"What's it like?" she enquired laying back on her pillows hands behind her head. Mojo sitting with his head resting on the bed looking at her.

"What's what like?"

"Being...you know. What you are".

I was not sure how to answer, such a simple question. "It's weird, mentally I feel nothing has changed" it occurred to me that I hadn't eaten or drunk since..well since it happened "I don't need to eat, I think I don't, I mean, I don't feel hungry or thirsty" I started to pace the room, wondering how to explain what I felt "it's hard to explain exactly.. I know I'm here, but I'm not …"

In a car, travelling fast, the sun, high in the sky was in my eyes, it must be about midday.

I could see the speedometer, 50'ish mile an hour.

The hands on the steering wheel I could see clearly, streaked with grass stains, the knuckles were white from gripping the synthetic clad wheel. Occasionally, the fingers flexed open on the right, as if they ached from physical exhaustion.

I could sense an air of arousal, but it didn't feel like it was of a sexual nature, more out of a feeling of completing a task, a feeling of being alive, the whole body pulsing with an electrical charge.

Looking through the windscreen, I hoped to see a sign, some indication of where I was, where I was going. Typical, nothing.

Flashing blue lights appeared on the opposite side of the dual carriageway. Sirens getting louder as they drew closer, then hurtling past without hesitation.

A hand reached up and adjusted the windscreen mirror fixed in the centre of the expanse of glass, the driver was wearing a hat. 'Damn' I thought, hoping to catch a glimpse of the drivers' hair, face, eyes.

The blue lights disappeared in the distance behind me.

"… not what?"

"… sorry"

"You went again."

"Did I? Yes, yes I did…I don't know where I was though…I see things, sometimes feel things. I don't know how, and I don't always know where I am. I don't have any control." Pausing, looking for a way to make myself clear in a situation that was strange to me "like this morning when I met you. That time when I wasn't with you. I could see you from across the road. It's like I'm in two places at once, but can only focus on one situation at a time. I have no control over it though. When it happens, I don't know what any of it means."

Ann-Marie sat there, silent, obviously thinking I'd gone

mad, or she had, by listening to me.

Mojo's head lifted sharply, ears pricked at the ready and alert followed by a sound of a key entering a lock.

"That's my mum" she reached over to the bedside table and picked up her clock, it didn't have any glass covering the face, and with her fingertips felt the position of the hands " she usually gets home about now for lunch."

Next we heard foot falls on the stairs and within a minute or so a tall slender woman walked through the doorway. She was undoing her overcoat, taking off her scarf. She must have been nearly six foot, long flowing straight brunette hair. She had a young complexion. A pleasant smile greeted us, a warm look in her eyes. Unfortunately for Ann-Marie, only I could see that, I thought that must be one the images of her mum that must be firmly planted in her mind, from the time she could see.

"I'm going to do some lunch. Do you want some? Or have you eaten?" her dulcet tones echoed round the room like a warm summer breeze.

"No I haven't. Yes thanks."

"Aunt Rose said she might pop in later.." she turned and walked back towards the top of the stairs "… as she's got to go to the chiropodist. Said she might take a breather and call in, take the weight off her corns".

Ann-Marie looked pensive "Yeah, ok" she called back, then clicking her fingers, turning and facing me "Yes" she exclaimed in whispered hush "Aunt Rose, of course, she should be able to help".

I was puzzled. Ann-Marie had an air of the cat that had got the cream. That this one person was going to solve everything, too strong a word, I think, but she could help with my predicament.

She didn't elaborate, but left me to fill in the blanks, I remained clueless, my brain throwing up all sorts of suggestions; maybe she was a spiritualist; a psychic; a witch. All seemed too far fetched for me to comprehend, but I was experiencing something completely unknown, so anything must be possible. I was fascinated by the subjects of ghosts, witchcraft and the likes, but had never encountered real ones so to speak.

Downstairs we heard the radio go on, a sudden blast of sound, before being turned to a more background sound and faintly, yet audible 'The TLR jingle'.

"I'm going to have some lunch, you can come if you like, or you can stay here" Ann-Marie exclaimed, getting off her bed, Mojo ready at her side.

"I'll stay here if you don't mind."

"Whatever, I'll leave the radio on. Come on Mojo, kitchen. I won't be long" She walked out of the room, one hand on Mojo's head, the other searching out the door frame, then the banister that would lead her to the top of the stairs then guide her safely down.

Left by myself, I surveyed the room more closely, now I didn't feel I was being watched, I relaxed and took in the surrounding details.

It was a plain looking room, one colour seemed to dominate, beige – a warm tone. On closer inspection it was not as plain as it initially looked, more thought had gone into the décor than met the eye. The detail was in the textures, that is what made this room different. I looked more closely at the patterns of the wallpapers, each wall being different, wanting to run my hands over them but knew it was useless, four walls, four patterns. The carpet had a heavy circular pattern on it. Even the duvet had a bold braiding round the edges. Anything that could be done to bring this room alive to touch had been done. The minutest of details, patterns were the colours for this room and for Ann-Marie.

Taking in the love and affection with which this room had

been furnished, my mind drifted back to the question of Aunt Rose, How was she going to help?

5

I sat down in the wicker chair that sat in front of the little window to the left of the big bay window. I wasn't sure if I was actually sitting in it, or just levitating on it, it seemed a strange concept, I could walk through solid things, yet still manage to sit in them or was it that I just believed I could.

I looked around the room, noticing more trivial details that made this room so much more. Details that separated this room from any other, bringing it to life, making it far from the plain soulless void it could have been. I thought about the love, the attention placed by an adoring parent.

I reflected on my own parents. What will they do when they don't hear anything from me? It would take a while, but they will miss me eventually. What exactly will they find out? Sadness filled my mind amidst the memories, both good and bad; I wanted to cry, yet the emotion didn't seem real enough, sort of disconnected, somehow half hearted. I sat there feeling cold, isolated, lost in a world I didn't belong to, not knowing where I was meant to be.

I was awoken from my slumber by footfalls, Ann-Marie and Mojo passed through the open doorway. Pausing for a split second, before continuing to the bed where she sat down casting her eye in my direction.

"That's my favourite chair. I sit there whenever I need a hug and no ones around. When I was young my dad used to sit in that chair with me on his knees and read stories to me... he did all the voices too" she said with an affectionate smile, hesitating to reflect on those times "Aunt Rose" she broke from her thoughts "is a bit of a spiritualist, she's a white witch. She won't tell that to mum though."

"Why not?"

"Mum doesn't really feel comfortable about that sort of thing. I remember we were having a chat once and the subject, just sort of came up; can't remember why" she thought for a second, then continued "never mind. But the subject came up and mum said 'she didn't believe in that sort of thing it's all sort of gobbledy gook and gave her the creeps so what she doesn't know won't hurt her. She's not really my Aunt you know just someone we met one day in the doctor's surgery, we hadn't been down here long…"

"Sorry… What was that Ann-Marie?" came the voice from the hallway.

"Nothing mum just singing along to the radio".

Her mother poked her head round the door "Aunt Rose's appointments about 2.30, she probably call in about 4pm, you know what she's like when she gets talking. I'm off now, I'll be back about 7ish, want to get a couple of bits of shopping on the way home".

"OK mum, see you later" Her mum vanished from sight, seeming to glide silently down the stairs, the catch on the door clicked securely in place. Her mum had left.

Ann-Marie continued making herself more comfortable on the bed, Mojo laying on the floor "Where was I. Oh yeah…we hadn't been down here long, we were just sitting there, in the doctor's surgery, and it was so weird. I can't even remember why we were there" Pausing as if the answer would magically appear "Anyway. I think mum had been feeling depressed or something. Anyway this lady just turns round to her".

'Terrible to lose someone so close dear, always hard on the young ones.'

'Excuse me' my mum said astounded by the woman's voice.

'It's always hard when you lose someone so close.'

"Aunt Rose spoke so softly that you couldn't help but feel at ease. The waiting room was empty, only three of us, mum used tell me about my surroundings to make me feel at ease. I didn't have Mojo then, not that we would have taken him anyway. The whole situation was so surreal, I'd never known my mum talk to people she didn't know. But she told me later that she just looked this woman straight in the eye. There must have been a connection 'cos without warning, the sluice gates just opened. All mum's pent up feelings came rushing out so fast I thought she wasn't going to take a breath. Up to that point, after dad's death she had always been so focussed, sterner that she had been before.

Then, for some unknown reason this woman, Aunt Rose, seemed to hold the key to unlock mum's deepest feelings, everything she'd wanted to say, but couldn't." reflectively "I wish I could've seen the Doctors face when he came out to call her in, my mum that is, I'm sure it must have been a picture when he said 'Mrs Lewington.'

My mum replied: 'Yes... no... (blowing her nose)... I'm fine now I think... yes definitely. Much better' in between wiping her eyes, regaining her composure. 'come on Ann-Marie let's go home. Thank you' she said to woman, then she did something which I would never have believed, if I hadn't witnessed it with my own ears, she invited her back to our house for a cup of tea. Aunt Rose accepted quite readily.

It was so funny I could hear the strains in the doctors voice, he sounded stunned.

'Miss Davies you're next then.'

'No I'm fine thank you Doctor.'

'If only all my patients could be cured so easily, I'd be out of a job.'

"Then he turned, huffed, and went back in his surgery totally perplexed" Ann-Marie smiled to herself and sniggered, "Well you had to be there."

"When we got back to the house Aunt Rose and my mum must have talked for hours. I was starving, but, I didn't want to interrupt, I think mum had felt so isolated up to this point, but now felt relaxed, at ease with life once again.

When I did go down to the kitchen, I felt Aunt Rose give me a knowing stare, mum left us to go to the toilet.

'You feel things don't you dear' she said.

'I'm not sure what you mean' I said defensively.

'I can sense it dear, you feel the spirits. You talk to them sometimes don't you? It's ok dear, I'm not going to hurt you. You don't know what to make of your special' she emphasized that word 'gift? I can help you master it. If you want to?'

I stood there silent not knowing what to do, I wanted to confess, it was so strange, a complete unknown person could know things about me, things I wasn't even sure about…

I was holding something close to my face, it was difficult to see. It wasn't something. It was someone. The back of someone's head. I was holding them tight, against their will, forced. Their hair in my face. My hand over their mouth.

This felt more unusual than before. I felt the cold on my face or the face I was seeing through. Before, it had always just been pictures, a blinkered view, but pictures. Now, I could feel, sense the coldness of the air.

There was struggling, we were walking, moving forward along a path I'd never seen. From my perspective it seemed secluded but I just couldn't tell.

We got lower to the ground, laying 'the someone' on the ground in front of me, then surveying the area around, this was definitely secluded, I didn't recognise it, but we were out in some fields by a cropping of trees. Then there was shot…

"Woh…. " I was back with a jolt, waking from a nightmare, I felt myself shaking " What's going on?"

"Was that another one…?"

"Yes, it was worse though" I was trying to calm down, my

voice shaky.

"What? How?" Ann-Marie sat bolt upright on the edge of her bed seemingly looking at me.

"It seemed more real. The cold. The hair. The person" I saw the images flash through my mind again.

"What actually happened this time?"

I explained as best I could what I saw, and what I felt. Verbalising the images just made me feel more agitated "I don't like this. Argh" I exclaimed. I wanted to scream rake it all from my head. I was living a vivid nightmare. Grabbing me when I least expected it to. I got up out of the wicker chair "What does it mean?" I paced the floor "What am I doing here? This is ridiculous, I'm dead, yet, these feelings, visions." Almost sarcastically, agitated "I always believed when you die, you become a ghost, you don't have feelings, just roam the Earth, day in, day out, the same place. But no, it has to be different."

"Aunt Rose should be able to explain things. She knows things, she helped me…" Ann-Marie said trying to ease my anxiety. I could feel her looking at me.

"How will she be able to help? I'm dead" I said punctuating the last words with venom, walking towards Ann-Marie just stopping short, aware that Mojo had sat up, baring his teeth at me to protect her.

"There's no need for you to be like that. She will, she knows things, can tell things… just give her a chance, it took me a while but once I let her in she helped me develop my 'special gift'" she lifted both hands flexing the first two fingers of each to emphasize that phrase "…believe me we'll help you sort this out…you've got to trust me though"

Ann-Marie sounded so convincing, I felt abashed for sounding so harsh, but it was the way I felt, frustrated, confused, lost, and angry.

I backed off from my oppressive position and let the radio fill the room again, an uneasy stand off this time. I paced a little more, trying to clarify the answers to questions I wanted to ask yet knowing no one could answer any of them.

I wanted to leave, I felt awkward, as if this was all futile. I didn't know where I'd go though, Ann-Marie was my best option, not that I had any different ones to choose from. An injustice to Ann-Marie, she had befriended me, she didn't have to, I would never have known. I couldn't understand why she was trying to do what she was, I felt ashamed that I'd even questioned her.

"You're not a normal spirit like the ones I usually speak to" she relaxed back on the bed, resting her head on the pillows pushed up against the bed head, feet outstretched.

"What do you mean?" I walked back to the wicker chair, stood in front of it, trying to picture Ann-Marie and her father sitting there.

"You feel things far too passionately. Spirits I normally communicate with don't feel the way you do, they know things, feelings they felt once. They are just stuck here in this world, they all have a purpose" she paused, swallowed slower, then looked directly at me I could feel her pupils digging into my back, I turned and looked at her "...my dad's purpose was to guide me when I first went blind. His spirit didn't crossover straight away... he hung around although I didn't know it at first. His purpose wasn't clear, that was until I suffered Meningitis... that's when I lost my sight. He... we started to communicate just after. It was like losing one sense and gaining another. I was scared at first, of the blindness and a little of him, but for the wrong reasons. He helped me come to terms with being blind. I s'pose I believed I'd gained something through losing my sight. I'd been able to speak to my father again, tell him that I missed him. He told me he couldn't stay, and until then he didn't know his purpose, once his task was done he went... for good."

She twisted her body reaching with her left hand taking a

small bear from her pillow, holding it tight in her hands, squeezing, affectionately, a tear formed in the corner of her eye.

I watched her, touched by her sign of affection, shaken by my own disrespect for all she was trying to do for me.

Once again the radio was the only audible sound to break the silence that rested between us. I knew I was bad company, on a one to one basis, it was only now that it was hitting home just how bad I could be, how thoughtless.

Mojo's head perked up, then the doorbell rang.

"That'll be Aunt Rose" Ann-Marie stated with certainty, placing the teddy bear back down on the pillow "come Mojo".

I followed them down the hallway, the stairs, to the front door in silence. I stood in anticipation of the person I was about to meet. Uncertainty. My imagination was up to its tricks again firing random images of films that I'd seen, putting together a formidable picture of an old hag, dark dirty clothes, a slight stench of some strange concoction that she'd been mixing in her cauldron. A picture of a woman who walked with a stoop, a hunch on her back, had buckteeth, long black straggly hair.

Instead, the face that greeted me was that of a very well dressed, pleasant looking woman, mid sixties possibly, she had young looking eyes, a brightness that is lost sometimes in the old. She did walk with a stick, however, she didn't have a stoop or a hump like I'd imagined. She was stern in demeanour, yet when she spoke the softness of her voice blew away that facade.

"Hello Annie dear" she said with affection "Ahh" she said looking in my direction.

I turned expecting to see someone else standing behind me like a shadow.

"This is Daniel" Ann-Marie closed the door, as Aunt Rose walked towards me.

I was breathing heavily. The cold air was hitting my warm face. I was running through a field of tall overgrown weeds. There was no obvious destination in sight, just hedges.

Looking down at the ground, it was muddy, I could see my feet, but not consistently to get a good look at the shoes, they were covered in mud.

Another shot.

Then another, this time it hit something solid to my right. A fair way off but close enough it seemed.

I didn't like this, even more than before. What was going on?

I saw the ground loom closer.

My face was in the mud. I'd fallen. Getting back up, slowly, wearily, breathing heavier than before. Each gasp deeper and longer than the previous, I could feel it. My throat was dry from the exertions of breathing. The exhaustion.

I heard a shout from behind, a long way off. I was expecting to turn to face it, but no, whoever I was; I was determined to outrun the danger. Battling on step by step. Finally reaching the hedge. Letting it guide us to a gap, a way to get beyond this field.

We were through, a section of hedge that had died, allowing a person to scrape past its ferocity without getting too tangled up.

On a road. A country lane. Walking. Walking with assuredness now, still breathing heavily, coughing occasionally as the cold air reached the warm cavities of my lungs.

A car horn sounded....

I was back in the hallway again.

"Oh dear!" said Aunt Rose shaking, fear in her eyes, putting her hands to her face in horror. Looking at me. I felt I was in a museum being viewed by the masses.

"What is it Aunt Rose?" spoke Ann-Marie anxiously.

"This is not good Annie dear, not good at all."

"What is it Aunt Rose? Aunt Rose."

Aunt Rose face had filled with a deathly paleness, her breathing laboured and she took a faulty step backwards putting out her hand to steady herself.

"I sense death Annie dear, death" Aunt Rose's voice was

trembling, she was pointing to me.

I didn't understand. I glanced from one to the other bewildered. Waiting for an answer. Anything. Ann-Marie looked at me. Aunt Rose was staring at me, like a rabbit caught in headlights, her hands still at her face; one covering her mouth, the other at her cheek, her eyes still wide, her stick fallen to the floor.

"I nee... glass of water, please Annie dear" she choked on the words.

"Mojo, kitchen" Ann-Marie said urgently and she walked through me, I shuddered although I felt nothing.

Aunt Rose and I stood there, a stand down before the fighters drew their guns.

"Need to sit down" she said to herself, loud enough for me to hear. Wearily she turned placing her hands on the door frame that was to her left, steadying herself, she headed into the living room, where she sat down on the sofa.

Ann-Marie came back with the water.

"Aunt Rose?" she called out.

"In here dear. I had to sit down." Ann-Marie followed the voice "just to your left" Aunt Rose reached up to clasp the glass held in Ann-Marie's hands, "thank you Annie dear"

Ann-Marie sat down in the armchair she had occupied earlier in the day, Mojo by her feet, her hand resting halfway down his back.

"Are you ok Aunt Rose?"

I had followed Mojo into the room and was standing next to the open door. Not sure if I should stay, the reaction by Aunt Rose caused me to feel awkward and question my presence there. Was I evil and didn't know?

"What was your name again?" Aunt Rose inquired regaining her composure.

"Daniel" I said as if I was talking to a school teacher.

"Whatever I felt has gone... but it's connected to you... I

could feel… death" she focussed on me, her voice taking on a more definite tone "the touch of death and it was through you, wherever you went for that short time, you were in the presence of evil, you had the touch of death" she drank some more water.

Shell-shocked, I didn't know what to say. I could feel Ann-Marie's stare penetrating me like a nail.

I explained the visions that I had seen, in as much detail as I could remember as both listened intently without comment, captivated. Even though Ann-Marie had heard them before she still took in every detail as though this was the first time.

A thought occurred to me, she could hear me too.

As if reading my mind she answered my statement, "If you are wondering, yes I can hear you, like many who have the gift."

6

Aunt Rose settled more comfortably on the settee "Now Daniel. Come and sit next to me dear" her voice was warm, caring, almost enchanting.

I sat as instructed, making no impact on the soft, pillow-like cushions, still she knew I was there.

"Yes" she said in the stereotypical way that you'd expect from palm reader you find in a fairground. I began to wonder what I was letting myself in for. "You have a strong aura, a strong, powerful force. I can see why you felt Daniel's presence Annie."

"It's like nothing I've ever felt before, I knew there was something different but I couldn't put my finger on it."

"Daniel just rest your hands on mine" Aunt Rose held her hands out, twisting her body towards me. Slowly, tentatively I responded, guided by her instructions. I had always been sceptical about this sort of thing, believing it was just mumbo jumbo. Now all my beliefs seemed to be tested, pushed to their limits. As I acquiesced to her, I felt a charge drive itself through me, an electrical pulse of energy, course its way to every fibre of my being. In an instant Aunt Rose was in a trance-like state. Eyes glazed, pupils dilated, staring directly at me.

I felt her presence grow stronger within me, exploring, searching for clues and information I became relaxed and comfortable as the process continued, all my initial scepticism fading. Slowly Aunt Rose's eyes widened taking on a different persona, a peculiar emotional state, an enlightenment, understanding, even bewilderment.

With a weak voice Aunt Rose spoke "A strong powerful force is consuming you. Making you weaker. You can't fight it. It's becoming stronger... and..."

Her body slumped backwards into the settee, her hands breaking the connection with my own. Arms flaying outwards, her left arm knocking over the half-empty glass of water she had rested on the arm of the settee. It fell onto the carpet its contents quickly dissipating into the deep brown pile. Aunt Rose's head flopped onto her right shoulder, chin barely resting on her chest, and she lay there motionless.

Glancing over at Ann-Marie; who had been listening intently. I half expected her to jump up to attend to Aunt Rose. She sat there, seemingly unaware, yet at the same time aware that something was not right, her face quizzical. Her Aunt remained unconscious on the settee.

For an endless split second, I stared from one to the other, not knowing what to say, what to do.

"Ann-Marie!" I exclaimed.

"What?" her voice calm.

"Your Aunt" I said with great urgency.

"She's not moving. Just laying there, passed out or something."

Ann-Marie sat there coolly facing towards where her Aunt slouched. I noticed she started to concentrate harder, her facial expression pained somewhat. Then she spoke "She's fine. Sometimes when she feels things, it can take a lot out of her. Sort of saps her mental energy. She'll be ok in couple of minutes."

"How can you be so sure? How do you know?"

"If I concentrate I can feel her aura. She taught me how to tune into her. She'll be fine."

"Oh. ok" I was learning more and more about Ann-Marie all the time; displaying a different side to her talents "She spilt her glass of water on the floor" this seemed rather trivial, but I wanted to let her know.

"I didn't hear it break."

"No, it's in one piece."

Ann-Marie got up and moved towards the settee to pick up the fallen glass, letting her hands feel their way over the carpet to locate it. Then she left the room, I could hear the sliding of her hand along the wall as she walked towards the kitchen Mojo following. She returned a few minutes later with the glass refilled, and a tea towel to put on the carpet.

Still groggy Aunt Rose came round putting her hands to her forehead "Oh dear... my, I haven't felt anything like that before." Her voice shaky.

"What?" I was desperate to know anything she had discovered "What happened?" She didn't answer me "What is it? Please. Tell me." I pleaded, my voice scared. I started imagining all the possibilities, I was concerned, worried, she'd felt something, what?

She still looked pale, almost confused about her whereabouts. Ann-Marie offered her the glass of water.

I wanted to shake her, making her come round quicker. I wanted answers. I wanted them now. In my frustration I got up and paced the room "Come on what was it? What did you feel?" I turned back on her "Please. Tell me..." My fists clenched in frustration.

Ann-Marie looked at me "It's no good talking to her. It takes her a while to recover. She won't be able to hear you. Give her a few minutes and then she'll re-focuss on you. Aunt Rose. I brought you a glass of water."

She looked at the glass being offered and took it "Thank you dear" she said struggling to form the words that should have come so easily.

The room fell silent, both Ann-Marie and myself looking at Aunt Rose as she drank from the glass; one large continuous gulp; we stared like expectant parents waiting for the first words from their child; a break from the silence.

The waiting, tiring, and frustrating. I wanted to know more. Find out about me. As I pondered that thought I felt a pain biting from inside, a pain that I'd never felt before...

...I was locking my car door, watching for any prying eyes in the shadows, hovering. It was a street that was familiar to me, yet I couldn't place it. I heard the thud of the central locking, clicking securely in place. I turned around. Scanning the street, no-one about, a cat was crouching on a wall, its tail flicking gently in the breeze, staring at me, him. Us!

I headed along the road 100 yards towards a block of garages set back slightly from the street. As I drew level with them, I glanced around once more; all clear, then entered a narrow alleyway that ran along the left side of one of them, it was overgrown with brambles, overhung with trees and climbing shrubs, creating a sort of natural tunnel. Without hesitation, I plunged further and further in, brushing aside anything that was in my way, with purpose. There was somewhere I was heading, but I was being kept in the dark about the destination.

There was a 'T' junction up ahead. Unhesitatingly I turned right and carried on, ploughing through the thicket ahead of me. A noise to my left caught my attention. I stopped and found a broken chair buried in the undergrowth, tugging it free I placed it next to the fence where I heard the noise. Standing on it I peered over.

It was a tall fence and I could only just see over it. Through the trees there was a child playing in the garden, about six or seven years old, I was never much good with ages.

"Psst" I heard. Where did that come from? It was someone trying to attract my attention.

It was from me...

"...ack within minutes. Daniel! You're back... see Aunt Rose, that's what happens."

"Yes" Aunt Rose said thoughtfully "I've never come into contact with this sort of thing, personally. Meg, my friend on the other hand, has told me of encounters like this. I'm sure, I'm sure I remember her telling me. Mmmm. Yes, I can't quite remember all the details. Let me think, there is a reason you're experiencing the 'Visions'. What was it that Meg said. Oh fudge, memory's not as good as it should be. I'll give her a ring".

She reached into the pocket of her cardigan she wore pulling out a mobile phone. Squinting at the screen she searched through the numbers that appeared one by one, all the time muttering to herself, eventually finding the name she was look-ing for and pushing the dial button. I could hear it ringing.

After five rings "Hello. Meg…it's Rose."

Ann-Marie and I listened as Aunt Rose continued her conversation with Meg relaying all she knew so far.

"Daniel, How long has it been now?"

"Less than a day… Why?"

"Less than a day Meg" she paused.

"When you first had these visions was there anything different about them, than now?"

"They were silent…" I thought a bit harder "…just pictures like a silent film I couldn't hear… or feel anything."

Again she passed this information to Meg.

"And now?"

That instant I suffered from what can only be described as an awakening, a realization, an awareness of what had been occurring; how the visions, and symptoms of the visions had changed.

"And now I hear things… and feel things… each time they seem more realistic. I feel heartbeats, adrenalin rushes. I have no control. I can't look where I want to, or turn round".

Aunt Rose busily relayed all this to Meg, then, there was a long silence.

"Thank you Meg. See you at Bridge on Thursday. It's at Maud's isn't it?… Bye" she flicked the off switch on the phone and looked directly at me. After a moments contemplation;

"Meg says that what is happening is that you are becoming one with the other being, two sides of the one coin joining together to make the whole thing. Eventually you will become one" she leaned in "Then the stronger half takes control" She paused as if more bad news was to come. How bad could it be? "That unfortunately will be the other half of you. You will lose everything you were, and everything you are. You, as you know will no longer exist. And that will occur in only eight days."

"But how can she be so sure?"

"My dear friend has experienced this twice before."

"What" I was gobsmacked "It happens all the time?"

"No dear. That is not what I said."

"But it can't be. It can't be."

Shocked, I didn't know what to make of any of what I'd just heard. I saw the events of the last day flash before me. Replaying at double speed, then repeating in slow motion. A well of emotion flowing up inside, I wanted to punch out, but knew I couldn't. The only two people who seemed to understand and wanted to help were here. I couldn't offend them and I couldn't stay. I bolted from the room, from the house without more thought. As if running was going to make a difference. That if I ran hard enough I could beat this thing. I was running for my life.

What life? I was dead already.

7

With darkness falling I hardly noticed the people around me dressed up in scarves and hats, collars fastened so tightly round their necks you'd think it would cut of the oxygen supply. I walked the streets aimlessly. Streets I'd known for years, familiar sights, places, memories. What was going to happen now? Inside a mix of emotions battled with each other. I wanted to punch something. Hit out. Strike someone. Something 'WHY ME?' I wanted cry at the top of my voice. It wouldn't have made any difference, no one would have heard me.

I wanted to speak to my parents; they wouldn't be able see me, they wouldn't be able hear me. I didn't exist to any to them anymore, and they didn't know it.

Is this what I'd been reduced to? My whole existence condensed down to, to this.

Again I ran. I didn't know why, just compelled to run. I hated running. I ran 'til I could run no more, as if that would change things. Street after street I passed, across roads not looking just running, head down, wanting to be hit by a car, end all the frustration, even though I knew it wouldn't make any difference.

When I stopped I was outside my parents bungalow, my security blanket I suppose, somewhere I'd always felt safe, a haven where I could find help. Good advice. A friendly face and a kind word, reassurance if I was ever in doubt. They had always been there for me, I couldn't remember a time when they hadn't, every fall. I was lucky to have my parents, the people they were.

What now? That thought echoed inside my head, a

pneumatic drill pounding every nerve ending inside my skull. Parents are meant to go before their children, one of life's hardships that make us stronger; not the other way round. I never had a chance to speak to them just once more even just to say goodbye, wrapped up in my own world, which now seemed a futile existence. Now I could see them, they couldn't see me. I could listen into every conversation they had, they'd never know.

What will they learn about their son? How he went? What happened? How is anyone else going to know? This is crazy.

It occurred to me, like the sun melting away the mist on a frosty morning that I didn't really know what happened to me. Surely, I should know how I died, if I died! I did die didn't I? Questioning my own sanity. Yes! Ghosts always re-enact how they died, that's what I believed, so they must know. I didn't. I have more conscious awareness, stronger feelings, so Ann-Marie said. Why?

How did I die?

I needed to know all the facts whether I liked them or not. I had to find out everything I could.

My fathers' car turned into the driveway, the headlights not casting my shadow upon the low front wall in the dark winter evening, my mother in the passenger seat. They pulled up in front of the white garage door and got out, chatting casually, as I had heard many times before.

My parents – both in their mid fifties had taken early retirement. My father had worked in the post office since leaving school. He had been quite lucky as well, occasionally having a flutter on the horses when he felt the urge. One time he'd won £35,000 on a five horse each way accumulator, each horse coming in first. This had enabled him to invest modestly in property, buying and renting – their retirement plan, they now owned six properties mortgage free, plus their bungalow, they helped me out when necessary but I had to learn the value of money. My mother still did the occasional bit of teaching she always enjoyed giving back to others what knowledge she had.

I was watching a TV reality program unfolding in front of my eyes. Except I was physically present in a strange sort of way, I smiled.

"Matthew... you can be so rude sometimes." Mother closed the car door and walked to the boot "that checkout girl had probably had a busy day, and you know what it can be like sometimes when it's busy."

Opening the boot and handing some full shopping bags to my mother "Well what do you expect? It was a stupid question anyway."

"There's no need to be rude though" shooting a glance at my father before walking to the front door "Have you got the front door key handy?"

"No" my father put the last carrier bag on the ground and closed the boot, locking the car with the remote key "Hello... I hand her the credit card...and she goes, 'Do you want to pay with this?'...errr no I want to pick my nose with it."

"Everyone's entitled to get a little confused."

"I think you've got to be alive to get confused. Where do they find these people?"

"You're so sarcastic" father joined my mother at the front door where she was fumbling around in her handbag for the key, shopping bags at her feet.

I watched my father struggling to hold the shopping and find his keys in his pocket while mother hunted for hers, then both together they found them. They smiled at each other, opened the door and went inside.

I stood there a while longer, enjoying the picture, seeing my parents together. I followed them in. The door closing on me, it made no difference though.

I stood in the entrance hall. Behind my parents.

"It's turned cold all of a sudden. Matthew. Did you turn the heating off before we went out?"

"No" looking at the thermostat situated on the wall by the telephone a little further down the hallway. "Still at 15."

"Strange, just felt a chill in the air" there was a pregnant pause and my mothers expression became one of seriousness "...something's not right... It's Daniel. Don't ask me how I know, I just know."

"What do you mean something's not right?"

"I don't know for sure. I need to ring him."

I watched as my mother quietly and efficiently went about the task at hand, trying to contact me, ignoring the shopping on the floor, she had stopped taking her coat off. She picked up the handset to the phone, which had been laying in the telephone holder attached to the wall, pressed the buttons, in what looked like a random manner, but there was sequence. All the time muttering to herself.

"Answer the phone, please answer the phone..." repeatedly.

My father went about the business of carrying the shopping into the kitchen, leaving my mother talking to herself. She seemed to know, but my father didn't really give it any credibility.

I felt guilty standing there, watching all this unfold, knowing I couldn't do anything to ease her mind, put her worries to rest. Knowing that if I didn't answer the phone she would fret until she heard news, a word, anything from me, about me. This was too much, I had to go. I turned about, exiting through the front door.

As I passed through the door I felt the pain that I had felt earlier, and I knew what this meant...

I was in a hallway, my hallway. I was staring at the wall. Standing, staring, in a daydream, either that or I was admiring the previous owners choice of wallpaper.

I could just make out the aerial to my phone, which was in my hand.

I felt a sense of mischief, a rye smile. I could feel the smile. I didn't know why!

I stood there a little while.

The doorbell rang out its pretty little charm. It always did sound dreadful, one of those small jobs I'd always meant to do, but had never got around to.

I turned to look down the stairs at the front door. I could make out the shape of a young person, the paperboy, through the non patterned glass panel immediately above the door.

I began to fear for his life. I couldn't justify why, a sense of uneasiness about the possible ways forward for this situation. Damn why didn't I leave the money for him last week?

Slowly, purposely I walked down the stairs. I still felt the rye smile on my face, the phone in one hand I turned the catch to the door and pushed it outwards.

"Excuse me, you haven't paid your papers for a couple weeks, and I was told to come and collect it, it's £6.32 with the magazines, only if I don't get paid, it'll get deducted from my wages."

I didn't say anything, just looked around. I wanted to shout out RUN, but couldn't, I opened my mouth, I heard another voice, a strange unfamiliar voice.

"Yes sure. Why not come inside and I will sort out the money?"

"No it's ok I'll wait here if..." the boy took a step backwards

"it is quite alright, you are safe you know, it is just I do not like leaving the door open" I shifted my position in the doorway, closer to the boy.

He stepped back a look of suspicion on his face "I've got to keep an eye on my bike."

Reassuringly "It will only take a couple of minutes, your bike will be safe" I reached out a hand as if to put it on his shoulder. The phone in my hand rang.

The boy looked uncomfortable with the situation. Allelujah I said to myself, just when you want a kid who stands up for himself.

"No I'm alright here mister" taking a further step back towards the outer door.

I started to lunge forward.

The next door neighbours' door opened abruptly.

Safe.

"Evening…"

I was back outside my parents place.

For the first time since finding myself in this half existence I knew what I had to do, I had to go back to the beginning. The theatre! I needed to discover what had happened to me. I had to start solving this riddle, this puzzle. Piece together the pieces and solve the mystery in which I was trapped.

I headed up to the main road, the quickest route.

Monday night I thought, the theatre would be closed, there was no show in this week, so no reason to open it up. That was my narrow minded point of view on the matter. Irrelevant that works still goes on when there was not a show in.

It didn't take me long to reach the theatre, I had purpose to drive me along with verve and a new energy, I felt alive again. Upon reaching the front doors I stood there transfixed, the imposing building stood like a formidable barrier that I knew I had to cross.

I was scared. I wanted to know. Yet. I didn't.

I rocked about on my heels for a while trying to steal the moment when I would make a dash, break through the locked doors. I was re-entering the beginning of the nightmare I had started only 24 hours before, this seemed impossible.

Finally knowing I had to do it I counted to three and went for it.

Once in I observed the lobby like I'd never been there before. I walked over to the stairs from which I had descended the night before, so innocently, only to discover the truth of my predicament.

It was dark. Only the light from the street lamps outside

spilled in enough to give me any light. The recess at one end, which contained the stairwell remained encased in formidable blackness. I walked over and returned to the beginning of my hell. As I moved up the stairs I became unnerved, losing my grip on the positive attitude I had acquired only an hour before. I stopped.

What could be the worst that could happen? Nothing more than had already occurred, I laughed nervously to myself, not that it would have made much difference if I had laughed out loud.

Without answer to this question, I gingerly proceeded, taking the steps one at a time... pain again...

Blackness. Nothing but blackness. A shimmering sheet of nothing.

For the briefest instant I thought I was back in the corridor again, where it first happened, I couldn't make out anything.

This felt different though. Something new. I tried to re-orient again. But all I could sense was that I was laying down. I was in bed. Sleeping? Vaguely feeling the covers moving around me, I was not in a restful sleep.

I was caught there with nothing I could do, I tried to relax and slowly I let myself drift too. I lay there listening, puzzling, thinking.

I was in a street. I recognised it, not from physically ever being there, maybe a picture I'd seen somewhere. Buildings looked new, dated new, I was in the past.

Streets of cobbled stone, gas lights. Looking around, I surveyed the shops, there was Mr Ridleys hardware store, it looked so different, so new, yet so old. All the new UPVC facade was gone.

Then I found myself spun round like a top at high speed, looking at a commotion going on about ten feet away.

There was a horse and carriage stationary. The horse was agitated rearing up on its hind legs. There was someone lying on the ground. A crowd gathered blocking the view. A policeman ran to the scene blowing his whistle pushing his way through the crowd, brushing people aside, like toy soldiers.

I caught a glimpse of some blood. Almost fluorescent as it stained the white blouse the lady was wearing. The horse was still rearing, driver trying his best to get it under control. The crowd wary of the horse stayed a safe distance away. Slowly, its actions became less pronounced as it settled, it's head making an occasional pull to one side, as if trying to break the reigns, another man started to stroke its nose as it calmed, soothing it further.

My sight was drawn to a girl standing just away from the scene, she was crying, sobbing her poor little heart out, there was a lady standing next to her with her arm around her, doing her best to comfort the little girl. For some strange reason it didn't look like a parent, just friendly passer-by.

Walking towards the scene, I could see a woman lying on the ground, motionless. I wanted to cry out. But it wasn't me this time.

I was bolt upright in bed, my bed, pearls of sweat dripping from the end of my nose onto the sheets. Breathing heavy, my chest rising and falling, I could feel every muscle, every heave as my lungs tried to fill with air, my hand clasped the duvet cover tightly, screwing it up into a ball. I looked at the clock beside the bed it was 3.35am. Gulping down water from the glass that I'd left by the bed.

Breathing returned to normal, I looked around the room before laying back down again, pulling the covers up to my chin, I felt a tear in my eye....

I was on the stairs again in the theatre, falling down them, I reached the bottom. I stayed put, trying to decipher the images I'd just seen, wandering which me was I?

8

I laid there contemplating, debating between fact and fiction. Losing track of where I was, who I was, and when I was. Even being dead I was finding this dis-orientating. I had to discover the truth, the truth of how I died.

I stood and marched up the stairs with renewed determination to where the door was. Extending my hand to the handle forgetting that I didn't need to use it just for the minutest second, then I hesitated. This magical barrier casting its spell over me, stopping me from entering the playing field I knew I had to cross, I thrust forward and beyond.

I was standing in the vast void of blackness, although I was not real I still could not see in the dark, I needed light, it was useless to rely on sense of touch. I couldn't feel what I was looking for, I needed to see it. Every step I took another obstacle, infuriating me, the anger inside boiling up, every obstacle notching up another point on the scale, a scale that would reach an end eventually.

I wanted to find answers; it was becoming apparent that I needed help as much as I didn't want to accept it. I knew getting angry was not going to help matters. I changed tack to something calming, something funny. I remembered one of the after show parties.

After-show parties were a tradition, some of us would get together and put on an after-show show, we'd spend time between the Saturday matinee and evening shows discussing what we would do and about five minutes before actually doing it, rehearsing, then just go on stage and perform. Normally we'd take the mickey out of the show that we had just performed, sometimes it was past shows, in particular the number 'Black Velvet', this held a lot of special memories, for nearly everyone, I was just glad to be part of it. The evenings entertainment was usually recorded, the laughter from the other cast members was most apparent when played back.

Smiling to myself, I felt calmer now and could think more rationally.

I needed Ann-Marie, although she was blind, ironically she could help me see.

I'd run out on her, hours previously. Why would she want to help me? She was trying then, and I disregarded her, threw her to one side like a piece of waste. I felt guilty as I knew I should.

If I went back I would have to make amends, How? I didn't know her.

I left the theatre knowing what I had to do, also a little scared of being turned away, with good reason. I had to put things right. I didn't know how. I needed to convince Ann-Marie to help me again. I doubted this would be easy. I ran different explanations of my behaviour around in my head, none of which really justified my actions. How could I apologise? This occupied my mind for the journey back.

Ann-Marie's place was 25 minutes walk from the theatre. The closer I got to her house, the further an explanation seemed, an apology was all I could offer.

'How was I going get Ann-Marie into the theatre unnoticed?' bearing in mind that she was blind. It hadn't occurred to me on the way, but now the thought sprang like a cat reaching for it's prey.

Ann-Marie's house was shrouded in darkness internally. Illuminated outside only by the street light on the other side of the road. I had no idea what the time was and didn't know how long I would have to wait for her to get up.

"More waiting" I muttered "Nope it's no good if I wait I won't do it" I had to act now. I walked through the front door and up to Ann-Marie's room.

Outside her bedroom door I contemplated what I was about to do, deciding it almost rude to just waltz in and wake her from her slumber.

Ann-Marie obviously hadn't closed her curtains, she didn't need to, and in the dim light I saw the door move slightly, rock on its hinges. Blinking I thought I was hallucinating then a hand appeared at the edge and pulled it open further.

Ann-Marie stood there in her pyjamas. How could she have known?

She walked straight through me, and for those few seconds I felt uncomfortable, she headed down the hall then stopped, turned and faced me.

Whispering "Go and wait in my room I'll be back in a minute, I need the bathroom."

I did as instructed, taking up residence on the corner of her bed, waiting. Mojo lifted his head in recognition, then lowered it again and carried on sleeping where he was on the bed.

Ann-Marie came back in the room a while later. Still she spoke to me in a whisper without any sign of anger or annoyance.

"I hoped you would come back" she was a little drowsy climbing back into bed, pulling the covers over herself.

"Why?" I answered in an imitating whisper. Had I blown everything out of all proportion?

"There's no need for you to whisper my mum can't hear you."

"Sorry, habit I guess… you know? When someone whispers I start to.." I didn't bother to finish the sentence, she knew what I meant. I could tell by the expression on her face lit by the light from the outside world.

Timidly I spoke "I'm sorry about running out earlier" my

feeble apology sounding even worse out loud.

"It's ok, I sort of guessed you were upset" she spoke without the slightest hint of displeasure.

"I didn't know what to think. I needed to get my head together" I started speaking, not thinking what I was saying just rambling on "You know everything that happened in the last twenty four hours, my parents, the visions. What do they mean?"

"I understand. Sort of. I can understand where you are coming from" she yawned "I'm sorry, I'm tired."

"Of course. I'll let you get some sleep" I got up off the bed.

"It's ok, carry on."

I didn't know where to start. I felt I needed to tell her everything that had occurred since we last spoke and I proceeded at a race, she listened intently. I paced the room, vocally and visually I ran through everything, my ideas, the theatre, my parents.

At the end I turned and saw Ann-Marie asleep, head resting on her pillow, one hand underneath it.

I walked over to her bed and looked on, Mojo lifted his head.

"Its ok Mojo, I'm not going hurt her" I looked at the clock on her bedside table, I could barely make out the fluorescent pads on the hands, it was nearly five in the morning.

I went to the window and looked out on the street scene below, an empty stage waiting for its actors to take up their positions for the opening.

I wasn't tired, didn't need sleep, time went by so slowly. However it did give me the time I needed to ponder the problems ahead. How was I going to get Ann-Marie into the theatre?

Ann-Marie's Mum called up "Ann-Marie, it's 8 o'clock, breakfast is on the table."

She sluggishly roused herself yawning and stretching,

throwing back the covers, hiding Mojo from view. He fought
with them playfully and jumped off the bed.

"How are we going to get into the theatre though?" she said
feeling around for Mojo he snuzzled her hand in response.

"I thought you'd fallen asleep".

"I sort of dozed off, but caught most of what you said".

"Oh. I've been racking my brains all night trying to think
of all sorts of ways. I'm not sure but I think I've come up with
a plan".

She yawned again. "I'm sorry."

"Forgot you need sleep."

"What's it like outside?" she asked.

"Dull, and cloudy, looks like it might rain again.

Ann-Marie got up from the bed and unhooked the
dressing gown that hung on the back of the door, putting it
on, tying it loosely about her waist "Oh yeah, Aunt Rose said,
after you went, that she needs to make contact with you again.
She thought that if she made contact with you when 'IT'"
punctuating the air with the first two fingers on each hand "You
know, when it happens, you see things, she reckons she'll be
able to identify who it is... who's eyes you are viewing things
through, when you see things. Does that make sense?"

"Kind of, I think, but I don't have control over them. When
they happen. They just…HAPPEN."

"We might just have to spend some time with her and wait
then" she left the room, Mojo at her right hand.

"Ann-Marie, who are you talking to?"

"No one Mum, just Mojo" she hunched her shoulders up
realising that she had been quite loud, forgetting her Mum was
still in the house.

"I'm going to work now, I'll see you lunchtime."

"Ok, 'bye."

A few moments later the front door clicked into place.

Ann-Marie disappeared into the bathroom and closed the

door, Mojo went in with her.

I waited in the room for her return.

"That's better" Ann-Marie said as she re-entered the room.

I turned to face her "Ann-Marie before we see Aunt Rose. I need to go the theatre. I need you to provide the light, a torch or something, so I can see. Then I can find out as much as I can about what happened and I think I've worked out a way to get in without being noticed."

"How?"

I became more animated as I explained my plan "There is a show there tonight and tomorrow night, so the stage door will be open, it always is. You can pretend you're one of the performers, it's a dance show. They'll be loads of young girls going in and out all day no one will notice."

"How about Mojo? I'm sure they won't allow dogs in there" she replied a little sarcastic.

"You'll have to trust me to be your eyes."

"But what about Mojo?" she stroked his back.

"We'll have to leave him here" this didn't go down to well judging by the look on her face. Mojo sat and looked up at Ann-Marie. He seemed to know.

"I won't be able to move as quickly without Mojo. Even if you tell me what's where, it'll take ages. It took me ages to build up my confidence to rely on him. I don't know if I can go it alone, relying on someone else who can't physically guide me" she paused "And another thing. How will I get to the theatre without him?"

I thought for a second, "Look I don't know any other way of doing it" I felt I was battling a lost cause. I understood her reluctance, if the situation were reversed I would probably feel the same. I sighed.

I slumped into the wicker chair whilst Ann-Marie sat on the bed, both in silence.

"How about if we take Mojo with us. We can tie him up

outside. We won't be that long, Will we? He'll be ok for a while."

"Can do I s'pose" Mojo lifted his head and glanced at Ann-Marie as if he'd understood every word she'd said. I sensed her displeasure at the thought of leaving her beloved friend.

"I'm still not sure it'll work but I'll give it a go" with that she got up and touched Mojo's head then left the room "I'm going to get some breakfast. What time do we need to leave?"

I called down the hall "If we go about 10am, it'll take us about half an hour or so, they should have all the set in by that time" we need to wait until the cast arrive anyway.

I decided to join her downstairs and followed at a slower pace, taking another look at the photos that lined the wall.

While Ann-Marie ate her breakfast I looked out of the kitchen window at the garden. It was small and compact, mainly concrete, a few flowerbeds broken up by a few shingle footpaths here and there. I heard the radio being switched on. But I was lost in my own daydream.

"Did you hear that?" Ann-Marie exclaimed.

"What? Hear what?"

"There have been two murders and an attempted murder, all in the local and surrounding area in the last 24 hours. Police wouldn't release too many details as they don't want to create a panic, but I believe they are hunting a single male in his late twenties. They are warning everyone to be vigilant. All the victims were young girls."

"Yeah, so?" I didn't see the relevance, I never did unless it involved me.

"Don't you care?"

I detected a hostile tone and tried to play it down "Yes. But what has it got to do with me, I can't do anything to stop a killer. Especially not as I am".

Ann-Marie obviously had a clue "Didn't you say in the vision you had yesterday, you were in a field, there were shots? Well.

One of the girls was abducted and taken to a field, the only thing that saved her life was the fact that a farmer had spotted two people in his field and fired warning shots thinking they were trespassers."

I thought for a second, I'd completely shut out whatever I could of the visions, when it suited me.

"Oh my god" I felt sick, even though I didn't think I was capable of being sick. All the pictures in my head became clear at once - everything I'd seen- everything I'd felt. I was viewing life through the eyes of a murderer! More questions ransacked my head like random explosions. Questions I wanted answers to, yet I didn't know how I was going to get them.

Then a pain shot into my body, cramps in my hands and feet crippling me...

I was walking down an alley. This time I knew why. It was clear to me what I was seeing. A slow torture as I could only watch in horror as the play continued to unfold.

I arrived at the entrance to the alley and halted, standing back slightly, enough to be hidden by the overgrowing brush. I was viewing a scene in Elizabeth Street. I recognised it, this was where I used to go to school.

A cold feeling flooded my heart quelling any possible beat that could have been there. A mixed up stew of emotions, anger, hate, love, came to me at once. I knew the outcome of this venture without seeing it unfold in front of me.

I was waiting, waiting for stragglers.

There had to be something I could do, I felt so helpless, a puppet, being guided by the power of the force that controlled me.

I heard a voice, a young girl's voice and I knew what was going happen next, I tried my best to shout out, nothing, my voice like a scream in a vacuum.

It was no good. Before I knew it the girl had been dragged into the alley kicking, she was trying to scream but my hand was tightly over her mouth, I could feel her saliva on my fingers. She was weak in comparison to me. She tried in vain to break free, kicking, writhing all to no avail. Her bag fell to the ground and I managed to drag it behind me with one foot.

I watched the grizzly scene unfold, every motion, every thrust of the knife into the body, the struggle of the girl to fight for her freedom in this no win situation. I couldn't avert my gaze or close my eyes, forced to look on.

Then it was all over. The body lay still in my arms. I could feel the warm blood on my hands, sticky. I wanted to break free.

Back in Ann-Marie's kitchen. I was crying without tears, the emotion was real.

Ann-Marie moved from the table towards me, like a friend would "What's wrong Daniel?"

It took a while for me to find my voice. I was choked.

"I've seen the next victim... I was... there... I couldn't stop it. It was... I... I don't know. I feel sick".

I saw Ann-Marie stretch out a hand for comfort. A hand for comfort that would not be felt.

9

By the time I'd gathered my thoughts and pulled myself together, it was nearly 11am. Ann-Marie had been good in trying to console me as I had become engulfed by feelings of inadequacy about preventing the actions I'd seen in my vision and knowing now that it had in fact been real. I was angry and frustrated and Ann-Marie was quick to point out that it would do me no good as there was nothing I could do to change what had happened.

We headed off towards the theatre. It was cold and overcast, luckily it didn't rain which was good as Mojo was going to be outside for a while. He had a thick coat but even so leaving him in the pouring rain I didn't think would bode too well with Ann-Marie.

On the way to the theatre I explained the procedure that most groups operated backstage. It was a simple one which only required the relevant person to place a tick by their name in the box on entering the theatre, and a tick in the next box on leaving, this was for fire regulations, also it let the stage manager know if any of the cast were late.

I did my best to describe the back stage area that would lead us up to the dressing rooms. There were many different levels, this was an old theatre and many additions had occurred over its lifetime, walking down two steps only to go up three steps a few feet further on, and then there was a slope.

It sounded complicated and judging by the look on Ann-Maries' face, she was daunted by the task that lay ahead, she had my sympathy. She was lucky in one respect that most people wouldn't give her a second look as she past each dressing room, each person busy sorting out themselves for the forthcoming show. However, she needed to appear competent at walking the corridors otherwise she might attract the unnecessary attention we wanted to avoid. It had occurred to me that the teacher would know their pupils. I had to pray they would be too busy to notice an odd girl walking about. I didn't voice my concern to Ann-Marie, and I hoped it wouldn't occur to her.

On the way I thought it would be an idea to stop at the library gardens, situated on Queen Street, and build what trust we could, between my instructions and Ann-Marie's interpretations, that way we'd have an idea of what to expect. Mojo sat on the grass looking on with concern to see his companion brave the first tentative steps with a different guide to the one she was used to, and trusted.

At first her footsteps were hesitant and very deliberate. She listened diligently to what was said, but interpretation is very different for different people and finding the middle ground we needed wasn't going to be easy. We didn't have a lot of time and this process whilst very important was eating away at what little we did have.

From where we were I could see the clock on the library building further down the road, an hour and half had past. Whilst we were not completely satisfied with the results, we both knew it would have to do. We left the park in silence and remained that way until we reached the theatre.

Tying Mojo's lead through some railings on the main high street she knelt down, held his head in her hands and tenderly, reassuringly spoke to him, stroking the top of his head. Mojo licked her face affectionately, but looked anxious. She stood up still resting her hand on his head. Ann-Marie had left the traditional harness at home to avoid any unnecessary attention it may bring to Mojo.

We headed off down Claret Street to the backstage door,

stopping just outside the pub next door. I told her to wait, whilst I went through the door to see how many people were milling around, and to estimate how many footsteps there were to the list that was hung on the notice board; where the pen was in relation to it; and the stairs. This was quite a revealing exercise. I'd always taken my eyesight for granted; now I was beginning to realise how difficult things could be.

I went back outside and passed all this information onto Ann-Marie as best I could. She looked worried and apprehensive. I spoke reassuringly to her, but little I could say would calm her nerves.

The cast had started to arrive. The scene was a familiar one, groups of two or three, walking down the street carrying bags and hangers with costumes on. I'd forgotten about the baggage. Ann-Marie would look out of place but there was nothing I could do now and if I didn't say anything she wouldn't know.

We waited outside the pub and I watched as a group of girls came walking down the street, carrying costumes and chatting excitedly about the pending performance. After they'd gone in we moved towards the stage door. Another girl came walking down the street, on her own, she was swamped with costumes, barely able to see where she was going. I guessed that she must have been one of the main performers, this would be the perfect one to follow in, and I alerted Ann-Marie that we would be moving off shortly.

"Ann-Marie. Turn left and start walking forward, there are no curbs it's a level surface, you have a lamppost on your right in about three paces, the gate is on the left, about five paces after that" she walked slowly and steadily "Now turn 90 degree to your left... bit more, move forward, there's a slight step; about six inches." Ann-Marie followed my instruction implicitly. "Another two paces and you are at the door, it is still slightly ajar, opens towards you, the handle is just above your waist height to the left of the door, bit further to the left and slightly higher. Grip and pull open to your right. As you go through there is another step of about three inches, then your feet will be on carpet."

This was working well so far, although I could feel the pressure. We both remained calm and focussed. The lead girl had gone through a few feet in front not taking any notice of Ann-Marie, who quickly as possible had followed behind.

"Right now move forward slightly, turn to your right. That's it. Lift your right hand up about shoulder height and touch the wall, it is about two feet away, if you move your hand slightly further right, up a bit, bit more. The pen is at your fingertips"

She fumbled at the pen finding the correct end to write with. The cast were all too busy dressing, chatting, and laughing to pay any attention to Ann-Marie. There was however, a security camera to fool.

"Now just next to that on the left you'll feel a piece of paper. That's the cast list."

She lifted her left hand feeling for the paper, she had great co-ordination putting pen to paper. "There is no need to mark the paper, just make it look real. With this task accomplished I guided Ann-Marie up the stairs, they were concrete, worn away over years by performers trampling up and down to get to the stage then back to their dressing rooms.

"Why was ticking myself in necessary? Why didn't I just walk straight up the stairs?" she whispered, sure that no one was within earshot.

"There's a security camera pointing at the back door. Although they don't know what every performer looks like, they might question one who doesn't sign in".

"Oh! But how abou…"

"Ssh there's someone coming. Look to your right and smile."

She did so. The girl coming towards her passed straight through me, I was concentrating too hard on the task at hand to give it any more thought than that, I was on Ann-Marie's right. The girl ignored Ann-Marie and carried on.

"Sorry about that" I said when the coast was clear. "I'll answer the rest of your questions in a second. We are at the top of the stairs, you need to turn left, then you have about, mmmm, 14 or so paces before you reach two steps down. The steps down are quite steep, I'd say about eight to ten inches" she moved swiftly only slowing to take the stairs "Go forward another 10 paces and the wall narrows from your right. Just go to your left a touch. That's it. It's wide again now, this corridor is quite long… aarghh".

I was somewhere dark. I could hear water dripping. Hear splashes as the footfalls landed in puddles. I was upright, and seemingly I knew where I was going marching at a brisk pace.

There was a damp, musty smell in the air. My hand was on one wall, using it as a guide, it felt smooth and cold.

I continued walking. The passageway seemed endless. The wall skewed at an angle guiding me in a slight deviation. To the right I could make out an illumination in the distance. Daylight. We entered a larger chamber. I could just make out the size in the dim light.

We carried on towards the light at the end of the chamber. A large wooden door lay between us and the outside world.

It was thick, covered in green slime which squelched under the pressure of my hands. I pushed to get the door open further, it didn't move easily and I put my shoulder to it, pushing harder, I could feel the softness of the slime as it oozed under my pressure. Gradually it moved, slowly inching its way open until there was enough room for me to squeeze through.

I put my hands up to my eyes to shade them from the glare of daylight, still too bright for my eyes after the darkness.

Once I'd emerged from behind a large thick bush I knew where I was. Ambleside Sunken Garden. First opened, in 1843, by the Mayor Bridgewater in memory of his wife who passed away while in child birth.

I heard a rip.

"Damn" I looked down at my trouser leg, there was a tear about seven inches in length. My clothes were dirty and I caught a waft as a breeze blew past. I needed a bath.

Back in the corridor Ann-Marie was crouching against the wall almost squatting on the floor.

"Are you ok?"

"Thank god you're back" she gradually stood up "I didn't know how long I was going to able stay here without someone asking me..."

"Sssh" I said putting my finger to my lips, even though she wouldn't have seen this.

"You alright dear?" said an harassed looking woman in her forties wearing black.

"Yes thank you I was... was just doing my shoelace up" said Ann-Marie thinking fast. The woman just nodded and carried on about her business.

"Technical run through in 15 minutes. We want everyone on stage in 10" the woman said sternly as she walked off. As she passed each dressing room she poked her head and repeated the message.

Ann-Marie whispered "I thought she might start asking me a few awkward questions".

"No. That's the beauty of show weeks, everyone so wrapped up in the show you can go unobserved. But before you do start getting some funny looks let's get going. You've got another three feet then the corridor turns 45 degrees to your right and up a slight but constant incline. When you get to the top you'll reach a door, which opens the same side as the stage door but this time away from you. When you go through turn immediately right and the door we need is just down some steps about 40-45 feet away."

We reached the door, up to this point we'd encountered no people problems except that once, even then due to

Ann-Marie's quick thinking we'd gotten away with that. We exited and were now closer to our goal. My goal.

Ann-Marie rested her hand on the wall, found the dado rail and used it as a guide down the stairs. When it changed elevation she knew she was at the bottom of the stairs. Finally at the door, we'd been lucky to get this far so easily, I had expected to encounter a few more minor snags, although I hadn't relayed this to Ann-Marie.

My heart sank as we stood at the door to the corridor where it all began.

"If you reach out your right hand, just about waist height you should feel a handle, this the door opens towards you and from the left. Have you got the torch?"

"Yes, it's here in my pocket" she got it out and switched it on "Is it on?"

"Yes. Thank you."

Opening the door we walked in. Now there was light I could see the corridor stretching out before us. I described to Ann-Marie where exactly to step. The corridor was full of various tut stacked up against the walls. I advised her to move carefully along, she did so, feeling her way with her feet, lifting them just enough to slide each one a few inches at a time as the ground was rough and uneven.

I asked her to direct the torch in certain directions, taking in every detail. There was no sign of any struggle. Nothing looked out of place, everything was still a mess, but the same mess it was when last I saw it with the light on. Then I felt a twinge of pain, I tried to fight it, knowing the possible danger I was leaving Ann-Marie in.

Once again I was outside, this time sitting down on a bench. Watching people go by.

I wasn't feeling any anger, or arousal of any sort, just calm. Something I hadn't felt up to now when in this view of things. This was almost restful.

It went dark. I'd closed my eyes. I felt myself recline deeper into the bench. Again the picture I'd seen the previous night flashed into my mind. A woman lay on the ground, blood everywhere, the little girl standing at the side of the street crying, commotion going on all around, the hustle and bustle of the people as they looked on.

I felt a tear start its journey down my cheek. At first slowly, then quickening as it followed round the outline of my face.

I brushed it aside, got up, and started walking towards Hotel Road.

Disorientated I found myself in the corridor. Ann-Marie was not visible at first. I noticed the torch laying on the floor. In my absence she'd taken a fall, I knelt down, she didn't seem to be moving. There was nothing I could do. I wanted to gently prod her shoulder to bring her round, check her pulse to make sure she was still alive, to touch her hand, anything. I could not do anything. I growled to myself, flexing every muscle in my body. What had I done?

I heard movement. It was Ann-Marie, she was alive.

"Are you ok?" I couldn't get the words out quick enough.

"Yes I think so" came the weary voice. Ann-Marie was rubbing her head with one hand, clutching her ankle with the other. As she moved the light rolled about on the floor. In the flicker of light I saw a hole, near the base of a wall near where Ann-Marie had fallen. As she fell she had knocked some of the chairs stacked against the opposite wall over and they'd dislodged a few of the bricks.

"Ann-Marie can you shine the torch over here please."

"Where's…"

"Sorry, straight ahead of you."

"No. Where's the torch?"

I turned to face her "Sorry, it's about two and a half feet from your right side" she reached out fumbling on the floor catching hold of the torch. "Can you shine it to your left. A bit more"

She did so. I heard her make a noise of pain. "Are you ok?"

"Yeah I think so. I'm just going to have a nice bruise on my leg."

"This hole goes right through the wall." I peered through and although I was in the way the light shone straight into the cavity, which was cylindrical in appearance and went downwards into a dark abyss.

"Can you bring it a little closer please" I asked rhetorically.

"What have you found?"

"There's a ladder in here, connected to the wall, it goes down."

Ann-Marie joined me at the entrance of the hole in the wall and shone the torch in and down the well-like shaft. It just kept going and going, I couldn't make out the bottom.

10

Ann-Marie directed the beam of light down the shaft, as I descended, the light was not strong enough to illuminate the shaft completely and when I reached the bottom I was once again shrouded in darkness.

I climbed back up into the light of the torch and called up to Ann-Marie.

"How do you feel about climbing down here with me? Can't see a damn thing. I think, there's a passage that goes somewhere but I need the light to explore it" I was half expecting Ann-Marie to balk at the idea.

"I'm not sure, what are the steps like?" Ann-Marie didn't let her disability stop her from doing anything. I admired her.

"It's basically a ladder, the rungs about 12 inches apart. It's quite a narrow shaft and goes down a long way. If you don't want to do it, that's fine, I understand".

"But you need the light, right?"

Pausing "Unfortunately, Yeah" I climbed up nearer Ann-Marie, the apprehension in her face was easy to see from the reflection of the torch.

She wouldn't be able to see where she was going, and after already falling down, she was not looking forward to this next stretch of our journey. Though prepared to make the effort and possibly put herself in danger, this was way beyond what I believed I deserved, she had more courage in her than I had. I doubted I would have done it if the situation were reversed.

Before she could enter the shaft Ann-Marie had to remove more of the loose bricks so that the hole was big enough for her to slip through whilst relying on my instructions to guide her onto the ladder. A situation which due to the nature of the conditions would prove difficult even to a sighted person, she put her trust in me, in turn I would not let her put a foot wrong. Why did she trust me so much? I hadn't exactly done anything to earn this trust.

After a few precarious moments, she was standing on the ladder, hands gripped tightly on one of the rungs, torch clasped in her mouth. I talked to her constantly, reassuring her of her footing, which I could just make out in the dim light. Efficiently she descended the ladder, easier now she could feel each rung under foot before she laid all her body weight on it, hands continually clasping the next rung before allowing her body to rest.

"Aaarrgh" I saw myself falling away from her.

I was strolling along the seafront. The wind was blowing in gusts that whipped up the rubbish, whirling it around in the air before allowing it fall to the ground, then the next gust would pick it up and hurl it up into the air again. There wasn't a soul about.

I didn't detect any anger or excitement, just a relaxed persona, strange, contemplative. This was unnerving in itself I'd only experienced the other side of this person, this murderer; now thrown into an emotional well, a coherence that made this person complete, and so real.

I think it this was easier for me to deal with when I didn't understand. Now I was confused, this was a real person, real feelings, and real emotions. Why the killings? Was I in the body of a deranged madman. No this seemed too controlled. My mind was wandering off at a tangent, like it sometimes did. Here I was viewing life through the eyes of a stranger, a murderer and I was starting to relax. In theatrical terms. I was starting to know my character.

I kept looking around, taking in the scenery, there was confusion yet understanding and recognition. Why? Was the thought that echoed round my head.

I was back in the passageway laying on the floor, Ann-Marie standing next to me, she'd made it down by herself, once again proving that she doesn't always need other people to help her.

"Did you see another murder?" she said calmly.

"We're at the bottom" I was still a little confused by what I'd felt "Can you shine the torch around?" My speech disjointed as I kept going over the emotions of my last encounter "Please... slowly... thanks. No I didn't see another murder. This time it was strange."

"Stranger than seeing murders committed?" I detected a note of sarcasm.

I looked around as Ann-Marie swung the torch in a slow arc. "No that's not what I mean. I was walking along the seafront, just observing, not looking. There was a sense of curiosity, I'm not sure why though. We're standing in a tunnel. Similar to the one I was in earlier, but only viewing" I paused "We can go left or right" as I looked both ways I tried to work out our location according to the streets above "If I've got my bearings correct, left we head towards Crescent Mews and if we go right, back towards Western Parade." Still going over my last vision in my head I looked one way then the other.

"I don't know where they..."

"What?" I snapped, then retracted it "Sorry didn't mean to..."

"It's alright."

She turned on the spot losing her footing, as she fell I instinctively went to grab her hand but mine passed straight through hers. Unlike before though, I felt a tingle, pins and needles.

"Ouch!" I said

In the dim light from the torch I could see her sitting on the ground...

"You ok?"

"What was that?" panic in Ann-Marie's voice.

"What was what?"

"I saw something briefly, bright light. It shone directly into my eyes. It hurt."

"I don't know. I tried to grab your hand as you fell, I felt a tingle in my hand and the light shone in my eyes. Then the torch fell to the ground."

"Where is it?" Ann-Marie started to get up brushing herself down "What did I see then?"

"I don't know. The torch is just a little to your left... bit more."

"I must be imagining things. It was weird though" shaking her head "Where are we going?"

"I don't know which way to go."

Ann-Marie continued to brush herself down "Er. The ground was wet. You're lucky you don't have to worry about that."

"Lucky. Hmm s'pose that's one way to look at it. I thought we'd head towards Crescent Mews, that's not far from the seafront, and that's where I last saw me, him, oh you know what I mean."

"Ok, don't go too fast, the ground's a bit slippery."

"I noticed. Ok" I saw her smile briefly.

Progress was slow along the tunnel, it was mainly dry, just the odd patch of water lay on the ground, shallow puddles. Onwards we went. I didn't really pay too much attention to the surroundings continually looking ahead to the lighted area where the torch shone. I could hear Ann-Marie behind shuffling, dragging her feet so she could feel the ground below them, one hand against the wall to steady herself, I glanced round occasionally to make sure she was alright. I tried to convince her that the ground was even but after her little fall she was understandably apprehensive as we moved along the tunnel.

The tunnel ahead turned right and the passage became narrow. We followed the path ahead, torch shining directly in front of us. I could make out the end and another ladder.

This ladder had been put here deliberately leaning against the wall, not fixed like the other one, it was old and covered in cobwebs; no use had been made of it in many years. The ladder stretched up about 25 feet to what looked like a tiny manhole cover.

"Wait here, I'm going up the ladder to see where we are." I climbed upwards. As I couldn't feel the rungs I wasn't sure of their condition and it was too dark to tell. At the top I pushed my head through the manhole cover. Through layers of mud and roots I went. This was a weird thing to experience. A totally new perspective on things I'd never given a second thought to, now, I could go through them and see them from a cross-sectional point of view. Daylight struck my eyes.

I was in someone's garden. I could see the back of a house, there was a patio area with garden chairs tilting, leaning against the table to keep the rain of the seats.

"Aargh" I was falling.

I was walking along a road. Cross Street. I knew this road, I often parked my car here when we had to bring costumes in to the theatre, they were always too heavy to carry, too many of them. One of the few times I brought the car it was free parking here, if you could find a space. Something I seemed to have the knack of.

I was looking round me, a dim recollection of a distant land.

I stopped at the junction of Cross Close and Cross Street. There had been some bombing in this area during the World War 2 and although the layout of streets and gardens had remained unchanged, the houses had been rebuilt. Turning on the spot, surveying the area, I tried to assess where I was.

A good few minutes passed. A couple of young lads passed by, they seemed to be staring at me. I didn't know why.

I turned down Cross Close heading towards the flats at the end of this dead end street. There was an alleyway to the left of the block and I headed for that.

It was a red tarmac alleyway with a light at each end, and those stupid bars the council put in the ground that look like small 'n's to prevent cyclists heading in and out at breakneck speed.

I stopped about halfway along. The fence on my right was six feet high with trellis along the top. The other side was brick, the bricks cemented together forming a sort of weave look; each brick just overlapping the ones underneath by barely an inch leaving a gap between the two ends of about six inches, plenty of room to get the toe of a shoe in without too much trouble. That's exactly what I did. Placing my hands on the top of the wall, putting my right foot into a hole, two feet from the ground, I eased myself up and over the wall. In a matter of seconds I was in the garden. I headed right towards the rear of the house, keeping a careful watch for prying eyes. I made my way to to, what looked like apple trees, standing 20 feet in height.

I slipped round behind them and started scraping at the dirt.

I was on my back, on the floor of the tunnel.

"Daniel. Daniel.....what's that noise?"

It took me a minute or so to focus and listen. Then I realised exactly what I was listening to.

Whispering, my voice full of urgency "We've got to get out of here quick, back the way we came."

"Why? What's going on?"

"That noise you can hear is me, him... it, trying to get in here" My heart sank deep within me. What had I'd done? I'd led Ann-Marie almost straight to him and now if we didn't get out of here quick I would be responsible for her death. I felt sick. Without thinking I reached for Ann-Marie's hand, which I could see in the dim light of the torch.

As I made contact I felt the twinge of pins and needles again. I retracted my hand immediately.

"I just saw myself" Ann-Marie said shocked.

"What?"

"I just saw myself. I wasn't dreaming. Just then. I saw me" she said in awe of herself.

"Ann-Marie there is no time We have got to get out here now, I can't protect you. You know that."

"Daniel I know, but I saw myself. How?"

"I don't know. Can we get moving before it's too late?"

This was insane. I was in a dark tunnel with a blind girl that I couldn't help and any minute now she would have a murderer breathing down her neck and all I would be able to do would be to watch.

Ann-Marie slowly made her way along the tunnel following my guiding dialogue, both hands on the wall, one over the other continually feeling the direction of the wall moving as fast as she dared. This was frustrating. A snails pace compared to what I wanted to be doing. I couldn't speed her up anymore, if she fell it wouldn't expedite our progress, and she could hurt herself in the process. I willed her on silently.

Behind I caught the sound of a metal clang.

"Oh no. He's in... move" I tried to sound calm, knowing that I didn't.

In the flickering of the torchlight I noticed a hole in the wall ahead on our left, I didn't know where it led, it didn't matter, just somewhere to hide, I hoped. It wasn't a proper entrance just where the wall had been smashed. There was a gap big enough for a person to get through crouching. It would have to do.

With no time to get back to the theatre we took our chances. I guided Ann-Marie to the opening and through it as quietly as I could to avoid letting the person that would soon be passing this way know we were in here.

The chamber we entered wasn't massive, a dug out, a primitive cave-like structure of earth and rock. There was a place we could hide, behind a mound of fallen earth and stones; without being seen, unless the chamber was searched thoroughly, which I prayed it wouldn't be. Ann-Marie settled in the deep chasm. I rested my hand on Ann-Marie's, wanting to reassure her it was going to be alright. She flicked off the torch and we were thrown into darkness.

We sat in the darkness. In silence, every sound seemed louder and more pronounced; her breathing, slightest movement of her feet or hands, the rustle of her coat; we waited. I feared for Ann-Marie's safety and was regretting involving her in my stupid idea to come down here. It was too late now though.

Foot steps approached the entrance to our hiding place. There was a light haphazardly glancing along the tunnel walls; it had no purpose. Then the source of the light became level with our hiding place.

I could almost feel Ann-Marie trembling with fright, sense her fears, her dread. I was helpless here, yet I was still cowering with her in hiding as if it was serving some purpose.

The light passed without actually entering our hideout. Relief filled my thoughts. We still sat there without moving for what seemed eternity.

"I saw the light, Daniel" Ann-Marie whispered.

"You what!"

"I saw the light as the man passed, I saw him, well the shape."

"How? You're blind."

"I know, but I did" I could hear the excitement building in her voice.

I had been staring dead ahead of me all this time still resting my hand on Ann-Marie's hand, I turned to face her.

11

"But that's not possible...How?" I didn't understand.

"I don't know either."

I felt a tingling in my fingers and retracted my hand at speed, automatically. All the time danger had loomed I'd been too worried to notice the strange sensation.

"Hold on" I had an idea, I wasn't absolutely sure what I was hoping for, but it was idea "Now turn the light on."

She fumbled around on the floor, her hands searching out the torch. Once in her grasp she switched it on.

"Can you see now?" I asked.

"No... but I could" she said puzzled.

"Now can you see?" I'd taken hold of Ann-Marie's hand.

"That's it" She said loudly.

"SSHH. He could still be in the vicinity" we sat still and quietly listened; the coast was clear.

"Sorry. Grab my hand" again I held her hand.

"That's it" she said trying to contain her excitement in a controlled whisper "... When you touch my hand I can see, I don't know how or why. But I can see through your eyes. Wow. This is awesome" she sat trying to comprehend what was going on "This has never happened before physical interaction! I've got to tell Aunt Rose."

"This is weird. I didn't think things could get any weirder" I stood up letting go of her hand, not sure what to do next, lost, baffled.

"Yes" I could feel the smile she was beaming from where I was. "This is so strange I'd got used to not having my sight, I'd almost forgotten what I miss."

I wasn't sure what to say in answer, so I chose to ignore it "Come on we'd better get going, the coast should be clear by now". My way of dealing with things is ignore them and carry on as though nothing had happened.

We made our way back to the main tunnel again.

"Daniel."

"What?"

"It'd probably be easier if you held my hand" she said tentatively. There was a brief awkward pause whilst I evaluated my own thoughts, before conceding.

I don't know why I was reluctant. Maybe everything was starting to get to me, it had all been so strange and kept getting worse. She could see everything I could see now, this made the journey back easier, and except for the tingling in my hand, which I believed I would eventually shut out, I couldn't understand my own hesitation.

She only tripped a couple of times. Seeing things from a different perspective, to her left, made her judgement a bit skewed in relation to her body. She adjusted well.

We arrived at the bottom of the ladder "Your going to have to be blind again for this."

"Yes. I know" she said uneasily "I'm a little scared of when I get to the top."

"You put your foot on the bottom rung now, your hand on the side of the ladder, I'll go up first and when you get to the top I'll hold your hand. That way you will be able to see what you're doing first hand; second hand; you know what I mean!"

"Ok" I could see her smile in the dim light of the torch.

Ann-Marie had no problem ascending to the top and once there we did as planned, except for the initial step of confidence, it worked well.

Our way out of the theatre, I hoped, wouldn't be a problem either. I had no idea how long we'd been down in the tunnel, so hoped that the theatre was still open.

I went outside the door we entered and checked that the coast was clear.

I couldn't hear any noise. I went down and looked in the foyer this would be the quickest exit, there was no one around. The monitor was on, the show was in full flow.

I went back upstairs and got Ann-Marie. This was a lot easier now with me holding her hand. She was getting used to seeing things from this strange skewed view, and we were no longer in the dark tunnels. As we were about to exit through the front doors I heard a familiar voice.

"Oi! Where did you come from?"

I'd forgotten about Mark, he often did front of house. He must have been in the back of the ticket kiosk, where I couldn't see him.

Before I had time to think what to do Ann-Marie was one step ahead of me.

"I was just looking for the toilets, I'm sorry I just really needed to go, I just dashed in, no one was here so... I went looking for them. Found them upstairs. Hope you don't mind?!"

He looked at her, sizing up her story "Ok" he didn't say anything else, his eyes followed her out the door.

Mark was a nice guy, I got on well with him.

Night had drawn in outside making it apparent how long we'd actually been down in the tunnels.

"Mojo" Ann-Marie said with great urgency and walked briskly forward, I couldn't keep hold of her hand. She was fine for the first few steps, then grazed the side of a wall. "Sorry I forget, but I've got to get to Mojo, he'll be worried."

I thought that was more the other way round. I could understand her concern for her four-legged pal.

When she came into view he sat up, tail wagging with delight. Ann-Marie knelt down put her face to his and nuzzled him, untying his lead. We walked back towards her house. She asked to hold my hand again, having never lived in the area when she could see she didn't know what the place looked like. On the way asking me to look at certain things, a child with an inquisitive nature sprang to my mind. She hadn't realised that she was talking quite loudly and people were looking on, probably thinking she was babbling on, talking to the dog.

I was in a tunnel, just barely lit by the torch I was holding, the battery fading fast. It was the like the tunnel I'd been in before, maybe the same one it was difficult to tell in the gloom, no distinct markings, or characteristics.

I stopped, turned to my right and felt the wall with my fingertips, I was looking for something. I had a feeling of recognition. Brushing away the dirt residue from the wall, feeling for something, I felt the smoothness of the brickwork, the coldness of the hard stone, I could have been there for real. I felt a round metal loop. Scraping the dirt away with my fingertips I fumbled around trying to lift it up the loop, it was stiff but moved with a little effort. I pushed my index finger through the loop and pulled. Nothing happened. I tried again, still nothing.

Scraping away more of the dirt from the wall I revealed a frame of some description. A door? Although it seemed too small for a door, I cleared an area about three feet across. Placing the torch awkwardly between my legs I tried again to pull it, it still wouldn't budge. Again, and again, I was feeling the metal loop burn its indentation into my finger. It wasn't big enough to put more than one finger in.

Looking around on the ground for anything that could be used as a lever, nothing. Again I tried. No use.

"Damn it" the voice reverberated round the walls fading in the distance.

I tried kicking it the door, grabbing the loop, pulling, and again kicking and pulling trying to free it. I kept repeating these procedures until, finally it moved, then slowly opened.

Shining the torch inside I could make out a knife, and a big canvas bag, I reached in and grabbed them, the torch precariously perched between my legs. As I moved them I noticed a picture hidden behind, I couldn't see it clearly, but it was a large wooden frame, the glass cracked and covered in thick black dust.

I lowered the bag onto the ground, resting the torch next to it, and untied the knot of the rope that was holding it closed. I reached in.

"...you ok? Hello" came an unfamiliar voice.

Back in the main shopping street I still had Ann-Marie's hand in mine. I turned to her, the look on her face gave away that she knew something.

"Sorry. What? Yes" Ann-Marie replied uncertainly "Yes. Thank you..." she continued more politely.

Ann-Marie moved away from the figure, an older lady dressed in a rain coat, head wrapped in a scarf.

"I saw Daniel, I saw" she whispered.

I was silent in response.

"I saw what you saw."

Marching on, her pace quickened, excited and intrigued by what she'd seen, finally she knew exactly what I meant by the visions.

"Stop looking at me" she said.

I turned away not realising I had been looking at her, her expression was one of puzzlement, intrigue, and excitement at what she'd seen.

Before long we reached her house. Her mother quizzing her about where she'd been as soon as we had entered and closed the front door, Ann-Marie lied convincingly saying she'd gone to the park and lost track of time. This also helped explain why her clothes were quite dirty, she said she'd fallen over. Her mother re-heated her tea prepared hours earlier while she went upstairs and got changed and cleaned up. She ate quickly and we went back upstairs to her room putting on some music to cover the conversation.

"I never knew those tunnels existed, they must have been

sealed up for years."

"I've never been so scared in my life, I thought he'd see us, it's alright for you he can't see you, but me." Ann-Marie sat on her bed, stroking Mojo, trying to make amends for leaving him for so long, she asked me to sit next to her and touch her hand again, this time so she could see Mojo, as she didn't know what he looked like.

"The one thing that's been bugging me is I can't see who I am, when I…. you know, go off into these dreams, nightmares, visions. Oh I don't know. Whatever you want to call them."

"I couldn't see what he looked like either."

The conversation stopped as we both fell deep in thought. With this new discovery came more possibilities of how we could move forward, but, what was the next step? There were so many questions bombarding their way round my head that I thought I might explode. What was the point of the tunnels? Where did they all go? How did he know they existed? Why had the entrance in the theatre been sealed up?

"I think we need to see Aunt Rose again tomorrow, she should be able to help us, she might be able to explain a little more about these visions. And now I can see them too. Maybe that will help. Maybe she'll be able to see them as well if you hold her hand." I could hear tenuous points of excitement in her voice, this was a big adventure, I had no idea what had occupied her time before I'd come along, and judging by her response, not a lot. Maybe I was just being cynical. I was beginning to appreciate her help.

"So we'll go round tomorrow?"

"Yes, after breakfast when mother's gone to work we can head round to her house. It's not far".

Ann-Marie had a bath and got ready for bed. She was quite tired after the experiences of the day. I settled on the wicker chair and replayed the day's events in my head, piecing together what I could.

The hours past slowly, before I felt what was becoming a familiar pain, ever increasing in intensity.

I was running, I could feel my chest heaving with the pressure of breathing, my legs were feeling like jelly, I was on the main road heading away from the main high street. I ran past the jewellers and ducked into the alley to my left. I stuck my head out and glanced back the way I had come, I couldn't see anyone else running, everything seemed normal.

Back in the alley ducking just a little bit further in to conceal myself from the light of the street lamps. I bent over resting my hands on my knees. Sweat was dripping from my face. I'd run a fair way. From what though? Police? Someone else?

It was too dark to make out any detail on the clothing. I was wearing jeans and what looked like a leather jacket judging by the sleeves.

After a few minutes I proceeded deeper into the alley. The alley ran to Bernice Street, parallel to the main road, and was concreted, clear from shrubs and bushes. I reached the exit. I stopped and looked out to see if anyone was about.

The corner shop to the right of the exit and opposite was open. I heard the sound of a milk-float to my left and I sharply turned my head. It was early morning. The shopkeeper put out the 'A' frame board that had the local newspaper heading on it:

'Another victim – Residents warned to stay vigilant'

Underneath there was a photo-fit of a man but it was too small to see at this distance. I felt myself smile and laugh. Casually I walked from the alley.

Back in the bedroom all was still, just like when you wake from a nightmare and find that it was just that. I looked at the clock it was only 4am.

I began to think long and hard about all the occurrences and what it was I needed to know.

It started in the theatre. I was seeing visions through the eyes of a murderer. The underground tunnels, like rat runs. The murderer uses them, Why? How does he know about them? They didn't seem to have been used in years, the dream I saw the other night. So much information. So many pieces that were part of this puzzle. How did they fit together? What was the key?

I needed answers and soon. What was it that Aunt Rose told me, 'That I was growing weaker, soon I would fade away and become this person, losing my own identity.'

I was disturbed by the sound of Ann-Marie stirring from her sleep and before she had time to gather her wits I was entertaining her with my thoughts, trying to explain what I was thinking. It was as if by telling her it would organise them into some sort of proper order, a starting point.

She yawned stretching her arms. Mojo looking up from his position on the floor.

"I've had a thought we ought to check out the library" she said halfway through her yawn.

"The library?"

"Yes. They've got a reference point, we can look up the history of Southend and the Theatre. Maybe discover where all those tunnels lead and who made them. Might be a connection somewhere. What was that dream you saw?"

"A woman lying on the ground, loads of people, there was a girl crying."

"Maybe it's not a dream. I told Aunt Rose about it and she said that maybe it's a reflection from the persons memory."

"Yeah. But it doesn't tie up, the horse carriage, it was Southend alright, but some distant past Southend. I recognised Ridley's hardware store, it was new, didn't look like it does today."

"Mmmm... I don't know then... If we go to the library though we can start by looking at the town maps."

"How? You can't see!"

"If you hold my hand I can see everything I need to."

12

After breakfast and leaving Mojo at home this time, we made our way to the library. Mojo fussed and whined a little, I could see the guilt on Ann-Marie's face as she closed the door behind us; he looked as if he was being punished. He'd always been there for her. We walked in silence initially not knowing what to say, me holding her hand so that she could see. This was starting to become more natural, arms swinging in time with each other, keeping the connection.

"When we get into the library I'll direct you as I did in the theatre. Can't remember exactly what it's like myself as I haven't been there for a few years. I think I have a rough idea though."

Ann-Marie nodded "Ok. I'll be alright. Just remember if it's crowded I might lose your grip on my hand if I get knocked by someone."

"It should be fine. There shouldn't be too many peop..."

A blur of images. A woman's face, a young face, long mousy coloured hair, soft features and bright eyes full of life. She was talking but I couldn't hear the words. She was speaking in a loving way, full of affection, her face so sweet. She leaned in to kiss me.

I heard a phone ringing. The woman's face faded. It was dark. The phone rang again.

I was in the high street, a girl crying, a woman comforting her, people running around, a commotion. I heard voices. The world is spinning.

I heard the phone ringing. I was back in my lounge, lying on the settee. My hand knocked over a glass but luckily it was empty.

Back on the street. We were standing still.

"What did all that mean? I'm confused."

"I don't know. I'm as confused as you."

"What happens if that occurs whilst we're inside?" Ann-Marie asked.

I didn't know what to say. Depending where it happened, on the stairs, in a crowd of people, it could prove to be dangerous for her. Not life threatening, just hazardous to her health. She wouldn't have Mojo as back up and we were in an unfamiliar place. I gripped her hand tighter although it made no impact, she didn't notice. "I really don't know" I said barely audible. In silence we walked on, until we reached the library. It was closed. It didn't open for another ten minutes.

There were some benches just outside, surrounding a small green area where during the summer I'd seen people sitting and reading. Ann-Marie sat down.

"If you're alright here I'll go in and have a quick look around to get some idea of where to go once inside."

"Ok."

"Sorry dear?" said the lady we hadn't noticed walking behind the bench.

"Oh, nothing I was just talking to myself."

The lady smiled and walked on by.

I went into the library leaving Ann-Marie waiting outside. It was a dry day, overcast, but dry. She had wrapped up warm so I knew she would be ok for a short time.

Wandering through the front doors, I was beginning to enjoy this new found freedom, able to view the world without being seen, adding a whole new perspective to my meagre existence. I could listen in on conversations without fear of being noticed; the librarians discussing last nights TV, whilst busying themselves for the days intellectual crowd to pass through the doors.

Mentally I ran through all the possible problem areas,

looking for solutions before problems arose.

The staircase spiralled up the centre of the building, each floor open plan like a department store. The area we needed was on the third floor tucked away in a corner and consisting of a computer on a desk, shelves stacked with reference material of the local area, books, maps, magazines, anything and everything you could think of.

There was a coffee bar situated on the first floor.

I heard the doors below being unlocked and the steps of the first few people as they entered this glass walled building that was considered modern, 25 years ago.

Ann-Marie still sat outside her arms folded across her chest, her breath forming cloud-like shapes as she exhaled. As I exited the building through the throng of people entering it I began to feel uneasy. We were in a public place, people everywhere. We had to pass as one and I knew Ann-Marie was not feeling confident about that.

I took Ann-Marie's hand and we headed for the doors. As always, when you least need it there was an explosion of people hustling towards the entrance from nowhere, like magic. Holding her hand proved difficult as she was jolted by people, students eager to find the reference books they needed, or to get to the CD section so they could hire the latest cd's, OAPs with carrier bags of books they'd just read.

As I lost my grip on Ann-Marie's hand she found herself blind again, this time in unfamiliar territory and without her best friend. I watched as she stumbled forward trying to appear confident. I tried in vane to grab her hand but the attempts were lost in the array of people and coats.

"Watch it!" said one of the younger male figures who was wearing headphones.

"Sor..." Ann-Marie tried to say but was pushed in another direction. The guy just looked at her and then carried on walking.

"You alright love" said an older gentleman as he grabbed her to prevent her losing her balance.

"Yes" she stammered "Thank you."

"It can be mayhem in here first thing in the morning."

"Yes, I can see that. Thank you" with that the gentleman nodded and walked away.

The rush ceased and she stood just past the entrance, gathering her senses not sure where to look, trying to appear relaxed. She unbuttoned her coat after getting quite warm in the commotion of it all. I rushed to take her hand and take her to a quiet spot by the day's newspapers.

"Are you ok?" I asked.

In a low whisper "I'm fine now. It's weird being without Mojo. I'm lost."

"I'm sorry. I'm sorry I got you involved."

If I could have walked out I would have done, but I couldn't leave her there. The silence between us was deafening.

"It's alright, I wanted to help, I'm just scared."

"I don't know what's it's like for you, I just know that I want my life back, I want to see my parents again and have them see me" Both stood there awkwardly.

"Come on let's go, just stay close and hold my hand."

We walked to the staircase and made our way up to the third floor. Sometimes Ann-Marie lost her balance as she tried to get used to viewing things from outside her own body.

The section we needed was kept in good order as expected and contained maps and books upon books plotting the history of the town, true stories of the buildings, an Aladdin's cave of information. Where to start? was the question that came to my mind.

"What shall we look for first" no one was in this section so Ann-Marie could talk more freely.

"I don't know… How about the theatre? That's where it started lets see what there is on that."

We scanned through the book titles, so many that were unspecific, then one caught my eye 'Theatre through the years in Southend-On-Sea' By Harvey Williamson.

Ann-Marie picked the book from the shelf and let fall open in her hands. Because of our perspective I moved behind Ann-Marie resting my head on her right shoulder, still keeping my hand on hers. Her point of view was now as direct as it could be. This made it easier for her to turn the pages and know what I was looking at. This book mainly focussed on the performances that had taken place within the theatres in the town, there had been five theatres in the local area at one point in history, The Academy being the largest. We browsed further.

Book after book. Taking out. Replacing.

Finally! 'How Southend Theatre came to life' By Alexander Partridge, published in 1963, seemed to hold the information we were looking for.

Sitting down at the table to our left we perused the pages of this volume. The theatre was owned and built by the Hughes family, they owned half a dozen shops in the town, scattered about in various locations.

During the first World War they connected all these premises with secret tunnels enabling them to get from one shop to another without being seen. Mr Hughes was paranoid about protecting his family and during the war, which he was sure would last for decades, he wanted to be sure that they could get together and escape using any one of the many external exits. It took years to complete the passages and by the time they were finished the war had been over for four years. They still proved useful as it made it possible to collect all the takings from the shops and deposit them in the safe at the theatre. The access point to the theatre was via the ladder in the corridor.

Not many people outside the family knew about these

passages, only the occasional member of staff.

We scanned through various pictures, past pages and pages of irrelevant dialogue, although in normal circumstances these would have been of interest. About three quarters of the way through the book there was a chapter about the mystery of the remains found in a chamber near the bottom of the ladder.

In 1957 when the theatre was to become a dance hall, the basement was being turned into a storage area with cloakroom facilities, according to the plans at the time there was another room hidden behind what is now the costume warehouse. When the builders knocked through the joining wall they discovered the skeletal remains of someone. Before the Hughes family sold the theatre in 1927 they had blocked up the entrance to the ladder unaware that they were burying the remains of one of their ex-employees, Mr Highway. Mr Highway had worked for the Hughes family for more than 12 years, served them, dedicated and content in his job. The Hughes family were a good family to work for, once they accepted you and you became part of their life. Mr Henry Highway got married to a nice young daughter of another wealthy businessman in the area, Mr Lansdowne. Unfortunately she was killed in an accident six months after they were married.

The loss of his wife affected Henry Highway greatly, he began to keep antisocial hours, drank too much, was rude to customers and staff. One day he struck the youngest son of Mr Hughes, Albert, who was learning the business. Mr Hughes had to confront Henry. This incident was just one of many contributing to the fact that Mr Hughes was thinking of selling up and moving out into the country, ill health was not helping, he already had an offer for his businesses, and this was the straw that broke the camels back.

Before he sold the business's he bricked up all the access ways in each shop, sealing the fate of the body, leaving it to decay over the next few years. No one would know any different.

Mr Hughes did file a missing person report on Henry Highway; deep down he had thought of Henry as a son which was why he took it so personally when Albert was struck, he didn't like fighting even less when it was his own family, no one ever saw him again.

Stories started to spread amongst the gossip mongers in the town that he got caught up in the occult, and the devil took him. There was a spate of murders around the same time which just fuelled the fire, especially as they stopped about the same time he disappeared.

"Maybe there's some newspaper stories, in the local papers of the time" I was sure this was the person we were looking for but was also intrigued. This story had fired my imagination.

We switched on the computer on the table and waited for it to fire up. In this modern time everything had been down loaded onto a central hard-drive for ease of access and storage.

We designated all the information we were looking for and let the computer do its bit.

I was in a building, derelict from the glimpses I was catching between blows. I was stabbing a body with such venom. I could feel the tip of the blade make contact with the floor. Blood was spewing everywhere. The victims struggles subsided. Still I carried on. I was angry, hateful, vengeful. I could feel it, I didn't know why.

I stopped. Tears streaming from my eyes, blood on my hands, clothes, pools extricating their way across the floor from the body that now lay lifeless in my hands. The knife fell to the ground, the metal blade striking the floor sending echoes around this desolate place. I threw my head into my hands and cried...

Back in the library there was a few people gathered around, talking to Ann-Marie.

'Are you ok?' 'You were screaming?' 'Can we help?'

Ann-Marie looked up at everyone. A rabbit caught in the

headlights.

"I'm... sorry... yeah... fine... I... just... mmmm".

"Excuse me, do you know where I might find 'Churches in Southend-on-Sea' By Cannon Thetford?" A middle aged woman said.

The focus of the librarian changed to address the question being asked.

"I need to get out of here" Ann-Marie whispered quietly, urgently. Standing up abruptly, I could see tears forming in her eyes.

"Ok" I said, she'd already helped more than was reasonable. I glanced at the screen, various articles were shown on the computer, I read on, forgetting about Ann-Marie briefly. There was a missing persons article about Henry Highway, also on the same page was a report on recent murders which seem to have come to an abrupt end, the only connection is that all the victims were young girls, stabbed repeatedly, these brutal crimes started for no reason and ended just the same. No person has ever been charged with these murders.

Out of the corner of my eye I saw a figure stumble to my right, it was Ann-Marie, she wanted to leave, yet I wanted to stay and read on.

13

I wanted to read more of the newspaper articles, but Ann-Marie needed to leave, forced to go with her so she could get out without hurting herself or giving it away that she was blind, I felt cheated although she had my sympathy as well. I held her hand as best I could. She was agitated and shaking like a leaf. We struggled but made it outside, walking to the bench so that she could sit down.

She looked pale, ill, obviously the horror she had witnessed was too much for her.

I'd begun to shut the horrors out, preferring to believe I was just watching a video nasty of real life proportions, this eased my mind. Ann-Marie had not seen them from the beginning and had not had time to adjust even slightly to some of the strange sights, I wished she hadn't seen that. Only her bad luck made her live through it.

Slowly the colour came back to her face and the tears dried.

"Is that what you always see?" the words struggled to form the sentence still disturbed by the vision.

"No. I've told you what I've seen. I may have left out a few minor details. I didn't necessarily think you needed to know. That's only the second time I've witnessed something so… so horrific."

"I feel sick" she bent over resting her elbows on her knees, forehead in her hands breathing heavily, vaporous clouds of warming air expelling themselves from within.

"We'd better get you ho…"

I was still in the derelict building, tears still streamed from my eyes. I hated myself for what I was doing, but felt compelled to do it, an insane justice going on in my head. It was clear to me and only me. I could see the sense in what I was doing although I didn't know why I was doing it.

I moved to a half boarded upstairs window and stared back at the macabre scene in front of me. The body motionless, bloodied. I wanted to go over and take a closer look. But I couldn't move my legs, they felt stone cemented in place.

All the times before when I'd been present, the feelings and emotions I felt were of strength and power. Now I felt the weakness, even confusion.

Slowly I walked to the body. I looked at it. Satisfaction came flooding back to me, swiftly. Followed by a sense of a duty achieved, somehow I'd justified my actions within. I dragged some loose broken pieces of wood and other dirty materials over to the body, doing my best to cover my work.

Once done I headed to the stairwell, and descended. I turned right at the bottom and headed across the large open room towards a doorway where I pulled back a piece of wood, and viewed the overgrown alley outside. I looked both ways, then down at my clothes. Thick red blood stained them. I didn't know what I was going to do. I couldn't exactly walk out like this, I'd draw attention to myself. I took of my shirt and threw it to the floor. I picked up a jacket that was laying on the ground, brushed it down and put it on, it was torn but it would do, it looked familiar. I picked handfuls of dust and rubbed them into my jeans to disguise the blood as best I could.

I left the building cautiously, heading deeper into the alley.

I was standing by the bench, Ann-Marie was gone. I looked around panicked and scared. She didn't have Mojo with her. I turned round on the spot, scouring every direction, expecting to catch a glimpse of her. 'Nothing. Damn' I said to myself.

I started to run in the direction of her house, it was the only possibility I could think of in that instant. I ran and ran. There was no where else she could possibly be.

At her house I ran straight through the front door. Mojo was laying on the floor, waiting patiently. He lifted his head, he knew I was there. From this I knew Ann-Marie was not there. I turned about and left.

At the front gate I stopped, looking left, then right. I didn't know where to go. I didn't know her that well. She could be anywhere, and with anyone, my pessimistic mind kicking in.

All sorts of thoughts pulsed through my head, worse case scenarios. There had to be a good explanation. Aunt Rose would probably be able to help, but I didn't know where she lived.

Helpless I went back inside and up to Ann-Marie's room. Mojo followed me, watching as I looked for clues as to where she would go, nothing, she was blind and on the street without her companion, she wouldn't be able to find her way about. Not on her own.

"Where is she Mojo?" I asked rhetorically.

Mojo just stared at me. Like Ann-Marie, he could always tell where I was.

I paced the room, wishing she would walk through the door. I needed her to.

There she was. I was watching her. She was with Aunt Rose. Aunt Rose must have found her outside the library.

What was I doing? I was spying on her. Not directly just generally, people watching from a secluded place, crouching, hidden behind some bushes viewing the scene waiting for the next victim, the next opportunity. I recognised the area, Roth Road. I had to be in the cemetery, the only place down that road that had any sort of bushes. There was a school about 100 yards along the road. The road seemed overcome by a relaxed silence, lesson time. I was watching Ann-Marie and Aunt Rose intently.

They walked slowly, reaching Wall Road and turning into it. I looked up and down the road from where I was situated, all was clear. Dread filled my thoughts as I moved out of the bushes and started to

cross the road. I reached the closed down bakers on the corner of the
street and observed the two figures walking in the distance.

A sudden colossus of noise behind me, school was out for lunch.

I sprinted out of Ann-Marie's bedroom, through the open
door and down the stairs. I felt fear, fear for her, Ann-Marie's
life and Aunt Rose's. Now I knew where they were I made
good progress no longer limited by my mortal constraints
of fitness.

Within minutes I was there viewing the same scene I had
witnessed only minutes before, school children scattered along
the road. I stopped and watched, looking, hunting, for what I
wasn't exactly sure.

I wanted to make sure all the kids got home safely, an impossible task I knew, I couldn't protect them all, but that didn't
matter. I was looking for him, without the knowledge of what
he looked like, so I was searching out any unusual characters
in the hope of catching a glimpse of Henry, anyone acting
strangely. I hoped he would stand out within this crowd.

I was wrong. The parents littered amongst the young
ones all dressed so differently, anyone of them could be
Henry. A scream. I spun round on the spot. Just a group of kids
mucking about. Another scream! Again just kids messing about.
My ears were acting like highly sensitive radars. I had to find
Ann-Marie.

I headed off down the street that I'd seen them enter, picking
up speed, running faster and faster. At the end of this street I
had to make a decision which way to go Crane Avenue to my
left, or Crane Close, a dead end to my right. I couldn't see them
in either direction I headed left, again at full speed, the road
bent to the right heading into Squire Street. When I got to this
'T'junction I still couldn't see them. I called out, Ann-Marie
would hear; me no response. I turned right into Squire Street
still calling hoping Ann-Marie would hear me.

Walking. Calling. Finally a familiar voice behind me.

"Daniel?"

I turned and saw Aunt Rose, she wasn't looking in my direction she didn't seem to pick up my aura the way Ann-Marie did. I walked towards her.

"Aunt Rose."

"Daniel, Ann-Marie is inside" I turned and faced the open door. There was Ann-Marie standing one hand against the door frame looking on.

"I thought I lost you. I came back but you weren't there, I went to your house. I didn't know where else to go. I had another vision. I saw you. I was watching you and Aunt Rose. I thought. I thought…"

"It's ok Daniel. We're ok. You went again, I didn't have your hand I couldn't see, I couldn't even sense you near me, you had gone completely, I was scared. Then I heard Aunt Rose's voice and…" she stopped suddenly, I turned, there was a mother with her two children walking past, she stared in Ann-Marie's direction as she went by.

We went inside, I wanted to comfort Ann-Marie for everything I'd put her through, I couldn't. We sat down in Aunt Rose's living room whilst she went and made a pot of tea. It was a darkly decorated place, very oldie-worldy type. Flock wallpaper, dark red heavily patterned carpet, the woodwork, once white now was a dark cream colour. The settee had lace work on the arms, lightly decorating the corduroy fabric. The large coffee table was hidden amongst a collection books and various trinkets including a crystal ball which sat in its stand on purple velvet swash.

Aunt Rose came back with a tray in her hands, on it was two cups, a tea pot with tea cozy on, and a plateful full of biscuits. I felt like one even though I had no need for food. She poured out the tea and set a cup down in front of Ann-Marie, taking the other for herself.

"Daniel dear, Ann-Marie tells me she has seen what you see.

When you touch hands she can see through your eyes. As you see it! I have never known a connection quite that strong. Now take my hands."

I laid my hands in Aunt Rose's as I had done before. She fell into a trance like state again. I didn't understand what she was hoping to achieve.

Then I felt myself being tugged. My whole body jerked forward.

"Dani..."

I was holding my hand, I was hurting. There was blood coming from a wound on my right hand. I was kneeling on the ground the pain from the wound gripping me like a shock of electricity. I pulled away my other hand and viewed the damage. It was a bite mark, from what I couldn't tell but it hurt like hell. Deep inside I was almost glad.

I was facing Aunt Rose again.

"My hand it hurts".

"What do you mean it hurts?" asked Ann-Marie.

"My hand. It stings. I've been bitten, I think" I looked down at my hand, nothing, no marks.

Aunt Rose was still in her trance.

"Your aura doesn't feel as strong as it did Daniel" Ann-Marie said concerned.

"Ah" Aunt Rose screamed and fell back onto the settee, there she lay still. This time I wasn't as concerned as before knowing this was normal.

"What do you mean my aura isn't as strong?"

"When I first felt your presence, it was like nothing I'd ever felt before, powerful, almost overwhelming. Now you feel almost like a spirit that I would normally experience. I can't really explain it. You seem weaker."

"But nothing's changed Ann-Marie..." I stopped mid sentence. Things had changed, of course. It had been a slow progression but now I was feeling more, hearing more. The first vision I had was silent. The dream. The pain in my hand, it had all become more and more real, every vision taking me one step closer. One step closer to what though?

"What is it Daniel? What you thinking?"

"I was just thinking how things have changed, the visions that is. They're becoming more real. Like the pain in my hand, I can still feel it now, yet it was just a vision. Why?"

Aunt Rose started to come round.

"Oh deary me."

"What is it Aunt Rose?"

"It's worse dear. More than I first thought."

"What is it Aunt Rose?" asked Ann-Marie impatiently.

I sat there silent, waiting for bad news. Not that I believed it could get any worse. I was dead anyway, I believed that now. I felt it better to believe that.

Aunt Rose picked up her tea her hand shaking the cup, taking a sip, before replacing the cup on its saucer.

"What is it?" urgency filling my voice.

"I'm afraid it is as I said before, and I have confirmed this with my friend Heather who is also a white witch. Not only are you connected to this person, you are becoming this person, eventually you will be no longer."

"What becoming Henry Highway?" Ann-Marie voiced with alarm.

"Yes dear, unfortunately Daniel is losing the battle. I could feel the strength of this other person, he is powerful, he wasn't always evil as he appears now."

"What do you mean 'NOW'?"

"I could feel that he wasn't always like this, there was a time when he was good, and a caring person. Daniel, according to Froxidian beliefs you only have eight days before you'll fade out completely, lost to the world. He would have won."

"I don't understand Aunt Rose who were the Froxidians?"

"According to Heather they were a cult quite strong in the

local area around the 19th Century, fairly harmless in themselves, no one could ever prove otherwise, a lot of people were afraid of them though and dared not cross them. I'm not quite sure of the exact facts, but, at the head of the cult were three Arcs, powerful Wizards or Witches, each representing a book of Froxidian belief; Naga, Tisar, and mmmm... "Aunt Rose thought for a while "and Degan I think she said. Well, together the power they could yield was phenomenal. I have heard myths of people going insane after crossing them. One of the things I do remember Heather saying is that in order for an Arc to be replaced he would be challenged by another follower, a challenge of strength, both physical and mystical. If the Arc lost physically he would try to possess the losers' body, throwing out their soul so it became a shadow. They had eight days to try and win it back before they dissipated. This also gave the Arc a new lease of physical life.

My heart sank.

14

It all seemed lost, the world span round in front of me, no way out, no way to win, the end looming closer.

"Is there any way that Daniel can fight him?" Ann-Marie really cared, you could hear it in her voice.

"I'm sorry dear I don't know how to help I'm a spiritualist. But maybe" she though for a second before speaking again "Maybe Heather can help, being a White Witch she knows a lot more about this sort of thing."

"A what?" I said brought back from my own thoughts.

"A white witch, a good witch. She may be able to help you. I'll go and speak with her, she's only lives two doors down the road." With that she got up and started to walk out of the living room.

"Aunt Rose, Why can I see through Daniel's eyes, when he holds my hand?"

She stopped and turned to face Ann-Marie "My dear, you have a special gift. You can never tell how strong a gift is until the time when it is needed, you can go a whole lifetime never knowing, or in one instant all will become clear. Daniel is not a spirit, he is a 'soulshadow', a stronger more physical entity than you have come in contact with before, and you've found a new strength." She paused thoughtfully "and now is the time when you need it."

I looked at Ann-Marie, she understood. Aunt Rose walked out of the house, leaving the front door ajar.

How much difference it would make talking to Heather, I had no idea. Part of me thought all was lost whilst another still held out some hope, some slither of a chance. What I expected to happen, I didn't know, some strange phenomenon that would put everything straight, back the way it was, back in that corridor on Sunday night. That night seemed so far away now, a distant memory. Yet it was still only Wednesday, three days had passed, I couldn't explain how.

"Daniel, what's the time?"

"I don't know" I glanced around the room for a clock "5.20pm. Why?"

"I've got to get home before mother, otherwise she'll worry if she sees Mojo still there and I'm not" with that she started to fuss around gathering her things.

"Good point" I agreed "Did you ever tell your mum about your... gift?"

"No. She'd freak out. She hates the supernatural and anything vaguely unfamiliar. I tried once to explain to her about Dad, that I'd spoken to him, that I thought he helped me through my transition. I think that's kinda what made her make up her mind about moving in the first place. She didn't say so. I could hear it in her voice. She seemed scared by it all.

When I first went blind, I started to pay more attention to people's voices noting the stresses, I missed all that when I could see. I didn't pay close attention to the highs and lows, I could see their faces, their eyes, and that was enough."

"S'ppose it would frea..."

Blood was dripping from my hand, the bite must have been deep. I'd made it back to my flat though, and was in the bathroom washing my hand, I was shaking with the pain, cold.

The reflection of my shirt shone back at me from the shaving mirror that hung on the wall, the shirt was covered with dirt, one of my work shirts, lumberjack style. I always bought large size; it would fit anybody. I leaned over towards the toilet the lid was down, bandages resting on the top, with scissors and a dressing.

I sat down on the floor in front of it whilst I tried to put the dressing on. It was not easy, and I was getting frustrated with it, the pain was intense.

After about ten minutes I managed to fasten the bandage with a safety pin flexing my hand slowly to make sure it would stay in place. I went down stairs to the lounge. On the floor there were local evening papers from the last two nights, to the left there were cuttings from them and a whole front page. Another paper to the right still lay folded in half where it had been thrown, covered in blood patches.

I sat down on the settee then slipped onto the floor with my legs spread in front of me, picking up the scissors that I had put on the settee at some point.

I glanced at the double glazed plain glass back door, a pair of eyes were watching me, next door's cat, I growled making a sudden lunge, the cat flinched, but stayed for a while longer.

Reading the paper, the lead story was about the murders. I laughed to myself. They had no leads to go on and were asking for witnesses to come forward.

The victim from the field who had had a lucky escape was still in shock and couldn't give a very good description, she had never actually had a chance to get a look at her attacker. I smiled then winced at the pain of my hand which still stung. I thought I was smart. The photo fit picture on the front page didn't look familiar.

Carefully I cut out the story and placed it with others on the floor, satisfaction was mine. I laid back resting my head on a cushion and drifted into a sleep that was made uneasy by the throbbing from my hand.

Ann-Marie, and a new face were staring at me.

"...derstand what you mean. Hi I'm Heather."

I felt like an object on show in a museum again, the strange thing was that no one could see me, they just felt my presence, and they knew where I was in the room, all this was unnerving.

"Hi" was all I managed to get out.

Heather was a shortish lady, about mid forties I supposed,

cropped hair and wearing a brown heavy jumper, jeans and trainers, she held a book under her arm. I couldn't see the title.

"You're right you can certainly feel the power that takes him Rose, it's strong, very strong" she spoke with a northern accent.

"He is getting weaker. When I first met him I felt an almost overwhelming aura now it's not so strong" Ann-Marie stated matter of factly.

I was beginning to feel I wasn't there, talked about behind my back, but in front of me.

"I am here you know" I said curtly without meaning to.

"It's ok Daniel, I'm here to help."

"Yes I realise that. Thank you. But, I'm not a child" I don't know why I was so annoyed, they were here to help, maybe it was because I felt helpless, I was used to managing for myself, not having to rely on other people.

Heather sat down next to Rose on the settee placing the book on the coffee table in front of her. We all watched as she flicked through the pages intently looking for something in particular, settling on a page. Then she opened her handbag, which was on the floor, lifting out a crystal ball wrapped in a silk hankerchief.

"Why don't you use that one" I pointed to the crystal ball already on the coffee table, forgetting that they couldn't see my actions. They understood what I meant anyway.

"Because they are very..." Ann-Marie and Aunt Rose said together.

Aunt Rose continued "Because they are very personal to each user.

Gently Heather caressed it in her hands, transfixed. Normally I would have laughed as I didn't have much faith in this sort of thing, however, I found my beliefs well and truly tested, and blown apart. She rested it on her lap, flicked through more pages of her book, muttering to herself. We all watched waiting with baited breath.

"What's she doin…"

I was woken with a start. The doorbell. It took me a while to get my bearings.

I walked out into the hall and glanced down the stairs. It was dark, I hadn't put any lights on. I looked carefully down the stairs, avoiding being seen by anyone standing outside my front door, the glass panel above acting like a large peep hole.

The doorbell rang out again. In the dim street light which oozed into the lobby I could make out the shape of my parents, one of their surprise visits that they threw upon me if they hadn't seen me for a while. Hesitant about answering the door, I stood looking on. With no lights on they could not be sure if I was in or not.

Again the doorbell chimed.

I switched the light on. 'NO' I wanted to cry out. It was too late. I made my way down the stairs to the front door and slowly opened it..

"Nooooo."

"What is it, Daniel?" Ann-Marie enquired.

"My parents, I've got to save my parents. They're there, at my flat now" I got up heading towards the door.

"Don't go" Heather said firmly "There won't be anything you can do."

I stopped in my tracks "What?" I said curtly "There's got to be something I can do" I continued the frustration boiling to the surface.

"There is nothing you can do about that" The edge of firmness in her voice compelled me to listen. I turned to face her taking a step closer, still het-up inside.

"You know that you have eight days before you completely become one. At that stage it will be too late, your soulshadow will be gone and your physical body and his spirit will be, forever. If you want to put this right you have to locate the physical body of the spirit and perform a binding ritual that will tie his spirit to his remains, therefore enabling you to take back possession of your physical self."

"My physical self?! I'm not sure I understand" My mind was a whirl.

Ann-Marie and Aunt Rose were listening as intently as I was, this must have been new to them as well.

"The spirit here present in this room is the soulshadow of your physical entity, which has been taken over by the spirit of someone else."

"Henry Highway" Ann-Marie interrupted.

"Unless you get possession of your body, within the eight days, Henry Highway will become your life…" Heather continued.

"You mean all this time he has been parading as me?!"

"Yes."

"So the murders have been committed by Daniel's physical side?"

"Yes Ann-Marie."

I was horrified. It was bad enough being a witness to the gruesome crimes, but now, there blood was on my hands.

"My parents!" I exclaimed.

"Wait" Aunt Rose said.

"But I've got to go and see what I can do, they're in danger."

"They are ok."

"What? How do you know?"

"They are not, what he is after. The shadows show they are sitting and talking, he is even at peace for a while" she spoke with such certainty that I found it hard to disbelieve.

"How are we going to find Henry Highway's remains?"

"Ann-Marie that I cannot help you with, for that you will have to consult town records, they should have all the information you need, since this town was just a small parish it shouldn't be too hard or take too long, providing..." she broke off in thought.

"...he is from around this area and died here too. There is too much mist... I can't give you anymore information."

"Providing that is the case, What do we have to do then?" I asked wanting to get as much information as possible, preparing to extract this evil person from my life.

"Then you have to find out where he performed the ritual that enabled his spirit to live on past the death of his earthly self. And destroy the very thing that made it possible for his spirit to take over another person."

"So we find the remains and perform this binding ritual. Then we have to find where the door is that opened this chain of events."

"That is correct Ann-Marie, in this book it says the ritual you have to perform is on the grave of the remains, also you'll need something personal of his."

Heather passed the book into Ann-Marie's hands open at the page we required. She felt the book in her hands and I saw her hands dip from the physical weight of it.

"But how am I going to do this?" Ann-Marie asked

Heather leaned forward.

"Daniel will be with you, you need each other for this. He is your eyes" Heather said with a calming gentleness that gave Ann-Marie strength, or at least made her look more relaxed.

There we all sat for few minutes, contemplating the future events.

15

It was too late today to go to the town records office, it would have to wait until tomorrow.

Leaving Aunt Rose and Heather talking, we headed back to Ann-Marie's house, the book in a carrier bag, hoping her mother had been held up and was not home before her.

Walking in silence we were lost deep in our own thoughts. 'We needed each other' that thought was so true I couldn't complete this without her, and she needed me to make it possible for her to fulfil her side of the bargain. I couldn't manage without her, such a perfect pairing.

Another thought that hung around in the back of my mind, like a nightmare waiting to pounce, was the dreaded thought that at anytime a vision could come and take me, inadvertently taking her as well, thus rendering Ann-Marie helpless in the street, alone in a trance like state. It was dark and these side streets were badly lit and not that far away from my own flat. The paradox of it all would be if he was watching us, worse was the irony that she and I would see it all but not be able to do anything about it, all the time she held my hand, a possible living nightmare.

We had to get back hers before anything happened.

"I'm sorry I shouldn't have got you involved in all this."

"It's ok, it's nice, in some respects to be needed. Sometimes I feel I'm a burden to my mother, she never shouts or rushes me but it can't be easy for her, having to look after a blind daughter. I've been learning braille, but it's not easy. I used to be able to see... and I find it hard to learn all over again" She paused reflectively "It's nice helping you because I get to see again, even if it is a double edged sword."

"What do you mean?"

"Whatever the outcome of the next few days, I'll be back to being blind all the time" I saw a tear form in her eye and I wanted to hug her "But I've got Mojo now. I'd miss him if I could see again. I often wonder how my life would have turned out if I could still see."

"Don't look at me it's still too weird to see myself, outside of myself, if you know what I mean."

"Sorry" we carried on walking in silence.

The lights were on in Ann-Marie's house, damn, her mother was in.

Ann-Marie got her keys out and slid them into the door as quietly as she could, turning the key trying to avoid the click of the lock as it uncatches itself, pushing the door inwards waiting for the inevitable squeak of the hinges, nothing. Carefully stepping forward over the threshold, closing the door behind holding the lock in the open position until the door was safely closed before releasing gently.

We stood there for a minute I guess Ann-Marie was thinking what to say.

"Hi mum" she shouted.

"Hi honey, you feeling better now?" came the voice from the kitchen.

"Sorry?"

"You feeling better? How long have you been asleep?" quickly catching on Ann-Marie slipped off her coat and laid it on the stairs ready to pick it up again when she went up, before her mother saw it. She walked into the kitchen.

"Yeah, I'm fine just felt a little tired. What's the time?" she stretched and yawned.

"About 6.30pm, dinner will be ready in about half an hour".

"Ok, I'm going to put some music on" she left the kitchen,

making her way upstairs to her bedroom, collecting the coat on the way. Mojo was waiting in her room to greet her.

"Sorry Mojo I had to leave you behind. I've got to do the same tomorrow." She gave him a big hug then sat on her bed. "Daniel, Do you know exactly where we've got to go tomorrow?"

"Not exactly, I ju…"

It was my lounge again, three mugs sat on the floor, empty. My parents! There was no sign that there had been any sort of trouble here. I was sitting staring at the TV set, puzzled. Of course all this was new to him. The TV was on, there was a home improvement program on, they were knocking down a wall. I was intrigued, captivated by it all. I sat there and watched the whole program without moving.

I got up and moved about my flat paying more attention to it now. The video unit, full of films; taking the odd one out and reading the back cover. The CD's, opening the cases and viewing the silver disc inside.

In the hallway taking in the picture gallery I'd created up the stairway, pictures from shows I'd been in. At the top there was a full length mirror hung on the wall. I stopped and looked into it, like I'd done so many times when I was getting ready for work. Now I viewed something far worse, I didn't want to see. I didn't have a choice. What greeted my eyes, sent a chill down my spine, the events of the previous days hurtling back and forth in my mind. The reflection was me. I didn't want to believe it. I screamed.

"…aaarrghhh."

"What is it, Daniel?"

"I just saw myself, for the first time I saw me. The me that is me now. Not who I really am." I struggled to get the words out. If I could have cried I would have done so. I sat in the wicker chair feeling like I'd had the wind taken out of me. I tried to think coherently "Why me?" Anger coursed through me, preventing me from resting peacefully and at ease even though the rest of the night passed uneventfully, I found my mind racing as I watched the dream sequence again in my mind. As it played itself out again and again I started to understand the twisted sense of sobriety that kept him going on killing. Why he saw things the way he did. I found myself torn between sympathy and hatred for this monster.

After breakfast when Ann-Marie's mother had gone to work, we walked to the Town Hall, a prestigious building, the focal point of the high street, faced with large fifty foot high pillars and ornate features carved top and bottom. There were steps running the full width of the building. It had rained during the night and puddles lay on some of the steps. A big revolving door led into the lobby with its fancy plasterwork and wooden parque flooring.

The reception desk was an add-on from the sixties, it didn't look right, but no one cared enough to change it so it remained. It was unmanned. Ann-Marie rang the buzzer.

She rang it again. A guard wandered out from a room at the back.

"Can I help you Miss?"

"Yes. Can you tell me where I'll find the records for all deaths in the area, I'm doing some research for my family tree and I know my Grandpa died locally but I'm not sure where he is buried."

I was taken aback, Ann-Marie had really thought her part out.

"Follow the stairs up two flights and take the second door on the right down the corridor" he moved his arm around doing his best to visually point to where he meant. He looked quite silly when he did, this in turn made Ann-Marie smirk.

"What's so funny?"

"Sorry, nothing."

"If you speak to Vivienne who is up there she'll point you in the right direction."

"Thank you."

We headed up the stairs as directed. It was a long winding staircase, the treads of which were about five foot wide, carpet just covering the centre three feet with stair-rods holding it in place.

Ann-Marie knocked at the door we required not sure whether to enter or wait for an invitation, she pushed it gently open revealing a big ominous room full of shelves upon shelves of books. In the corner was a lady sitting at a computer, there was a couple talking to her, sitting opposite. We marched over and stood waiting for her to finish with these people, looking round viewing the archive of information.

"Hello, can I help you?" this was a young lady, mid twenties, large build, long brown hair, and glasses, dressed in a business suit.

"Hi, I'm looking for a record of my Grandpa's death, I'm researching my family tree, and trying to trace where all my relatives are buried... and born."

"Well let me see, what was his surname?"

"Highway."

"Do you know when he died, just the year."

"No I don't." she bit her lower lip nervously "His first name was Henry, Will that help?"

"Let's try and see what the computer brings up."

I was in my car. Driving out of town, a country lane, heading towards Woodsea, a little village about three miles from the edge of town, a population of about fifty, with the requisite pub and church but not much else.

Within a few minutes I was in the main street. It ran fairly straight until near the end where it veered left to a dead end. This was where the church stood.

A small quaint church, headstones on all sides, bordered by a slowly crumbling dry stone wall, which wound its way round the grounds, the entrance was through a gate that was in need of repair.

I parked up outside, got out and walked into the churchyard. Surveying the headstones, I studied the names written upon them. I was looking for someone in particular. I knew they were here, but could not remember the exact location, it had all changed so much over the last, how many years? The trees were larger, bushes fuller, even the lay of the land looked different.

I perused through the headstones like pages in a book, I started to remember, it was coming back to me. With more haste I made my way behind the church.

There it was a small oak tree. I'd planted that when I was here.

Had it really been that long?

The grave stone I was looking for lay underneath the foliage, leaning to one side, not as I remembered it, the stone discoloured with yellow moss, the inscription hard to read.

I knelt down in front and brushed away the dirt and moss with my bare hands as best I could to reveal the name of 'Violet Rose Highway, 1887- 1915, My sweatheart'. I started to cry.

"Are you alright?"

"MM,yeah. I'm fine, I , mm, I sometimes suffer from, from a form of epilepsy, where I just blank out. I'm ok, honest. Sorry. You were saying?"

The lady began again "There is no record of a Henry Highway being buried anywhere around this area."

"Not at all, he's got to be buried around here, his wife, my Grandma was buried out in Woodsea, the little church out there."

"I'm sorry there's no record of it here, and we have pretty much got everything on computer now, all the details of the deaths. All the books contain now is the original hard copy information. If you knew what year he died we might be able to narrow the search."

"No I don't I'm afraid."

"Maybe he moved abroad, or died in the war. Was he in the services? We could do a nation wide search of databases."

"No I don't believe he was."

"The only other place you could look is through the records over there" She got up from behind her desk and walked us over to an area of the room that had only a few books on a table. "If for any reason when he died he couldn't be identified by the police of the time his records would be filed here. There might be a possibility he could be amongst these, but without knowing more of the circumstances it will be like looking for a needle in a haystack."

"Thank you" Ann-Marie said. I could hear the sadness in her voice.

16

We sat on the steps outside the town hall, avoiding the puddles.

"What do we do now?" Ann-Marie whispered.

"I don't know. He can't just have disappeared, he's got to be buried somewhere. But where?"

"Maybe we should go back to the …"

"Hope you don't mind me asking, Was she a relative of yours?"

I looked up, there was a tall man in his mid fifties wearing a long black gown with white collar standing behind me. I just stared not saying a word, tears rolled down my cheek.

"Maybe I had best leave you alone" the vicar said, a calm relaxed caring look in his eye "No I…" The vicar stopped and turned about. Then a long silence.

"In your own time… Maybe you'd like to come inside" he indicated towards the front entrance of the church.

"She was my wife… once. I miss her so much. We only had a short time together, she was everything to me. Why? Why was she taken from me?"

The vicar started to explain "Everybody has their time. The reasoning is not always fathomable, God…" he broke off staring at the headstone more closely "Excuse me for saying… but this lady died in 1915, she can't have been your wife."

"Are you calling me a liar? You think I don't know where my own wife is buried?" although I remained kneeling on the ground my menace grew as I felt the emotional rage grow within me before I stood to face up to the Vicar.

"I'm sorry." The Vicar withdrew slightly abashed "No. I merely

wished to point out that you can only be about your mid twenties, this la…"

"She WAS my wife… a long time ago…" I turned back to the grave stone and knelt down resting my hand on the top "she was" caressing the letters that spelt out her name.

"Of course" he remarked apologetically "please accept my apologies I didn't mean to doubt you" he looked bewildered but didn't want to pursue the matter further.

"I always blamed the little girl. She was only playing she didn't mean any harm, but I couldn't see that. I had to blame someone. I couldn't see clearly. Please forgive me" I pleaded to no one in particular "Now I'm confused" sorrow infused my voice "I don't know where I am, my crimes seem so worthless, they have no reason. But I can't go back. Why didn't I just die?"

I felt a hand on my shoulder "Come inside with me, son" I looked up and…

On the steps again, Ann-Marie was still sitting there next to me.

"What happened this time?" she whispered wanting to be kept informed but also knowing how horrific these visions could be.

"The dream, of course! The dream is the reason for all the killing."

"What do you mean?"

I repeated the whole conversation to Ann-Marie, suddenly the picture was becoming clear.

"I think we need to investigate the papers from 1915. He mentioned 'The killings'. This is just a continuation from then. If he had been caught and sent to prison, maybe his death was never recorded, or the records are held somewhere else."

"So we've got to go back to the library?"

"Yes" pausing, seeing the discomfort on Ann-Marie's face "I'm sorry I know you probably don't want…"

"No it's fine" she interrupted with a deep sigh.

"Maybe they won't recognise you" I tried to make the previous visit sound less memorable than it was.

"I think I made a big enough fool of myself for them to remember alright."

"It probably wasn't as bad as you imagine."

"Yeah right. It's ok Daniel, I'll go."

"Thank you" I said humbly realising the embarrassment that Ann-Marie would feel.

We made our way across the main road directly behind the Town Hall towards the library. It only took a few minutes, now we seemed to work comfortably as one, Ann-Marie using my eyes and me holding her hand.

"Are you ready?" I looked at Ann-Marie and saw the apprehension on her face, she took a deep breath.

"As ready as I'll ever be, if I didn't have to see it, it would be easier. How's that for irony?" she smiled.

We walked through the doors and made our way straight to the stairwell past the returns desk.

"They're staring at me" she whispered.

"It's probably just the toilet paper hanging from the back of your jeans."

"What?" she gasped throwing her free hand behind her back in automatic reflex then realizing I was joking, she smiled.

"Only kidding, made you smile though."

"Yeah now they think I'm completely insane talking to myself."

"Well be quiet then."

"I'm trying to but you keep talking to me."

I smiled to myself. For the first time since we'd met I found myself relaxed enough to allow a smile and a bit of friendly banter, it broke the tension.

At the top we turned left and headed to the computer on the table. Ann-Marie sat down and I settled into the position we had assumed previously allowing Ann-Marie to punch in all the details of what we were looking for.

Various headlines flashed up, some minor stories, other major stories, We didn't exactly know what we were looking for, except, that from what I'd heard I had to assume that there had been more than one death at the time, a spate of deaths.

Ann-Marie typed in various parameters to narrow our search. By now she was getting accustomed to seeing the obscurity of the differing perspectives. The computer raced away in the background, highlighting stories, and then storing them to one side whilst it searched for some more.

Finally grinding to a halt, search completed, 257 records. From this, and assuming that they had to have all been young girls, another 163 records were eliminated, just 94 to view and draw our own conclusions from.

Slowly we started our search, closing any we thought inappropriate, gradually shutting out whatever was going on in our own surroundings consumed by the search, a kind of sadistic excitement at other's misfortunes.

In my car driving back towards town, I was calm, collected, no sense of anger possessed me, guilt was the only emotion that empowered my thoughts. I was confused.

The demeanour of the person I first felt had changed, the brutality and rage gone. This was a human being, not some monster I'd made him up to be, it had made it so easy for me to hate him. I was beginning to feel compassion, an understanding of what he must have gone through. The tragic loss, the injustice a strange kind of reasoning for doing the things he had. There was a reason. Albeit, a twisted one.

Even so I, he had still done wrong both here and now, and way back then.

A police siren broke me from my thoughts. It went rushing by. A deep rooted evil rose within me again, I flexed my right hand contorting it into a ball, I was remembering, a murder, nearby. All my sense of reasoning ran from me like wild horses. I smiled, the pleasure had returned. I'd enjoyed it. Wrong or right didn't matter any more, I enjoyed what I did. It had taken a hold, an animal I couldn't subdue, when I tried it fought back...

We tried to ignore the visions as best we could in order to work towards our goal. The picture in front of us was of a girl aged 11, long blonde hair, she wore a pretty little summer bonnet. She had been killed, her body dumped in an alley, off Ambleside Gardens, there were no witnesses, brutally stabbed in what was a violent crime, no motive was known.

We collected a map of the local area from one of the shelves, photocopied a section and brought it back to the desk, plotting this first murder on it, we had no idea how many we were looking for.

The next couple of articles, a 19 year girl old raped and murdered, a six year old girl attacked by a dog. We closed them down. Next was a murder that took place in Waterwell Gardens near the seafront, again a young girl, no motive. Ann-Marie marked the photocopied map.

Time was passing and I forgot that I didn't need to eat, but I could hear Ann-Marie's stomach rumbling, we went to the canteen on the first floor, where she sat and had a coke and a sandwich, we took the map with us to peruse.

Ann-Marie had marked 17 murder scenes in all on our map, not all relevant, as had been proved by a little further research. We had filed through newspaper articles until it became clear that we were following the trail of a serial killer, we believed it to be that of Henry Highway. A couple of the murders we'd managed to disregard once it became apparent the papers were focussing on one steady stream of killings, a certain criteria.

They'd started in March. March 13th the first one was discovered. Next, March 29th, then April 17th, April 27th, April 30th, May 4th , May 17th. There was no regularity. Local residents were scared to let there children out to play alone.

There was a rumour bandied about at the time in the bars

that it was a religious thing, a devil worshipper, a witch. Stealing the children's souls and using their blood for spells. There was no evidence to substantiate this, but the people felt happy believing something out of the ordinary was to blame, rather than not knowing.

There was such a group in the area at the time, but nothing could ever be proved. Although the members were treated like outcasts those that were thought to be involved always pleaded their innocence.

No one had been seen at any of the crime scenes. No one had been seen leaving them either. He was good. He had audacity, some of these crimes had to have been committed during daylight hours. Some of the headlines that we had read called 'him', they believed these crimes could only have been done by a man, 'The Slippery Slasher'. Police were baffled by the whole affair.

In August 1915 they stopped. The streets settled into peace again. No crime with such ferocity was reported again for another two years and then the murderer was apprehended and no connection to these crimes was made, although the police tried. No murder weapon was ever recovered either.

The locations were all over the town. We both looked closely at the map and the locations that Ann-Marie had marked. An idea occurred to me.

"Ann-Marie look at some of the locations, Waterwell Gardens, Ambleside Gardens, Claret Street, Weston Road, Hotel Road."

"What about them?" she whispered conscious that the canteen was filling up with people.

"Are they close to some of the exits of the tunnels?"

"Are you trying to say that he used the tunnels as escape routes?"

"Well no one saw anyone leaving the scenes or hanging around. If the entrances were concealed enough behind shrubs and the like, no one would ever know."

"Surely the police would have checked the areas out thoroughly though."

"Only if they knew the tunnels were there and where to look. If you think about it, when you had your sight how often did you not notice something that was in front of your eyes. The crime scenes weren't necessarily in front of the entrances, just close by, enabling…"

"Enabling him to be in a completely different part of town quickly with a change of clothes, if prepared."

"The bag, the canvas bag that I saw him take out of that hidden hole in the wall must have contained a change of clothes. Maybe even the weapon."

A lady came and took Ann-Marie's tray from the table. We sat there pondering, feeling pleased with ourselves, we were getting somewhere.

"How?" Ann-Marie said loudly before remembering no one could see me "How does this help us find his remains?" she continued whispering.

"I don't know."

We sat again in silence whilst she drank the remainder of her coke.

"Let's go back to the computer see what else we can find out" Ann-Marie said.

Making our way up the stairs to our research area, we found someone else using the computer we had been using. There was only one computer in this department.

"Damn" I said.

We walked around the floor level and found another machine to use.

"What are you doing?" I asked.

"I'm looking for missing persons reports."

"Why?" I was perplexed.

"The killing stopped abruptly. Why did they stop? There is

no death record for him, according to the records, assuming that he stayed local, and we have to for now."

"Right!" I agreed

"Well there must have been a reason why he stopped killing, maybe if we follow the papers through in date order for missing persons, we might be able to establish a location where he was last seen."

I thought for a second while Ann-Marie carried on typing on the computer.

"That's not going help though is it?!"

"Why not?"

"The missing persons report will only acknowledge that he was missing, not where or when he died."

Ann-Marie stopped what she was doing resting her hands on the edge on the desk. "Damn."

"I've got it, we are trying to establish where he went missing, when we should be locating where he was found."

"I don't get it."

"There is no record of his death and we have to assume that he died somewhere. Now through the natural course of time, one would like to think that a body would've been discovered, maybe badly decomposed, or a pile of bones, some way shape or form that meant, due to bad medical records that he couldn't be identified."

I looked at her expecting a note of coherence to what I was saying, nothing. I tried a different tact.

"What are the chances of a body's remains laying undiscovered somewhere to this very day"

"Unlikely. Depending on where they are buried."

"Exactly. But if we make the assumption that they have been found then we go through the newspapers looking for stories about remains being found."

"I think I get it" her hands leapt to the keys of the computer, her fingers moved over them as if possessed "then we can cross reference the locations with possible locations where Henry could have been."

"Exactly."

I almost lost my connection with her as she set the search to cover the period from 1915 to present day.

Fortunately there were only three unidentified remains found in the local area. One in Lamdon Road, one in Albert Street, one actually discovered at the bottom of a shaft in the Empire Theatre in 1962 when it was being renovated and converted into a Dance Hall.

An air of satisfaction came over both of us as we read on.

The grizzly discovery was made by builders, as they hammered their way through the wrong wall in the basement. They were trying to connect two adjacent chambers to create a large storage area, and getting their bearings wrong found themselves in another chamber. On the ground lay a skeleton, now known to be male, approximately 30 years old. The few rags that were still attached gave no clue as to the identity of the person.

Police were called in to investigate, there seemed to be nothing suspicious, the broken leg bones forensics date as occurring 35-45 years previously, there was no evidence of anything sinister, the investigation was short, the remains removed for burial in a local church.

"It doesn't say what church."

Ann-Marie smiled.

"What are you looking so happy about?" I said gruffly.

"We know the year and location of where he was found."

"We can't be sure it is him though."

"It has to be, the theatre connection, the tunnels, it can't be anyone else."

I didn't share her enthusiasm, I had no better ideas.

17

Heading out of the Library, back to the town hall, Ann-Marie suggested that because now we knew what year the bones were discovered we could narrow our search through the books listing the burials of anonymous remains. Hopefully there wouldn't be many.

The weather was wet and miserable again making it feel like night time.

In the Records room we only had half an hour to spare, before they closed, Vivienne pointed us to the correct set of books then left us to get on with our search. The large record books held all the information we wanted, records not just for the local area but the whole of the county of Essex. The books were in chronological order, which made it easy to find the relevant year. Their were 127 books to view covering all the church constituents in the county, narrowing our search to the immediate area left only seven books to look through. As time was tight we had to make certain assumptions therefore expediting our search, and rely heavily on luck. In the fourth book we found what we were looking for, the remains from the theatre, buried in a graveyard, in Hockley. Now we knew where we had to go.

We left the building and headed back to Ann-Marie's house the question that was on our minds was, how are going to get to the remains? We couldn't exactly go into the cemetery and simply start digging them up.

"So have we got to dig up the remains?" Ann-Marie asked hesitantly.

"I don't know."

We walked on.

"There has to be another way. I'm sure Heather and my Aunt can't have wanted us to dig up his remains. There has to be a simpler way."

"Why don't you give her ring tonight and ask her, see if there is another way."

"Ok."

We got in before her mother returned from work, giving us enough time to telephone her Aunt. She relayed the conversation to me as it progressed.

"Hello... Aunt Rose... Fine thank you. We've discovered where the remains of Henry are. But when you said we needed to find them. Did you mean we had to dig them up as well... she says no... thank god for that... we just need the location because that's where we need to perform the binding ritual ... What binding ritual?... And we need something personal of his to tie his soul with his physical presense... Right... Thanks... yes I will" she put the receiver down. "Did you follow that, Daniel?"

"Yes, I think. How are we going to find something personal of his though?"

"The tunnels" we both said simultaneously smiling.

"The canvas bag that he got out of the little hiding hole that must have contained some personal stuff" I felt relieved.

"Yes, but is it still going to be there though? If you remember he removed it, you didn't see him put it back. So if he took it with him we won't know where it is now!"

Ann-Marie had a good point, a point we couldn't ignore. Our only starting place was the tunnels. Our task was made easier as we now had knowledge of other entrances, so we didn't need to go through the theatre. This eased Ann-Maries' mind.

"I'll go and search tonight while you sleep, this will speed things up as I don't need sleep"

"Ok. Wait you won't be able to see in the dark."

"Shit."

I had someone in my arms, I was holding them tight. They were struggling. Their hair was loose and shaggy, strands straying into my mouth. I was making my way into an alley, it was overgrown with vegetation; progress was slow.

The body in my arms was struggling less and less, my grip was powerful. They could only have been young. I had one hand over their mouth to keep them from screaming. I had tears in my eyes.

I changed direction. I knew where we were heading. Towards my flat. Why? This seemed ludicrous. All the other crimes had taken place in various sites around the area, but now I was heading home. Taking a victim with me. I couldn't see the logic.

As my flat came into view, I hesitated, just out of sight in the bushes. Just to be sure no one was watching. When I felt the coast was clear, I made my way to the stairs that led up to the balcony and my back door, I had a key hidden underneath a flowerpot. I always believed in having a back up plan if I got locked out.

I laid the girl down on the decking, she had fallen unconscious with the exhaustive struggle, fright aiding. She appeared to be only about eleven years old. My heart sank to the pit of my stomach.

In through the door I lifted her limp body, closing the door and locking it behind me, drawing the curtains for privacy. I placed the body on the floor leaning it up against the wall after taping her hands and feet together, and placing a gag over her mouth.

I stood up and looked at her, just stared. She looked so helpless, so innocent. A victim of something from another time. I couldn't do anything. Mixed emotions running through my mind.

Ann-Marie had gone down for dinner and was just returning when I returned from my vision.

"There was nothing I could do Daniel and mum kept calling me, hope you don't mind, I had to have my dinner otherwise mother would worry."

"No no that's fine" I spluttered out "I don't expect you to

wait, when there's nothing you can do."

"I'm actually really tired, so if you don't mind I'm going to bed. These active days are wearing me out." With that she yawned and left the room with her pyjamas in her hand. Mojo stayed sitting on the floor, he looked sort of dejected. Poor thing for the last year or so he had been Ann-Marie's eyes now I had taken that away from him.

When Ann-Marie re-entered the room Mojo didn't even raise his head, just stayed where he was.

"Mojo, come here boy" he lifted his head, but hesitated. "Come on Mojo" she re-iterated in playful tones "Ann-Marie does love you, she doesn't mean to leave you on your own, Come on boy, give me a hug." Finally Mojo jumped on the bed and laid on her legs, licking her face. She cupped his face in her hands and reciprocated the affection.

"Are you alright Ann-Marie? It's a bit early to go to bed isn't it?" came a voice from the door.

"I just feel really tired, spent longer than usual going through the braille books, it's getting easier, anyway night mother"

"Night dear, sleep tight"

After she heard her mother walk back down the stairs, she asked what I'd seen in the last vision. I could tell from the tone of her voice, the way it broke, the look on her face that she didn't like to ask and the disgust that emulated from her when I told her the details; she felt obliged to ask, a little curious.

"So he's there now, this minute. With another one?"

"Yes."

"What are we waiting for lets call the police we've got to help her."

It hadn't even occurred to me. That such a simple thing like that could save her life and put an end to all these crimes.

I was back in my flat the girl was conscious, fear in her eyes.

"I guess you're wondering what I am going to do with you" I detected a sick note in my voice, toying with my victim.

She nodded her head yes, fear shining like a beacon in her face.

"I have got to do it, you understand?" I drew closer to her, my face in hers, I could see the tears of fear rolling down her cheeks "I do not want to but I have to. It is the only way. I loved my wife. It is not fair. IT IS NOT FAIR. You understand" his voice pitched from calm to agitated.

The girl shook her head. Her jeans were wet. Fear driven right to her core.

I got up and walked around the room thumping the walls with my fist.

"You are all to blame, you took her life. Caused her death. If you had not been playing in the street she would still be alive today."

There was the canvas bag, behind the door. I picked the girl up so she was standing on her feet. Tears filled my eyes.

"It is your fault the horse reared" my voice broke "...and killed my wife, she never did anyone any harm. She loved everybody. So much love. But no. Now she is gone and it is your fault. Do you hear me? Your fault" I shook her she tried to cry out but only a muted sob came from her, the gag doing its job "You are all the same. Never think about the consequences just do whatever it is you want. Well what about me?" I could feel the raw energy of anger welling up inside "I had to live with your mistake. Do you know what that was like?" I picked up the little girl and thrust her like a rag doll, back against the wall "DO YOU? Do you?" and with that I thrust the knife I was unaware of in my hand straight into the belly of the girl. Tears streaming down my cheeks. Each thrust of the knife followed by a sob from myself "I am sorry". The girls eyes widened at the first blow almost in surprise then the eyelids gradually grew heavy and closed. The life force relinquishing from the body.

The body fell in a heap on the floor. Blood covering the carpet.

I stood there, one hand against the wall, supporting my weight, the other still holding the knife. Slowly my grip released the knife allowing it to fall to the floor.

I was back in Ann-Marie's bedroom.

"What's happened? I wanted to call the police but I couldn't tell them where you live."

"William Street, 159a William street" I said automatically my voice cold emotionless, my mind still on the little girl.

With that she reached onto her bed where she had already placed the handset of her phone and dialled 999.

It suddenly became clear, the canvas bag.

"Wait, we need the canvas bag."

"We've got to help the girl" she retorted.

"It's too late." If I was physical I think I would have been repulsed by my own inability to prevent the crime from happening, saddened that another life had been wiped out.

She paused. I could see, feel she was gutted, upset.

"We need to retrieve the canvas bag, it's our only possibility" I pleaded, half sobbing myself.

"What about the girl?" her voice almost empty of hope knowing what I was going to say.

"I'm sorry there is nothing we can do."

I wanted to put my arm round her for comfort, mine and hers, Mojo edged his way up the bed and licked Ann-Marie's face, she put her arms round him and hugged him like never before.

I daren't say anything else just let her deal with this the only way she knew how, with the one that was closest to her, Mojo. Eventually she fell uneasily into sleep and I watched as if I was some sort of guardian angel.

Morning came round with a whole new urgency to sort this situation out. Ann-Marie was not hungry and skipped breakfast.

As soon as her mother had gone out we headed for my flat. This could be dangerous. I hadn't had anymore visions and didn't know whether I was going to be in and what danger, if any, awaited Ann-Marie.

Walking down the road I kept a watch out for my car, preying that it wouldn't be there. I didn't see it. I sighed with relief.

I guided Ann-Marie to the alleyway that would lead us to my balcony and the back door. I kept believing that I would have put the key back where I normally kept it. This would allow us entry into my flat.

It was still there. Ann-Marie retrieved the key and unlocked the door, opening it hesitantly, afraid of the awaiting scene. I didn't want to hold her hand, I wanted to protect her from the grizzly scene.

The body was gone, blood still stained the carpet, no attempt had been made to cover this. The canvas bag was still behind the door.

I directed Ann-Marie to the bag, it wasn't light but she managed to carry it and we left as quickly as we could leaving the back door unlocked. Heading back to Ann-Marie's house.

18

Safely back in Ann-Marie's room she opened the canvas bag. Everything was wrapped up in rags for protection. Before laying everything out on the floor we went downstairs and got some old newspapers from the recycling cupboard. This was the first time Ann-Marie had viewed her home, knowing the time limit that we had to adhere to she didn't make a fuss about wanting to see more, although I could sense she wanted to.

Laying the newspaper on the floor, Ann-Marie proceeded to empty the contents of the canvas bag.

Mojo observed the proceedings from his place on the bed whilst Ann-Marie carefully lifted out each parcel, not sure whether they were fragile, depositing them on the paper, some parcels were small, whilst others seemed heavy and large, particularly one which was book shaped, larger than A4 and as thick as a jumbo file. The array of shapes and sizes, made it feel like Christmas, lining up all your presents in order, deciding which to open first. Somehow I didn't think we were going to find any pleasant surprises.

"What shall we open first?" Ann-Marie asked.

"Don't know, s'pose it doesn't really matter, might as well start with the nearest."

Ann-Marie gulped, hesitantly picking up the first parcel and unravelling it. As it proved difficult to hold her hand she opened each bundle blind, describing the feel of each one, more for her benefit than mine, constructing a picture in her mind. The wrapping just kept going and going until finally a knife fell out, onto the floor. I then held Ann-Marie's hand. The blade was jagged, approximately seven inches in length, different shades of black coloured it. The handle was made of bone. I saw Ann-Marie physically shake as she tentatively picked it up, placing it on its own wrapping. We followed this procedure until all the objects were laid out in front of us on their respective wrappings, eyeing them in silence.

There was the knife, a couple of lockets, a wooden jewellery box, a pair of worn out gloves, some letters, a large book titled 'Frodixan Book of Incantations', two pairs of men's shoes, and one bundle that was just men's clothes, they were dated but the material was of reasonable quality, although now it was a little fragile.

The photo I had seen earlier, but didn't get a good look at, was not there.

The wooden box contained a collection of jewellery; a pocket watch, five rings - silver and gold, a silver hand held mirror (broken) and a pendent which Ann-Marie picked up to read the inscription engraved on the back

"My true one, always, H" I read "I wonder" an idea occurred to me "Can you pick up the pocket watch? Has it got anything inscribed on it, something that proves it belonged to him" Exploring it in her hand, she flicked open the case "You are my one, forever V. That's it. Something that has to be his."

"Can we be sure?" Ann-Marie questioned.

"As near as damn it" I looked at the objects in front of us. "I think it's our best choice. We need to go to his grave and conduct this ritual, and put things right... at last" I let a sense of premature relief wash over me.

Ann-Marie clasped the watch tightly in her hand and looked towards me.

"Will you ever speak to me again?"

"What?" I was taken aback by her question.

"When we've done the ritual, will you visit me again?"

"Of course I will you've done more for me than I could

ever have wished. I could never, not see you again, I owe you so much"

"I think I'm going to miss my eyesight all over again when you've gone, it's been weird, but nice to see again, where I live".

There was an awkward silence, the sort of silence when no one needs to speak, but often people spend time thinking of something to say anyway.

"We'd better head off if we are going to get to the cemetery and get this finished. I think Mojo better join us this time." I stated matter of factly.

Ann-Marie got up gathering everything we needed for the ritual, despite working without her sight again she made it look effortless and put them in a rucksack which she got from her wardrobe, including the book Heather lent to us, candles, and the pocket watch, and another small box stored in the bottom draw of her bedside cabinet.

"I need something to mark out the 'Sign of Olizan'. If the grave is grassed I won't be able to draw 'The Sign', so I'll need something to mark it out. I don't like the colour of my room much, it's a bit bland" I looked at her then we both smiled.

"You can't exactly tell your mum though. Can you?"

"No not really" there was the briefest pause for reflection.

"Have you got any sand or pebbles that you could take in a small bag"

"I don't know, we could look out in the garden before we leave, mother often spends time there. I don't know what she does or what it looks like as I've never seen it. But the paths are gravel of some sort."

Once we'd gathered together everything we needed upstairs we went out into the garden. It was only a small terraced house garden made to look like a courtyard. I held Ann-Marie's hand while she viewed it, taking in as much as possible, as quickly as possible. Being winter there was not a full bloom of colour. The evergreen bushes and shrubs painted a good enough picture that enabled her to fill in the blanks.

The path that wound its way up the centre of the garden consisted of small white stones, just a few millimetres in diameter.

"These should do" we went and grabbed a couple of plastic bags from the kitchen, doubling them up, she put a few handfuls of the stones in them, before twisting the bags a few turns and placing them in her rucksack.

Leaving the house there was an ominous air about what we were about to do and silence prevailed for most of our walk to the bus stop.

Hockley was three miles north of the town, a pretty village, although it had grown over the years, it was still very picturesque as all the new buildings had been forced to keep to the architectural nature of the existing buildings, using similar materials.

"How are you going to get back? Maybe we should see if Aunt Rose can come too."

"I'll be fine. I think I'm capable of catching a bus, Mojo and I have been getting about quite well for the last year or so without too much of a problem"

"Sorry, I only mea…"

I shut up before I put my foot in it anymore. She hated people thinking that she was incapable and useless because she wasn't. That was my tactful side coming out again!

"Daniel where are you?"

"I'm here."

She had not wanted me to hold her hand, her eyes was Mojo's task today, she felt she had hurt his feelings more than enough, I walked behind her. I hadn't realised how much further away I was from her than normal.

"Ah, that's better, I can feel you again."

"I was only a few feet away, no more than usual."

"You're getting weaker then."

"I don't feel any different."

"You won't but your soulshadow is growing weak, it's been how many days? Five? Six?"

"Only four."

"Come on we need to get this sorted" urgency and direction in her voice.

After just the short couple of days, I had observed how quickly she had got used to seeing things through my eyes, a different perspective. Now back to her normal way of life I noticed how clumsy she had been initially and understandably why she didn't want me to take her hand. Also, I thought she was proving to me that she didn't need my help, which I knew, it was always the other way round.

Catching the bus wasn't a problem, Mojo was a highly trained dog, Ann-Marie just gives the correct instruction and Mojo responds. Then it was a case of asking someone if she was at the right bus stop. As I was there this was easy.

"Aren't you ever worried about someone guiding you in the wrong direction? I would be" I asked knowing how I would feel.

"You're very pessimistic aren't you?"

"No... not really, just think that some people might... you know."

"You can hear a lot in someone's voice, you have to listen. People are a lot more trustworthy than you think."

I really did underestimate her, for all her disability, I began to wonder whether it was a disability or not, she was more aware of her surroundings than I was.

We didn't have to wait long for the bus, the driver was helpful and said he would let her know when we reached Hockley village green. Ann-Marie took a seat at the front, so she would hear the driver. This gave us no opportunity to talk, I could but she wouldn't reply.

It was one of those times when I wanted to say something really touching, I don't know what, just something to let her know how much I appreciated her. Everything I thought of, felt honest, but also, felt too contrived, at least that's how it sounded in my head. So I kept quiet.

Upon reaching our stop the sun was shining, the day had started dark, cold and grey, now it seemed autumnal.

The church and graveyard stood just the other side of the green set amongst a backwash of trees and fields. This was the head of the village. The houses and other buildings ran away from it like a carpet stretching out for miles widening in a wedge shape.

The church was huge for a village, the cemetery encased the whole building spreading out like a sheet. It had a well kept hedge forming the boundary, and an ornate archway framing the way in. There was no gate, they didn't want to keep people out. We walked through…

I was sitting in my car covered in dirt. I started the engine and pulled away.

I was heading along a dirt track of sorts, two channels in the grass the only evidence that vehicles travelled this way with some regularity. The surroundings, thick with trees. I didn't recognise the area. I didn't believe I'd ever been there before.

I'd just dumped the girl's body from last night. This revelation hit me like a tidal wave. Things were becoming clearer. I was beginning to feel the consciousness of my possessor, his thoughts. I'd left early in the morning to avoid being noticed. I'd parked my car in the block of garages down the road out of sight. There was an alley which led from my flat to these. That's how I'd got the body out. I was now heading home again.

"Daniel, Daniel"

"I'm here"

"I wasn't sure if you'd gone completely or ju…"

I turned right off the stretch of track onto a more prominent dirt track. *I knew where I was going, but I didn't I was gathering speed. Looking round to make sure I wasn't being watched. This was a long track.*

"Ann-Marie. What's happening?"

"I don't know. Help me locate the grave, quick before it's too late."

"What are we looking for? Do we have any idea at all."

"No I guess something discreet, it won't be very…"

A horse and rider came out of nowhere, I swerved in reaction. The horse reared, I crashed straight into a tree. Everything went black.

"Don't go Daniel, don't go. Please don't go. Not yet I can't do this without you."

"It's alright I'm here. I crashed. I think. I've blacked out. I'm not sure."

"How are we going to find the grave?"

"You wait here I'll have a quick search, maybe there'll be something obvious, anything."

"Ok, don't be long though."

"I won't"

I could see blood on the steering wheel. I could hear a horse thrashing about somewhere in the vicinity. I looked around, there was steam coming from the engine. I wearily opened the drivers' door and got out stumbling to find my feet, holding onto the car for stability.

The horse was on its side, the rider underneath, not moving.

I watched and did nothing.

I turned about, I was feeling disorientated.

When I focussed Ann-Marie was talking to an old lady. I resumed my search, randomly checking grave after grave, trying to locate something, something that would just be a mark of respect, anything. Nothing.

I went back to Ann-Marie as I didn't know how long I'd been away, I promised I wouldn't be long.

I was walking along the dirt track, limping. My left leg hurt. I could still hear the horse thrashing about. Now though, I heard a human voice as well.

"Ann-Marie" she was still talking with the lady. I ran to her "I can't find anything" I listened to the conversation knowing Ann-Marie couldn't speak to me without appearing mad.

"…66 or was it 63, I can't remember. My Albert would know. Always particular he was, took great care in his duties you know. They found the remains in the theatre at the bottom of a stairwell. Shame. They gave whoever it was decent reading though, Father Grace was very good, believed everyone deserved a proper send off, whether he knew who they were or not. He called them the lost souls. He laid a special area for them all so they wouldn't get lonely or lost amongst the others. Just to the right of the church, by that chestnut tree. Silly me you're blind, I'll lead you there. This way dear."

With that she grabbed Ann-Marie's hand and led her to the patch she meant, sure enough, there were eight or nine small stones, just a few inches square, each marked with a date and where the remains were found, apparently with the foresight that if they ever got identified they could be reunited with their correct families.

"Here you go dear."

"Thank you…"

"Irene. My names Irene. I'll leave you now."

"Thank you Irene."

With that Irene walked off leaving us to do what we had to do, the binding ritual. Ann-Marie laid her rucksack on the ground.

19

The cluster of small stones looked like a fairy site tucked neatly under the shade of a chestnut tree. Dates and locations made it easy to find Henry's grave.

Ann-Marie knelt on the ground and unloaded the contents of her bag onto the grass surrounding the stone. It was difficult to keep hold of Ann-Marie's hand, so I let go until the bag was empty of its contents. She identified each object by touch, the pebbles, the book, the candles, all neatly laid out. The last parcel to be taken was the plain brown box, opening the lid and unwrapping the contents, which were enveloped in tissue paper, it became obvious what they were, they chinked as she held them in her hand.

"My father gave them to me when I was eight. I used to like sleeping in a tent in the garden at night in the summer, but I was scared of the dark, so my father bought me these glass holders, they rest over the candle to stop the wind blowing them out. I used to put them outside the entrance to the tent weighted down with small stones in the glass bases. I'd watch them for ages before I fell asleep. In the morning the candles were all but gone...

Still stumbling along the dirt track, the horse cry was just a distant sound, barely audible. The pain in my leg was stifling, cutting me like acid, I had a pain in my head, behind my eyes, throbbing.

A few more steps, I fell to the ground, I cried out in pain, rolling over onto my back clasping my leg in my hands.

As I tried to get up I felt the strength drain from my body. My eyelids became heavy, body not responding to what I was telling it to do.

Darkness.

"... up and come back Daniel. I need you. I can't do this without you"

"I'm here" I interrupted, all too aware that I was fading in and out all too frequently.

"Daniel I'm scared, my vision is going, you're too weak for me to hold on to. When you go I don't see what you see anymore. It just goes dark."

"Did you not see any of it?"

"No."

Fear started to ease into me. What if I become too weak for Ann-Marie to use for her vision. How will she read the book? The incantation.

I felt a pain in my leg.

"Arrgh."

"What is it?"

"I can feel the pain in my leg. The same as in the vision."

Ann-Marie visibly shuddered, she picked up the book shaking. There were post-it notes protruding from the pages she needed. As I wasn't holding her hand at the time I watched as she felt for them, this was the first time I'd seen her struggle, as she deciphered which one was first and which was second, rather than helping I just watched. She opened the book at the first marker and I rested my hand on hers. There was a diagram, a symbol; an octagon with a square inside touching alternate angles, a triangle within that, drawn up from the bottom two corners, dissecting the top horizontal line in the middle.

The instructions detailed the positioning of the candles. One on the uppermost point of the octagon, with two either side on the next points down. A fourth candle was to be placed just inside the bottom most point of the octagon.

Ann-Marie untied the bag of pebbles, picking a handful out.

I opened my eyes, daylight shone directly into them, squinting I shielded them from the glare. I was still lying on the ground. I felt the moisture soaking my clothes, the cold. Pain shot through me like a bolt of lightning. I rolled around, again clutching my leg.

Finally I struggled to my feet. Dazed. Incoherent. I leaned up against a tree and took a closer look, I struggled to focus clearly.

Dirt, blood, I couldn't make any detail out. I ran my hand gently down my leg, I felt the rip in my jeans, and the open gash that was causing so much pain. I winced again. Then I became warm, the pain abated somewhat.

I took a few deep breathes, composing myself, and forced myself onwards, not sure where I was going, aimlessly I went on.

I could hear sirens in the distance. Not trying to locate the direction from which they were coming, I limped on.

Re-orientating myself.

"Ann-Marie, what's happening?"

"Daniel is that you?"

"Yes."

"You're faint."

Raising my voice slightly "Is that better?"

"Hold my hand" I did as requested "You're getting even weaker, my sight isn't as clear as it was. Look at what I've done so far... not bad for a blind person."

I looked at the gravestone where she had been working.

"Not bad at all" I agreed smirking, acknowledging the attempt to lighten the gravity of the situation and trying to hide my own fear knowing that this would not work.

Now she could see what she was doing she lit the candles, covering each in turn with one of the shades then turning to the next marker in the book. A page with the heading, 'Spiritual Binding'.

I had never believed in witchcraft before. Now, here I was, my existence depending on it. I had to smile, the irony.

Ann-Marie retrieved the pocket-watch from her bag, carefully unwrapping it, placing it in the centre of the triangle.

"I think we are ready now."

"Are you sure you can do this?"

"Heather said it is easy to do, providing you have the power and belief. She seems to think that I can do it, but I must believe" she paused, taking a breath and with more confidence continued "Yes I'm sure I can do this. Scared to death though, in case something goes wrong. But I'm sure it won't."

"I didn't mean to doubt you, I'm..."

I was laying on a stretcher, paramedics attending my leg, a collar round my neck. They were cutting away my jeans, cleaning the wound.

"Aargh, that hurts."

"Can you tell us what happened?" the paramedic was ripping open a dressing.

"I don't remember. I woke up just over there" I tried to point to the edge of the track.

"Do you remember ringing for the ambulance?"

"No" I felt the dressing being laid on the open wound.

"We are going to take you to Southend General Hospital and get you checked out. There doesn't seem to be any broken bones. You seem to have hit your head pretty badly and we need to get that checked out" she spoke confidently and I just let it wash over me.

There was silence.

The paramedic spoke to her partner.

I didn't hear the reply as I faded into unconsciousness again.

"Ann-Marie we've got to get this done quickly, I'm in an ambulance."

"I can't do this without you Daniel. Where are you? Please come back quickly. I'm scared."

"I'm here, next to you."

"That is you isn't it? I can't feel you."

"I'm here."

I covered her hand with both of mine and concentrated, hoping it would make the connection stronger. Mojo watched the events unfold from his seated position a few feet away behind Ann-Marie.

"You're back. I'm ready. Let's get on with it."

She started to read the incantation:

> Abyssium, Contortium
> Tresyteria
> Crytada
>
> Power of the Octagon
> Take back the force
> That set itself free
>
> Power of the square
> Give back life
> To the Soulshadow
>
> Power of the triangle
> Restore the three levels of life
> Heaven, Earth, Hell
>
> Entortius, Cryssedius
> Attoria
> Implata

As Ann-Marie said the incantation we felt the ground jolt. The pocket watch started spinning fast on the spot, stopped, then the lid flicked open and shut in quick succession. Heat began to radiate from it, intense heat.

I felt less and less as I watched the events unfold, it became more difficult to see things, vision blurred, then cleared.

The candles went out, one by one in sequence, middle top, bottom, right top, left top. Then they re-lighted in the same sequence, this occurred three times.

I don't know what I was expecting to happen, but I began to feel this was useless, and we were just observing some special effects.

I was in the ambulance, on the move, awake again, just. The pain seemed to be subsiding. My vision blurry. The paramedic was saying something, I was too drowsy to make it out. I felt sick. Then I felt a warmth.

The pebbles were glowing, candles burning brighter than I'd ever seen before.

The watch began to hover a few inches above the gravestone.

Mojo barked, Ann-Marie didn't react.

"What's going on there? Excuse me. What do you think you are doing? This is church not" the Vicar came rushing towards us, then stopped in his tracks.

Ann-Marie had turned to face the figure, her eyes wide and wild, as though she had seen some terrible event. The figure hesitated a while, turned and walked away without uttering another word, then at the corner of the church I saw him make the sign of the cross on his chest with his finger, his lips moved but we couldn't hear anything, he looked like he was praying.

I looked at Ann-Marie her hands were resting over the two bottom corners of the triangle, there was a channel of light running from her palms to the corners.

"Ann-Marie what's happening?"

She didn't hear me. She just carried on doing whatever she was doing.

Repeatedly she said the last line of the spell

"Entortius, Cryssedius, Attoria, Implata" her voice getting louder and stronger.

The back doors of the ambulance flew open, I felt the bed move but was not fully aware of what was going on around me, weary, I had no strength. I tried to take it all in. I couldn't place where I was, or who

I was. People were talking around me as if I wasn't there.

"Ann-Marie what's happening?"

Dread filled me, whatever was going on felt powerful, I was still doubtful it would work.

The watch still hovered above the centre of the triangle. The lid open, spinning fast, and faster still, then vanished in a burst of busy red light leaving only a scorched patch on the grass.

I could see a policeman walking behind me, he was explaining something to the paramedic. I don't know what.

I wanted to move. I was being held in, the nurse on my right was speaking to me, her words were just a mumble of noise. We entered a curtained cubicle where I was lifted onto another bed.

The policeman stood outside whilst they closed the curtain around me.

In the graveyard Ann-Marie was flat out on the ground, Mojo whimpering beside her licking her face, pawing at her shoulder trying to wake her up.

I hadn't got a clue what had happened, I didn't feel any different. I turned to the symbol on the grave, the individual pebbles were vibrating, then they shot up in the air about two feet before crashing to the ground where everything became still, all the glass candle shades had melted into a molten mess on the ground.

I stared at the scene. Not comprehending what had occurred. Not sure what to make of any of it. Ann-Marie still flat out on the ground. Had it all gone wrong?

Ann-Marie started to come round.

"Daniel, what are you still doing here? Didn't it work?

"I don't" I stuttered "I... I guess not."

"But I did everything right, I'm sure I did... I don't remember much but I'm..."

"It was scary you should ha..."

I felt every particle in my body contort, every muscle cramp at once. I felt I was going to explode. Then a flash of blue light pierced my eyes.

"AARRGGHH."

I was in the hospital bed, nurses all around.

"It's ok, You're in Southend General Hospital. You've been unconscious. You've been in an accident, we are just making you comfortable, then we'll take a few X-Ray's just to be sure there is nothing more serious and transfer you onto a ward".

"NO, it can't be."

20

"It's ok just lie back sir and rest, you'll be fine. A doctor will be with you shortly."

The nurse pushed me back down on the bed in a firm but gentle way, all the time reassuring me that I was in safe hands.

As I laid there I started to flex all the muscles in my body, individually, savouring every movement. The simultaneous feeling of relief and anxiety that came over me was overwhelming, knowing that finally I was back in control of my own body. At first I didn't want to believe it, half expecting to find myself back in the graveyard with Ann-Marie. I wanted to let myself be submersed in the desire to relax and sleep.

Something niggled in the back of my mind, something still didn't feel right. I was hoping I would find myself back at the beginning of this whole nightmare. I became more aware of the commotion going on around my cubicle I began to feel that I had been thrown further into the breech.

The course of events was still a little blurry in my mind, but slowly tiny details flashed back into my head, teasers, none of which made much sense. I could remember my time with Ann-Marie well, the visions, also, clear in my memory.

Henry Highway's time when I couldn't see what he was doing, this was not obsolete, as I expected it to be, it was there. I could sense it there in my head, yet not make it out with any clarity. Over the next few hours images flashed at me, like the visions, except this time, it was of past events.

Once all the doctors were happy with my condition they transferred me onto a ward, which was all but empty save one other patient who was asleep.

I rested uneasily. My thoughts scattered with images from the previous Sunday to now. My concerns were for Ann-Marie and her safety. Did she get home alright? After lights out, the dark took me into its slumber. My night was restless, fresh images replaying new memories.

Breakfast came round early the next day. I had forgotten how nice it was to eat. I liked my food. I wolfed down breakfast almost without a breath, before I noticed that I was now the only one in this six bed ward, sometime during the night my co-habitee had been taken away.

There was a TV at one end of the ward. I pushed my break-fast table to one side and got out of bed, careful not to jar my hurt leg which now only ached with a dull pain. I went to the TV and switched it on, easing down into the not so comfortable easy chair. Breakfast TV 'oh bliss' I thought to myself sarcastically.

News, great I could catch up on world affairs, I wasn't an avid fan of the news, yet it was nice to know what was going on in the world, and after the last few days a welcome relief. I relaxed, sat back and put my feet up, my left leg heavily bandaged and feeling a little stiff.

'NOW THE LOCALS NEWS' said the presenter followed by the jingle and title sequence, 15 seconds of nothing.

'Police who have been hunting a killer in Southend-On-Sea, who has been responsible for a spate of murders of young girls, are now holding a suspect who is helping them with their enquiries. The man believed to be in his early thirties was arrested following various tip-offs from the public after a photo-fit picture was released in the local press.

The vague description given by one of the victims, lucky enough to survive, after the attacker was disturbed by a vigilant farmer, led to a number of calls, with one name repeatedly turning up in the list.

His arrest followed a dawn raid this morning. He has been remanded in custody at an undisclosed police station for further questioning.'

The door to the ward opened, in walked two police officers. A cold sweat gripped me. I realised that I must have looked guilty even before anything further happened. They walked towards my bed, then turned to face the chair where I was sitting.

"Daniel Stephens?"

"Yes" I acknowledged, eyeing each in turn nervously.

"We'd like to ask you a few questions about yesterday."

"A-ha" I was try to act calm but not succeeding.

"I'm WPC Woodcote. This is PC Hamble."

They walked over to the chair PC Hamble standing directly behind me, WPC Woodcote standing to my right. I craned my neck to look at PC Hamble. Then set my eye on WPC Woodcote.

"Mr Stephens, in your own words, can you explain the events of yesterday, leading up to the time your car crashed into the tree?"

I gulped, a thousand thoughts rushed through my brain, guilty flashed like a neon sign, even though I knew I wasn't. I cleared my throat, voice trembling I began to speak. "I can't really remember exactly what happened. I remember swerving and then hitting the tree... next thing... was... coming round. There was steam rising from the bonnet of my car. I could feel pain in my leg, I don't remember getting out. Just a little while later walking, well, hobbling along the path, then it sort of goes blurry after that."

Both police officers were watching me intently, I could make out PC Hamble's reflection in the TV screen as he stood behind me, I switched off the TV set and this reflection became more intimidating on the blank screen.

WPC Woodcote continued the questioning "Can you explain

what you were doing in Belfairs woods yesterday?"

"Err... mm... I think I was just going for a drive, I was looking for a spot I know, but I took a wrong turn. I think. I'm not too sure." It was all coming back to me now, a flood of pictures, a film sequence developing before me. The events that I had no control over, but I was there. "No, I'm not sure, I know I left my house about 7am."

"159a William Street?" said PC Hamble.

I twisted my body to face him "Yes."

"It was a bit early to go out for a drive wasn't it?!" said WPC Woodcote as I faced her again "Carry on" after a pause.

"Well I couldn't sleep and didn't feel like staying indoors. I just fancied going out somewhere quiet, away from the world, my own little space. Yes I think my neighbour downstairs was being quite noisy. I couldn't get back to sleep. I thought I'd do some writing. Thought I'd look for somewhere inspirational, there is this place I found by mistake once and I thought I'd try and find it again. I couldn't remember the exact location though. I knew it was there somewhere in that general direction. I sometimes do things like that if I'm not in a hurry, just chuck my guitar in the car and find somewhere to write" I felt I was starting to find my footing now.

"Not exactly ideal weather at the moment for outside writing" PC Hamble interjected.

"Just songs, ideas. Different places, different inspirations, I do my writing all over the place really, depends on what I feel like. Sometimes I just sit in the car" I was beginning to convince myself that this is what had happened. It struck me that if they had checked my car they would not find a guitar! I was playing a dangerous game of bluff, relying on the fact that they hadn't checked my car thoroughly.

"So you didn't know where the track actually leads?" WPC Woodcote walked round to the other side of the chair. PC Hamble took up WPC Woodcotes position. I now had one on either side. The pressure was mounting, but my belief in me, that I was convincing them, that this was just an innocent jaunt, was growing with each lie.

"No I got to the end of the track, it was a dead end so I turned round, I was on my way back. I knew it was one of the tracks off the main road. I wasn't in a hurry that day so I thought I'd try that one, you know, see where it went."

"Right" WPC Woodcote carried on writing in her pad.

"Do you know what made you hit the tree?" asked PC Hamble.

"I don't remember. As I say I remember coming round."

"And your leg hurt" PC Hamble finished.

"You have no recollection of the events immediately prior to the crash?" finished WPC Woodcote.

"As I said, no it's just a blur. You've already asked me this" I was becoming more and more conscious that my body language was probably telling a different story "just a blur" I was replaying things. I sounded guilty to me.

"Sometimes you have to ask these questions twice because it can help trigger a memory. We just want to make sure we've got the facts as clear as they can be." WPC Woodcote paused and threw a glance at her colleague, it had a purpose "So from your statement, you are not aware that you narrowly missed a horse and its rider?"

I swallowed hard "Are they ok?" the words almost getting stuck in my throat.

"The rider was lucky, just sustained a bump to the head and badly bruised leg, however, the horse was not so lucky and had to be put down. Landed on a tree stump" WPC Woodcote fixed me with a stare, her eyes piercing the very masquerade I was trying to create. I could tell she was questioning everything I was saying, the only witness was the rider, so as long as I played it cool I'd be ok, my word against theirs.

There was silence, while both officers eyed me, putting me

on edge, they seemed to suspect something but had proof of nothing.

"Well Mr Stephens, thank you for your time. If we have any further questions for you we know where you live" WPC Woodcote stated with an air of certainty that they would be seeing me again. Then flipping their notebooks closed and putting them back in the pockets from which they came, turned and walk to the door.

As she opened the door WPC Woodcote spoke once more.

"Your clothes were covered in mud when you were brought in."

This was an odd sentence to throw in.

"Nothing else you want to add is their Mr Stephens?"

"No."

"If you think of anything else, don't hesitate to give PC Hamble or myself a call. Thank you again for your time."

They left, leaving me to sweat it out so to speak.

The door closed behind them.

After a few seconds I got up out of the chair and headed to the door to listen to the conversation as they wandered down the corridor.

It was a waste of time, I couldn't make out their voices clearly. I went back over to the bed.

I stood there, hands resting on the mattress, pondering the events of the last few days. The questions.

The murders now came cascading back in a flourish of vivid pictures, my stomach cramped and I felt sick, as if I had indeed actually committed them myself. Whilst in body I had, in spirit it was not me. How was anyone else to know that? How could I convince others?I could hardly start to describe the events from my perspective. They'd have me locked up and committed. Maybe that would be my only way out, plead insanity, tell the truth. They'd believe it then.

"Wait" I said to myself, "They can't prove anything,

can they?"

My real problem was I hadn't been witness to every second of every crime so I didn't know if I had been reckless and left loads of clues. Had I been careful and left none, in which case I could play ignorant if ever questioned about a possible link between me and the murders? In some instances that would be easy, but in others I would have to lie through my teeth.

Then a thought struck me like a sledgehammer to the head.

My flat.

That was one of the murder scenes, the carpet, the blood soaked carpet. Had it been investigated yet? No it can't have otherwise they would've arrested me.

Who did they have in custody then? Where was the dawn raid?

I was dealing with a killer with no sense of covering his tracks. Was he stupid?

I started pacing the ward. My leg still hurt but I could walk with a limp.

My finger prints, various DNA in the abandoned warehouse, forensics were so clever these days. Talk about making it easy for the police, I've framed myself, every way I looked at it I was guilty.

Sooner or later they would locate the body I buried near the car accident, sooner or later, probably sooner the way things were panning out. There was no way on earth I was getting out of this without going to prison for the rest of my life.

A lifetime in prison for crimes I didn't actually commit, knowing that someone else did this using my identity. I felt even more useless than I did before as a soulshadow, at least if I'd stayed like that I would have faded into non existence. I wouldn't have known any difference then. So intent was I to get my body back I didn't think of the consequences.

I stopped pacing and stood still in the middle of the ward.

My only conclusion was I had to run. Now. Go and hide

somewhere, until I could figure out what to do.
Who was the bloke they had in custody?

21

I checked the bedside cupboard for my clothes. There was no sign of them.

A middle aged lady in uniform, not a nurses uniform, entered pushing a trolley, she'd come to collect my breakfast things.

"Excuse me, Do you know where my clothes might be?"

"No, sorry I just do the meal runs" she cleared away my breakfast tray.

"Yes. Well. Will the nurses know do you know?"

"The Sister might know" she said sliding the tray into one of the rack slots.

"Thank you."

With that I followed the dinner lady out of the ward towards the Sister who was sitting at the desk.

"Excuse me, I'm Daniel Stephens, I was wondering where my clothes might be".

"They should be in your bedside cupboard. If they're not then, they might not have come up from... You came in yesterday didn't you!" she stated matter of factly "In which case they might still be in A&E. I'll see if I can locate them for you".

She picked up the phone that sat on her tidy desk and dialled an extension number, leaving it to ring.

"Doesn't seem to be anyone around to answer right now. When the Duty Nurse comes in I'll go and have a look for you."

"Thank you."

With nothing more I could do and a little frustrated I went back to my ward.

I found it difficult to sit still, uneasy at the way the course of events was unravelling. I paced the ward. Occasionally staring out the window not looking for anything in particular, as though it would provide me with all the answers, there was something I was not getting and I just couldn't put my finger on it.

It was quite a while before the nurse turned up with my clothes in a clear plastic bag, all neatly folded, they looked dirty and horrible.

"Here you go, they were a bit dirty so we stored them offsite. No, only joking, one of the nurses was going to bring them up last night at the end of her shift, but things got a little hectic."

"Thanks" I said smiling. I felt relieved just knowing that I had my own clothes to hand.

As the nurse left the ward I contemplated my next plan of action.

I needed to leave the hospital, although I wasn't a prisoner here I didn't want to cause a fuss or draw unnecessary attention to myself, I just wanted to slip out unnoticed. I needed a plan.

I casually walked out of the ward into the corridor paying close attention to the layout of the corridor, I was in full view of the Sister as she sat at her desk, like a sentry on guard, she smiled. I turned and walked in the opposite direction investigating my surroundings, pretending just to be on a casual stroll.

The gravity of the situation flooded over me, giving me an overwhelming sense of awe. I knew it would only be a matter of time before the police arrived to question me further, this time about the murders. This could become my prison.

I couldn't walk past the Sister dressed or she'd ask me where I was going. She couldn't stop me from leaving and checking myself out, she may insist on calling the Doctor though, which would draw attention that I didn't want.

Casually I strolled back into my ward and thought about it a while longer.

Finally, I decided it would be best to wander out to the toilet with the gown on over my normal clothes, my dirty blood soaked jeans rolled up above my knees. Although my clothes were dark maybe from a quick glance she wouldn't notice. Next problem was to conceal my shoes and socks. I puzzled this issue further.

Then it came to me. I got dressed, carefully rolling my jeans up tightly above the hem of the gown. I undid my shirt buttons allowing my shirt to freely hang and avoid being seen above the neck line folding the collar down underneath itself. Picking up a magazine and holding it in the hand that would be furthest away from the sister, slightly hidden by my own body, I collected my shoes positioning them in my grip so that they were held in total seclusion behind the magazine and I prayed this would work.

I checked all my pockets to make sure I had everything, especially my keys. Then I stole my moment and went for it. Trying to look as casual as possible.

The Sister had her head down, this was going to be easy.

"Everything alright Mr Stephens?" barely glancing up.

"Yes" I sharply replied, then easing "fine thank you just going to the toilet".

"Just straight down the corridor fourth door on the right".

"Thank you."

Fourth door on the right. 'Damn' I said to myself it didn't take me through the double doors, out of her immediate sight. As I came level with the door I glanced back, only a further ten feet to go, she wasn't at her desk. I didn't hesitate, I went through the double doors, making sure that I stopped them from moving after my exit, I couldn't believe how quiet the corridor was. I hoped there would be people about, anyone to help conceal me.

I looked around for directions to the nearest exit and followed the arrows. Corridor after corridor, left then right, then left again, down a flight of stairs, another flight of stairs, left again. This place was a maze.

I made ground level. Before I went through the final double doors into the corridor to the exit, I ducked behind a stairwell out of sight and put my shoes and socks on, taking off the gown and throwing into the deepest recess under the bottom step.

Through the double doors, turn right, daylight, then over the prison wall, as I described it in my head. They probably wouldn't even notice I'd gone, if I'd waited til they changed shift it would probably have been easier but I wasn't sure how long that was going to be. I felt guilty, guilty about the murders, they were my fault. I started this charade and now I had to finish it. I didn't know how.

The final push. The breakthrough of the perimeter fence then exultation.

Another quick glance back to make sure I wasn't being followed. No. Out on to Crescent Boulevard, a dual carriageway, it had a long grass and tree lined track running down the middle separating the two carriageways.

Heading left, first thought to go home and get a change of clothes. Then to see Ann-Marie, make sure she got home alright yesterday. I hoped it was only yesterday. Yes, the police officers had referred to it as yesterday.

I didn't live more than a ten minute walk from the hospital. I was limping quite badly, the pain from my leg making its presence known the more I walked. It took me nearly 25 minutes.

Nearing my flat, I stopped and observed the area. I was nervous about entering my road. I knew what had occurred there and it chilled me to the bone.

I decided in the end that it would be better to enter via the back door. I could not help feel that this was overcautious, after all they had a man in custody, they weren't looking for me, yet they suspected I was hiding something. I let myself smile, this would provide me with breathing space.

A feeling of unease washed over me as I reached the back door. I pulled my keys slowly from my pocket. I paused. It seemed too perfect. Something wasn't right, didn't sit easy.

I caught a movement inside my flat. I pulled away from the glass back door, flinging my back to the wall adjacent the entrance. 'Shit that was close' I thought to myself.

The curtains twitched, I heard the key go into the lock from the other side. Looking round I tried to decide my best option. Fear pushing the adrenaline around my body, like a train at full speed.

I jumped over the railings that separated my balcony from my neighbours balcony, stifling the cry of pain as I landed on my injured leg, clasping a hand over my mouth biting down hard. Crouching down I hid behind the brick built shed that was there, the same as on all the balconies in this run of flats. Tears streamed down my cheeks from the pain, inside my head I was letting out a stream of obscenities.

I heard the door open, then abruptly close. No explanation. No voices. Someone just changed their mind.

I waited a few minutes before I dared look. Slowly I peered round the corner of the shed. The balcony was clear. I couldn't go in now. I didn't know who it was. I had to leave.

I made my way to the garden below using my neighbours stairs, heading once again into the alleyways that thread their way behind the gardens. I didn't want to leave the way I'd come in case it was being watched, so I took the alley further along that lead out into the road behind and ran parallel to mine. All the time paying attention to what was going on around me and aware of the throbbing pain in my leg.

At the edge of the alley I looked out before crossing the threshold, making sure the coast was clear. It was.

I had to get to Ann-Marie's house, that was the only place I felt I could go now. No one knew about her.

I was desperately trying to shut out the pain from my leg, I was unsuccessful, the odd tear making its way gently down my cheek, before being brushed away with the side of my hand. I felt a warm sensation around the wound in my leg, without checking I guessed that it was bleeding again.

I was not going to take the most direct route to Ann-Marie's in case I was seen. Again my imagination was my own worst enemy. I was beginning to doubt my own sanity. Maybe I was being sensible.

A car pulled up curtly by the curb across the road, tyres screeching. I jumped, turned round almost ready to run. False alarm. A boy racer got out and went into the house he was in front of.

I proceeded along the road, all the time aware that my limping was getting more pronounced, trying to conceal it hoping the pain would subside.

An eternity seemed to pass before I made it to Clock Street. I could see the yellow door of Ann-Marie's house. The pain seemed to fade away replaced by a feeling of security.

I rang the door bell. Again. And again. I didn't know what I would do if she wasn't in. I heard movement within.

The door opened and I saw Ann-Marie, I wanted to hug her, not sure whether it was relief she was safe and in or just the fact that I was pleased to see her.

"Thank god you're in, I was beginning to wonder what I was going to do, I wasn't sure if you'd got home alright yesterday or anything."

"Daniel, is that you?"

"Yes" I said with resignation.

"You sound different than before."

"Do I?"

We stood there poised, like two friends meeting for the first time in twenty years.

"Come in. Sorry, I didn't think I would meet you again" she closed the door behind us "it worked. I can't believe it worked."

She smiled chuffed.

"It worked alright. But now I'm the murderer. For real! The one the police are hunting."

"No the police have a man in custody. I heard it in the news this morning."

"That may have been this morning. But someone was just at my flat, I didn't get a proper look, but I think it was them. As soon as they see the blood stain on the carpet, then find the body buried near the car accident yesterday my days are numbered for sure."

"Oh" she exclaimed.

"Exactly. I thought the ritual would put everything right, but it hasn't, this is worse. If..." I corrected myself "...when they catch me I'll go to prison for the rest of my life."

Silence issued in the hallway.

"We need to see Aunt Rose, she might be able to help. I'm sorry. I thought it would put everything right." She looked if she wanted to cry.

"So did I" I looked at her then opened my arms to embrace her "I'm sorry, it's not your fault. You've helped me so much and I'm just throwing it back in your face."

I felt her reciprocate the embrace. A warm feeling penetrated every fibre of my body.

"I'm sure Aunt Rose, or even Heather will be able to help. They must be able to do something."

"Is there any chance they could come round here, I'm not sure how wise it would be for me to go out on the streets. Especially during daylight."

"I'll give her a ring."

She released her grip from me and picked up the phone, dialling the number she knew by heart.

22

Ann-Marie took her time and explained the situation as best she could to her Aunt. I took the opportunity to make myself at home and went and made a cup of tea for us both, afterwards settling down in the lounge, it felt good to be able to do things I'd taken for granted before.

I half listened to the telephone conversation taking place out in the hallway while switching the TV on. It was about 11.30am. Flicking through the channels I couldn't find anything of any interest to watch. I heard the phone being put down and lowered the volume on the TV.

"Aunt Rose said she'd be round shortly, she is going to speak to Heather, to try and find out what went wrong." Ann-Marie announced as she entered the room before settling down in her favourite armchair "The ritual should have returned you to the moment of the original transfer of power. That's why I wasn't worried about going to the cemetery, I didn't expect to still be there afterwards. Everything should have been as if it never happened. I don't know what went wrong. I did everything as I was supposed to. Heather said I had enough power, and." She stopped mid flow.

"And what?"

"And it had to be done by someone who..."

"Someone who what?"

"Someone who... had the power... and strength enough to see it through" she looked almost embarrassed.

"I'm certainly glad you do. But why didn't it work?" this was a rhetorical question on my part. "I hope you don't mind I made a cup of tea, it's just on the table where you normally have it."

"No, of course not. Thanks" she picked it up and drank slowly "Yuk!"

"What?"

"No sugar."

"Sorry I didn't know you took any."

"Two normally."

"I'll go and get some."

"Thank you."

I left the room and headed for the kitchen. I heard the volume go up on the TV.

I re-entered carrying the sugar bowl and a spoon, proceeding to add two teaspoons of sugar.

"I guess you got back ok yesterday without any problems."

"Sort of. Thanks." I stirred her tea "A little while after I'd done the ritual I was gathering up my things when I heard the vicar. He was saying something, I wasn't really listening, I just wanted to get away from there. I think it must have been some sort of protection. He probably thought I was trying to conjure up the devil or something. I thought he might have tried to grab hold of me or something, he didn't until I tried to leave."

"I think you scared him when you stared at him, your eyes were wide and wild."

"What do you mean?"

"Your eyes, you looked as though you were possessed when the Vicar first came out and saw you".

"Oh. Anyway I quickly grabbed my things and put them in my bag. Called Mojo and we left in a hurry. When he did grab my bag I struggled, he started calling me the devil's child... the handle broke and it fell to the ground. Mojo growled at him, he let go then" she patted her companion, who was laying by her feet, on the head. Her voiced softened "I didn't register at first that the shades had melted. Not 'til I got home. I just instinctively picked them up and put them in my pack as carefully as I could" She sniffed.

I just sat there and listened. I realised those lamps meant a lot to her and she'd sacrificed them for me.

"Anyway at that point I made a hasty exit, chanting gibberish at him" she smiled " I think he must have been scared because his voice became tense."

"Did you catch the bus home?"

"No, I decided to walk, it wasn't raining. And. And I wasn't sure if it had actually worked I just fancied the walk."

"That's Belfairs Woods" I caught out of the corner of my eye the fact that the lunchtime news had started. "Quick turn up the volume."

"Where is it?" she said searching the coffee table with her hands.

"Sorry, I've got it."

I reached for the remote and turned up the volume.

POLICE HAVE DISCOVERED TWO MORE BODIES OF YOUNG GIRLS THOUGHT TO BE THE VICTIMS OF A KNIFEMAN WHO HAS BEEN TERRORIZING THE LOCAL AREA.

THE FIRST DISCOVERY WAS MADE, IN BELFAIRS WOODS, IN THE EARLY HOURS OF THE MORNING WHEN POLICE AND A RECOVERY TEAM WERE INVESTIGATING THE SCENE OF AN ACCIDENT FROM THE PREVIOUS DAY. TYRE TRACKS WERE TRACED TO A SECLUDED SPOT WHERE A SHALLOW GRAVE HAD BEEN DUG.

POLICE ARE NOW HUNTING THE DRIVER OF THE VEHICLE WHO WAS TAKEN TO HOSPITAL BUT LATER DISAPPEARED. POLICE HAVE TAKEN THE UNUSUAL STEPS OF RELEASING THE NAME OF THE SUSPECT THEY WANT TO QUESTION 'DANIEL STEPHENS' POLICE ARE APPEALING TO ANYONE WHO KNOWS HIS WHEREABOUTS TO CONTACT THEM. DO NOT APPROACH HIM AS HE COULD BE ARMED AND DANGEROUS.

IN ANOTHER TWIST TO THIS STORY EVIDENCE OF
MURDER HAS BEEN FOUND IN A FLAT OWNED BY MR
STEPHENS. POLICE FORENSICS ARE TAKING DNA SAMPLES.
A SECOND BODY WAS DISCOVERED IN AN ABANDONED
WAREHOUSE IN GERALD STREET.
POLICE DO THINK THE MURDERS ARE CONNECTED.

"It was the police at the flat his morning."

"How did you get away?"

"I climbed onto my neighbours balcony. And hid. Then when I thought the coast was clear used the back alleys to get away. I wasn't exactly running though, more like limping"

"You'll be ok here for now, you'll have to be gone by the time mother gets in. If she sees you she'll call the police for sure."

"It's ok. I understand" I said as I thought of my options.

Ann-Marie got up and turned the TV off. "Do you have any idea where you can hide?"

"Nope. I can't exactly go to any friends. Not if they've seen the news. Hold on."

"What?"

"The tunnels, I can hide out in the tunnels, if they were good enough for Henry they are good enough for me. Not exactly the Ritz but they'll have to do."

"They'll be a bit cold and dark though."

"I don't believe I've got much choice. Have you got some candles and matches I can borrow?"

"I don't think I have, I used the last few when we went to the cemetery. I'll check" with that she headed towards the kitchen. I settled back into the chair letting my body relax completely. I felt all the aches and pains rushing back to me like mini explosions. The wound on my leg throbbed. Through the rip in my jeans I could see the bandages were blood stained. I would have to ask Ann-Marie for a clean dressing, if she had one. All energy drained from me as the adrenalin that had got me this far dissipated leaving me feeling tired. My eyelids grew heavy and I drifted into a restless snooze.

"... got any candles."

"Pardon? What? Sorry I fell asleep."

"That's ok. No we haven't got any candles."

"I'll have to get some on my way to the tunnels. Damn. I haven't got any money. Have you got any money you can lend me? I promise I'll pay it back as soon as I can."

"I'll go check" she left the room for a second time. I felt guilty, all I kept doing was asking for favours. How could I ever pay her back?

The doorbell rang. I went to the window, and discreetly peered through the net curtains to see who was there, it was Aunt Rose. I breathed a sigh of relief then went and answered the door.

"Hello."

"Daniel, I presume?"

"Yes, in the flesh this time" Aunt Rose walked past me and went into the lounge. I closed the door and followed.

"Where's Ann-Marie?"

"She went upstairs. Be down in a minute".

I didn't know what to say at this point. Although she'd helped thus far, it was a meeting between two strangers.

"You're different to what I'd imagined, quite a handsome fellow really."

I felt my cheeks go red. I didn't normally blush so readily.

"Thanks, I think."

"Have you seen the news, this morning?"

"Yes."

"So do you know who the other person is then?"

"Other person! What other person?"

"They've discovered two sets of unidentified fingerprints at your flat. So the police believe they are looking for two people".

"They are probably my parent's fingerprints, they have got a key."

"They have already eliminated them."

"I don't understand."

"This is all the money I've got, there's about £23 and some small change. Aunt Rose?"

I took the money and put it in my pocket thanking Ann-Marie.

"Hello dear."

"There is... two of us, now" I said half stunned.

"How can that be? I thought you were the murderer. So how can there be two" Ann-Marie was just as perplexed as I was.

The whole situation seemed to have changed in an instant. Not only had my life been turned upside down by the events of the last few days, but now there was someone else involved who's identity we had no idea about.

Maybe it wasn't the police at the flat this morning when I went back. It could have been the other person, I should have looked to see who it was. That must have been who ran from the police this morning, after I'd already gone. These thoughts ran round my head.

The question was, how were we going to find out who this other person was?

"Aunt Rose, is there any way we can track this other person?"

"I could use my crystal ball but that will only tell us what it wants to. I will give it a... " she paused looking at us individually "there is something else you should know which might tell us who exactly this second person is."

"What's that?" we both said in unison.

"First, Ann-Marie have you got the book of incantations that Heather lent you?"

"Yes, it's upstairs. Why?"

"Heather said one reason the ritual might not have worked

the way it should is that you might have not followed the instructions accurately and possibly not set up the DoxTrident Octagon correctly."

"But I followed the directions and the diagram" she said adamantly.

"It's alright dear, I'm just trying to establish a few facts".

"Sorry" she lowered her head abashed.

"It would appear that if the candles are placed at the wrong points it gives life back to the spirit in its own form. That's why I need to know what you did exactly."

I looked at Ann-Marie with disbelief, she gulped.

"So we could have brought back a murderer from the grave?"

"Yes, I'm afraid."

"And that's why everything is still carrying on rather than reverting back to the beginning?" I rhetorically asked.

"Yes" Aunt Rose confirmed.

"I did my best. It was difficult, Daniel you kept fading and…"

Ann-Marie didn't finish her sentence.

23

Ann-Marie fled the room using her hands to guide her, footfalls heavy on the stairs. We heard a door slam shut upstairs.

I eyed Aunt Rose with questions I couldn't verbalise. Dread pulsing through my veins like liquid nitrogen, sending shivers along my spine. She sat on the settee quite still, spinning a thought around her head.

Silence echoed through the room, only broken by a faint sob coming from upstairs.

At first I didn't know what to do. I looked at Aunt Rose then I followed the sound to the bathroom, the door was closed. I lightly tapped on the door with my knuckle.

"Are you alright?" I knew this seemed like a stupid question, I knew the answer, it was my way of letting her know I was there.

"I'll be fine in a second" came the reply amidst the sounds of sniffs, and blowing of nose. I heard rushing of water from a tap, followed by the flushing of the toilet. A few seconds later the door opened and I put my hand on Ann-Marie's shoulder as a sign of comfort. Her eyes were red from tears, cheeks flushed.

"Are you ok?" I enquired with softer tones.

"I feel sick."

I gave her a hug. She rested her head on my shoulder and reciprocated. "I'm sure there is something we can do" I was not convinced. Come on, let's go down stairs and see if Aunt Rose has any ideas"

I released her from the hug and took her hand, leading her slowly down the stairs.

We entered the lounge where Aunt Rose had taken out her crystal ball and was gently caressing it with her hands as if polishing it, intently staring, her eyes glued in place. We sat silently on the settee, I let go of Ann-Marie's hand. Mojo raised his head, cocked it at a slight angle then settled down again.

"I can see a man. Rugged face, slim build, dark eyes, neatly kept hair. He has got a red shirt on, blue jeans, black anorak. Cold, he is very cold. Sitting in some gardens, watching the people go about their business. He appears to be waiting for someone" she paused, the concentration on her face intent "No it's gone."

"Is that him?" I said.

"Yes it is" replied Aunt Rose replacing the crystal ball on a stand on the coffee table.

"How can he sit there so calmly. Waiting. I've got to hide. He openly goes about his business like he hasn't got a care in the world" I was agitated and logic had escaped me.

"You must remember that he has been living your life for the last few days. He knows the police are looking for you. They thought it was you running from the flat this morning. He has the advantage. His face has not been seen for nearly eighty years. No one knows him."

"So I can end up in prison for the rest of my life while he walks away scot free." I got up and paced the room clenching my fists "Can you tell whereabouts in the town he was?"

"No I'm sorry, it was just a garden I couldn't see too much clear detail. But there was a fountain, behind where he was sitting."

"Aunt Rose is there anything that can be done to put everything right? Correct my mistake."

"It's not your fault Ann-Marie. You've done everything you could, it was a difficult situation in the first place, with me fading in and out, you needed me to see the diagram. It can't have been easy for you."

"Thanks" she took my hand and held it in hers.

"I need to locate Henry. But I can't exactly go out during the day. And I don't recall seeing a fountain in any of the gardens in the area. Would your mum have a map of the area Ann-Marie? Do you know?"

"I don't."

"I have one at home Daniel. I could go and get it. It may take a while though."

Aunt Rose had a motherly way about her, always helpful, always had a solution to a problem.

"Hold on. Now I think about it. I think I recall a newspaper article, about a year ago, one of the local freebies. Yes a fountain being erected in memory of some local famous person, name escapes me, a politician I think. What was the name of the gardens though?!" I closed my eyes trying to picture the article in my head, believing this would help me remember the name of the gardens. "Oh what was the name?" I could have kicked myself. I could picture it but not see the name clearly. "Parry, Parly, Farley... Falley... Farry..."

"Farndon Gardens, near the town hall" said Aunt Rose.

"That's them. Yes. Of course the fountain was erected as the final piece to the gardens which were in memory of Ex Mayor Charles Farndon who served Southend-On-Sea in 197...2, I think, until 1988 when he retired because of ill health. He died in 199..." I added.

"1999, and they decided to commemorate all the good work that he'd done. I remember him. He was a good Mayor. Shame. He always cared about the local community, not like the ones nowadays, who just want to make a name for themselves. He didn't, just wanted to do the best he could." Aunt Rose obviously felt very passionately about his accomplishments.

"Didn't they..." Aunt Rose continued "... discover an entrance to a tunnel that no one seemed to know anything about. That's what caused the big stir. It was only about ten, fifteen feet long, blocked by debris. No one could explain its presence, nothing untoward was ever discovered so they sealed it up again."

"I wonder if he realises yet!"

Beep beep, it was a mobile phone. Aunt Rose opened her bag and got her phone out.

"Ooh I've got a message. Oh bother, I can never remember how to work these things."

I went over and showed her, it was a message from Heather. Aunt Rose struggled to read the little screen:

'HAVE FOUND WAY. WILL CALL LATER. H'

"What does that mean?" I asked.

"Before I came over I explained the situation to her and asked if she knew of anyway we could correct what had happened. I suspected straight away, as soon as I got the phone call from Ann-Marie, what had happened and the possible consequences."

I went and watched the world outside the window while listening to the dialogue. It was starting to get dark, the fact that it had remained overcast all day just helped the night sky form it's shadow over the town sooner.

"I'm going to try and find him. I can't stay here and do nothing it's driving me insane. It should be dark enough now. If you've got a coat or top with a hood on it that I can borrow I should be able to get by without being recognised."

"But what are you going to do?" questioned Ann-Marie.

"I honestly don't know but I've got to do something. Maybe if I find him I can stop him."

"There's no point if you can't do anything, you could get caught, and that won't help at all."

"Ann-Marie I've got to go. I'll simply have to be careful, that's all, and not get caught" I left the room. "Have you got a coat I can borrow?" I said from the hall.

"Yes. I'll go and get it."

"Thanks."

Ann-Marie headed upstairs to her room, returning minutes later with a coat. It was lucky for me that Ann-Marie was a bit of a tomboy, the coat was ideal. A three quarter length Parker, fake fur lining the cuffs, and rim to the hood.

"Thank you. Your mum will be back soon, so I'll see you tomorrow. Bye. Bye Aunt Rose and thank you."

"It's ok dear. Be careful."

"I will."

With that I headed out into the dark night, immediately putting the hood up. I heard the door close behind me. It was coldish so I didn't look out of place with the hood wrapped tightly round my head and my hands thrust deep into my pockets. I knew my destination and I walked there as fast as my limp would allow.

15 minutes later the entrance to the gardens was in view. I stopped just outside and took a deep breath. I had no great description to go on, so wasn't absolutely sure who to look for. In the depths of my mind I just thought I would know the moment I saw him, a feeling I couldn't justifiably explain.

There were a lot of people milling around now, the town clock showing it was half-past four, some people were already heading home from work, to snuggle up in their warm houses in front of the TV.

I should have been going bowling with some friends tonight, a few drinks, a bit of fun. Instead I was playing the 'Game of my Life', tails I lose, heads I lose, that's how I felt.

Searching even a small crowd of people was no easy task, every male face could be him. I just didn't know. I walked into the gardens, which were not very large, barely 200 feet long and 60 feet wide. No obvious hiding places visible here; not even during daylight, it was dark so I couldn't just look from one position I had to wander round.

No one. Deserted except for me. I stood there deflated just

the breath vapour which formed clouds in the air in front of me to keep me company. I didn't know what I expected to find, but it wasn't here.

Before leaving I glanced round once more.

Over in the far corner to my right there was movement, I could just make out a dark shadow in the bushes. My heart jumped into my mouth, I gulped down another mouthful of air. Slowly I limped in the direction of the movement.

I felt my nerves rattling on edge, fists clenched, I was ready for a fight. It was what I wanted, after everything that had happened, to let out my frustration. The closer I got to the bushes, the more the adrenalin was pumping through my body fuelling my actions.

I took a step off the path and into the bushes, careful to be observant for any sudden movement.

I felt the force of a wrecking ball strike me across the back of the shoulder blades, throwing me to the ground. Winded I lay there. My arm went numb where I'd banged my elbow as I hit the ground. Looking around to see where the force that had hit me had gone I made out a figure running through the gates of the gardens, a tear in my eye from the cold.

I rolled over onto my front thrusting my right foot to the ground to help bring me to full height. Pain issued, a reminder that my leg was hurt "Aaarggh, Damn, Shit" I said falling to the ground again. I didn't know what to grab first, elbow, leg, or shoulders.

I stood up trying to avoid putting too much pressure on my leg, which until now I'd almost forgotten was hurt. The limp was comfortable now, pain minimal.

I proceeded to the entrance of the gardens as fast as it allowed, when I got there whoever it was, was gone. Standing, I looked back to the corner where I had been knocked over and walked back hoping to find something, I entered the bushes, nothing. I found nothing. It was dark and I wasn't sure if I was expecting to find a body or an entrance to some tunnels. That was a thought, maybe he was looking for the entrance, which had once been there. My shoulders started to feel stiff. I rolled them around to loosen the aching muscles.

That thought firmly planted in my head I left the gardens to the night. I was hungry and needed food as well as candles. There was a chip shop not far from the gardens, also a selection of fast food outlets.

My one problem was to avoid being recognised, all the shops were well lit. I needed to conceal my face, that would prove difficult. Fish and chips sounded nice, I could almost taste it already. It was no good I couldn't risk it. I would have to find a shop where I felt I could get away with it.

I made my way along the high street keeping in the shadows, passed one of the pubs, I noticed a kebab van down the side street. I didn't like kebabs, but I was hungry and I needed to keep my strength up, it was cold, and it was going to be a cold night, so I was left with little choice.

When I reached the van I found they did quite a selection of foods, so I bought a burger and chips. There were no crowds at this time so it was easy to conceal my identity. Walking away I ate quickly, quenching my hunger.

Ambleside Gardens was where I was heading, there was an entrance to the tunnels there, the place should be deserted about now. On the way I passed a corner shop closing up for the day; half the lights were already extinguished I decided to take my chances. I persuaded the owner to sell me my requirements just before he closed for the night, some candles, matches, and a few snack bits for my overnight stay.

Once in the gardens I looked round to make sure I was not being watched, then disappeared into the trees and bushes. Locating the entrance which I had observed a couple of days previous, through the eyes of an exiting murderer. I pulled the cover open, it was not easy, the growth of vines on the walls held it tight. Once it was prized open enough for me to squeeze through, I did so, pulling it closed behind me finding myself thrown into complete blackness.

24

I opened the box of candles and lit one. Beyond the realm of the light the darkness seemed like an abyss of nothingness. I felt scared, cold and alone, only these damp walls as my companions, my ears like radars picking out every sound.

Something about the blackness made me feel uneasy, feeling safer staying near the entrance even though there was a draft penetrating. For some strange reason, because it was night, the tunnels appeared even more sinister. Daylight had no effect in here, so why it made the difference I can only surmise as being psychological.

I was probably more at risk from an unwelcome visitor staying here, but going further in sent a chill down my spine. Noises punctuated the darkness, firing my imagination to create all sorts of images, sinister things lurking in the shadows ready to pounce at me. My mind was in its element here, furtive with ideas, strange goings on.

Inching my way along the tunnel, the small flicker of light that I carried seemed useless in the vast array of black. It was the best I could do. In some respects it was better than the torch which was directional as this illuminated the whole area immediately surrounding it, making me feel a little more comfortable, the tiny bit of warmth enveloping my hand.

I was looking for somewhere to settle down for the duration of this long night. I was looking for somewhere clean and cosy, I laughed to myself, I was expecting the Ritz in a damp horrible tunnel. Lowering the candle I surveyed the ground to see what the conditions were like. The ground looked damp and mushy, a sandy type soil that looked like it would get everywhere if you sat on it. I had not brought anything to rest on, so I was at least looking for somewhere dry. I had an idea.

I emptied the carrier bag that I'd be given to carry the few snacks I'd bought, filling various pockets in the coat. I took three more candles out of the box and lit them, burying them a little in mounds of dirt to keep them upright. I then split the bag as carefully as I could down one side and along the seam at the bottom. Opening it out I laid it on the ground. That was best I could do to keep myself clean. I settled down, trying to get comfortable resting my back against the wall, moving the four candles closer to me, trying to make the most of the little heat they gave off.

Closing my eyes I tried to sleep, taking deep breaths, expelling the air slowly, trying to relax. Every time I was near to falling asleep a noise from the darkness would stir me, making me alert, ready to defend myself if necessary.

I was not wearing a watch so did not know how much time was passing. I was relieved in a way, as I would have constantly been looking at it, getting more and more frustrated that the hands would not have moved, wondering if the battery had stopped.

After what seemed an eternity the cold started to affect my toes and fingers. I put my hands in my pockets but this felt uncomfortable because of the position in which I was sitting. Weighing up my options I concluded that at least they were warmish. I wriggled my toes about to generate a little warmth. The heat this generated would only last for a few seconds before dissipating quickly leaving them back where they started, the cold biting back with a vengeance.

With back ache starting I tried to sit bolt upright, stretching every tense muscle, lowering and raising each shoulder in turn, just to get the blood flowing again.

As I moved it reminded me how cold it had become, every

movement emphasizing the warm patch of my body that I had uncovered. I rocked on my backside, side to side, clenching my knees into my chest, hands buried in the alternate sleeves of the coat. 'Is the night ever going end?' was the thought that rallied round my head as I sat there wishing the night away.

After a while sleep finally consumed me.

It was not a restful sleep, full of visions, replaying scenes in my head, the past few days echoing in silence.

Unfamiliar faces started to haunt my dreams, I felt they should be familiar to me, but I didn't know them, strange situations. Men in long red hooded cloaks were kneeling on the floor, a dozen or so. Two were standing at the front before a table. A naked man lay on the table. The ones kneeling were chanting the same thing over and over again.

Candles lit the whole room. There were no windows.

Symbols had been drawn upon the walls behind the table, an upside down cross in the middle on the right of what looked like a cutlass with an eye in the top of the handle. The image on the left was a moon or a sun, could be either.

The two men standing at either end of the table held the hands and feet of the one laying down.

A priest type figure entered, dressed in the same cloak, carrying a staff in one hand that was at least six foot in length, white and with an upside down cross at the top. In the other hand he carried a silver chalice with what looked like the handle of a pestle in it.

Standing behind the table he said something in a language I didn't recognise. The room fell silent, resting the chalice on the table he lifted the pestle out and drew a shape on the chest of the man, all the time saying something I couldn't make out, repeating it continuously. The man was conscious, seeming relaxed, the candles burned brighter.

All was silent, the pestle was replaced into the chalice, his left hand was now hovering above the man's chest.

The man began convulsing, his whole body writhing around in spasms, the two men holding his feet and hands struggled to keep them still. Steam rose from the marks on the man's chest. Then all went still. Every single pair of eyes in the place suddenly focussed on me. I stood up and began to run, but I felt hands grabbing at my shoulders, my ankles, my waist, I was being lifted above their heads then I was placed on the floor, held down by four men. The priest's figure shadowed me, standing above my head, he was saying something, tapping the staff rhythmically on the ground first to the right of my head, then to the left, then directly above it, finally raising it to about two feet above my face. I saw it move towards me. I screamed.

I was awake, cold sweat running down my face. It was pitch black the candles had long since exstinguished themselves, my breathing heavy and laboured the cold air penetrating my lungs. Shaking, I glanced in every direction, checking that I couldn't see anything. Cramp caused my left leg to spasm I took it in both hands and massaged the calf muscle gently. I stood up, started to walk around to get the blood flowing through my veins again, slowly it eased.

As I walked around in a tight circle I tried to make sense of the dream, or was it a nightmare? I must have watched too many horror films and with the latest events it was starting to twist my mind. That was my prognosis. It made me feel better.

In my rush to go to the gardens I hadn't brought anyway of contacting Ann-Marie. I was on my own.

'How careless' I thought.

I decided not to stay where I was, it was too cold, I would investigate the tunnels further. I lit two more candles from the box, one for each hand, this would give me more light. I headed in the only direction I could, this time paying more attention to my surroundings than I had done on my first visit here.

I walked slowly but steadily. Within 100 yards the tunnel took a sharp right turn. Every now and then I stopped and looked carefully at the walls to see if there were any markings, or even any more cupboards like the one before, nothing, just brick.

The passageway narrowed to about three feet wide and remained like this for a way, then I came to a step ladder fixed to the wall. Raising one of the candles above my head I tried to see where it went. The ladder disappeared into the dark. Debating whether to climb up or not was easy. I had the whole night to wile away, and was in no hurry.

I placed one candle at the bottom of the ladder and climbed carefully, holding the other. From the entrance where I'd entered the tunnels, I wasn't aware that I had travelled down further underground but the ladder seemed endless. I hesitated briefly because of the pain in my leg; the cold had numbed it, now I was generating heat it was reminding me of my injury, I pondered whether I should continue. I hooked my left arm round a couple rungs of the ladder and held the candle up with my free hand. I wasn't far from the top.

I proceeded upwards, although now I could feel something sharp on the rungs, they looked like barnacles, similar in colour and texture in the dim light. The ladder ended abruptly. It had been cut, and in place directly above my head was a concrete slab. I tried pushing but knew it was hopeless. I didn't waste anymore energy, I descended the ladder.

I continued along the route I had already started. The passageway widened again to approximately five feet, there was a spur tunnel to my left and a little further along the tunnel appeared to turn right. In the dim light I could make out another entrance on the left. My eyes were starting to adjust to the darkness.

In my head I tried to work out approximately where I'd be in relation to the streets above, calculating distance as best I could in strides. By my calculations I was either under the high street or the other side of it, not far from the railway station, town hall to my right, theatre to my left. I went left.

Something in my subconscious made this seem the appropriate way to go.

This tunnel went on for an age, without passageways off it, or diversions to the route. Dust started to fall from the roof of the tunnel, vibrations ran through the ground, a low rumbling sound reverberated round the brick walls, quickly the vibrations became more severe, the light flickered in my hand, dust fell on my head. The noise was horrendous. The tremors seemed to reach their climax, and then started to settle until all was still. I stood still contemplating what that were. It took me a while to realise it was a train. I was definitely near the station.

Moving on, the passage narrowed again, barely 18 inches wide. I had to go through sideways.

There was a recess on both sides. On one side the wall was smooth, no signs of anything. The other had bolts sticking out of it, evenly spaced, two parallel lines of them running upwards out of sight. In the dim light I could see the entrance to another chamber but it was about ten feet above me and I had no way to get up there.

Further along, another tunnel ran off to my left. I followed it. Within twenty paces my progress was barred due to a tunnel collapse.

I turned about continuing on in the general direction of the theatre.

I passed a chamber on my right, glancing in, shedding some of the candles light in. A small bundle of rags lay on the floor in the corner. I studied them from a distance before walking over to investigate further.

A couple of blankets had been laid down to make a makeshift bed, a small bundle of clothes at one end to form a pillow. A knife stood upright, point thrust into the ground. Bending down to unwrap the small bundle of clothes I heard a noise behind me. I froze, then blew out the candles instinctively.

A slight glow of light became visible in the entrance to this chamber, gulping, I slowly stood upright, doing my best to be as quiet as I could, feeling round for somewhere to hide.

The light grew brighter. Finally coming into view.

It was an old style oil lamp in a four-sided glass housing.

"I know you are there, so do not hide from me" came the rather well spoken voice.

I stood quiet, not moving, hoping this person was just bluffing, knowing he probably wasn't, all the time trying to look for some means of escape.

"This can be easy or hard. The choice is yours."

"Who are you?" I said finding my voice.

"Aah, so you have a voice, well sir, first may I enquire the name of your good self."

"Daniel, Daniel Stephens" I heard him laugh. A hearty laugh that filled the chamber.

The lantern he was carrying had remained at his side. Slowly he walked towards me lifting it up to chest height, stopping just short of where I was.

"Who am I? Well there is a question?" smirking." I could tell you yet I think you know the answer" he raised the lantern upwards to just above head height and leaned in towards me, illuminating both my face and his "I am Henry."

25

I stared at Henry in silent contemplation. Emotions ranging from anger to intrigue, rage to curiosity spinning through my mind like tiny whirlwinds, each instant being replaced by a new state.

Henry stood there. Not the man I'd imagined, a distorted, twisted being, rough features, dirty, eyes angry, but a well spoken gentleman, clever, sharp looking, wearing ill fitting clothes, which looked as though they had been taken from the nearest available washing line. He didn't look like he could be responsible for the crimes that I had been witness to. They were so malicious and brutal, they seemed to be the work of one out of control, yet the man that stood before me was calm and collected.

A million questions raced into my thoughts, I wanted answers. I couldn't connect the person and the crimes.

"Why?" as I said it I thought it sounded stupid, yet so logical.

Henry walked over to his bedded area turning his back on me, confident, cocky in his manner. He picked up another lantern, and lit it.

"Well, why?" I repeated. I heard the tension in my own voice. I continued "Why did you kill those girls?" my voice almost breaking trying to hide the anger "What was that dream about? The horse? The carriage? The little girl crying? How did all this happen?" questions ran from me like shots from a gun, echoing round the chamber.

Henry stood there still looking at me composing his thoughts

"Where would you like me to begin?" he said rhetorically, a hint of accomplishment in his voice, pausing as if expecting me to answer "I suppose the beginning would seem the choice place." He continued calmly, innocently, not even the slightest hint of hatred for anything or anyone.

I didn't know what to say. The nerve of this person, standing there, like this was a game and none of it mattered.

"I should start by thanking you for what you enabled me to achieve."

I took a step forward, fists clenched "What I've enabled you to achieve?" I stated defiantly, he didn't flinch, just stood his ground.

Carrying on oblivious to my emotional state "Yes. If it had not been for you, I would not be standing here at all. Yes things have certainly come about better than I could ever have planned. I must admit I did have my doubts. It is really quite remarkable what one can achieve" he smirked pleased with himself. He paced the chamber, circling me. I stayed where I was looking at the bed, and the knife.

"What one can achieve! What sort of sick plan did you have in mind then?" I felt repulsed being there with him. This was a game, a sick game to him.

"I did not have one. Just revenge... at first. That is the strange thing. In the beginning after each killing I felt guilty. I started to drink and it suppressed the guilt. I started to enjoy what I did. It took over gave me a thrill. Surprising how short a time it takes before you establish a twisted sort of moral justice, the drink helps of course although at the time you do not realise it."

"I was down on everyone and everything. I think that is what brought me to the attention of the 'Froxidian Fellowship'. A local group with high hopes, they were quite something. Many feared them. The truth is little was actually known about what they did. That is what scared people. People are always scared of things they do not know. I suppose ignorance can be a blessing sometimes" he continued ironically, smiling to himself "I was just the sort of person they liked to recruit. They thought I could be easily persuaded. I played them at their own game. I knew that it probably would not be long before I was caught so I wanted to make sure I had a back up plan.

"It is... was rumoured that there were judges amongst them and I thought I could curry favour if I was one of them. Well it was not like that. Then I caught a glimpse of their book and heard whisperings. Froxidian magic is powerful when it works... and if you have the power to wield it of course" He stood back behind me "Guess I do. Looks like I was right as well. They suspected what I was up to. I do not know how. There I was enjoying my nice little killing spree when they set me up" He stopped, looked at me "You have heard of the Froxidian Fellowship?"

I shook my head, then recalled the book, and nodded.

"Believed they could cure the world of all evil, the low lifes, scum of the earth, beggars and rich alike, they had their ideals. They met in secret in the basement of the warehouse just off of Hotel Junction.

"They cornered me one night held me captive. They did not like people going about things on their own. They had ways, formalities shall we say. I escaped. I stole one of only three copies of the Froxidian Book of Incantations that they had spoken about. You should read it sometime... I guess you have".

"What?" I said perplexed trying to take in every detail of what I was being told and still formulate a plan to hold him captive.

"You... have got my things?" pausing, he knew but was waiting for my agreement which I gave.

"The book proved to be quite interesting. As I had not been a member that long and they had only told me what they thought I ought to know, I read the book with some excitement. The Arcs are the powerful ones, not many people posses their power. Well that is what they would have you believe. By the results I would say I do" Henry sat down on the bedding, placing the lantern next to him. "I guess I probably would have become an Arc if I had stayed around long enough and followed their rules.

It was not a case of magic, more a case of connecting two ends together, connecting your spirit with the belief, a key, something to unlock the spirit returning it to the physical being. I had nothing to lose. I feared it would not be long before they caught up with me and my life would be over. So I set up my own little magic, I am so very pleased it worked, all I needed to do was write an incantation, there were certain words I needed to use and particular rituals in order to invoke it, but the rest was up to me.

I did have one problem I had to be sure the incantation would be visible to someone. I had no idea how long it was going to be before some person might invoke it. I did need time for the dust to settle. The theatre seemed a good place as it was always being used, and the people were normally quite curious, often I had heard people discussing the writings on the walls in various places. I did not expect it to be this long although it has done me quite a favour really.

"I am intrigued by how much things have changed."

"So why carry on killing? You've got the chance to start again, put the past behind you" distaste in my mouth, I felt like a psychiatrist saying it.

"Well that was just it" he got up and started to pace around me "at first I did not really know where I was. To me it was like; one instant you are dead, the next you are not. I was a bit disorientated, the anger from all those years ago still fresh in my head."

I looked around still confused about how I should react. The knife just a few feet away. I could end it all now. Something was stopping me. Morbid curiosity.

"So. Why did you start killing?!" I asked. "By all accounts you were an upstanding citizen of the local community" I was being brash now and mimicking him "you had a good job, an ok boss and family, treated you well by all accounts. Oh that's it! Your wife died!" I saw the anger boil in his eyes he stood up abruptly "'cos you're the only one to ever have experienced that aren't you?" I paced the chamber trying inconspicuously to get close to the knife "No one else has ever had to go through what you went through, HAVE THEY? No it's just you" I had turned physically on him, facing him, staring into his eyes "POOR OLD YOU" I punctuated.

The anger drained from his face, he laughed at me "You have done your research. BUT YOU DO NOT KNOW WHY SHE DIED DO YOU? DO YOU?" his voiced raised, staring into my face his eyes wild, voice echoing round the chamber.

"Actually I do" I took a couple of steps away from him, facing away. I was being brave showing him my back "she was run over. By a horse, trampled under foot".

"IT WAS HER FAULT!" I could almost feel the lunge that he made towards me, and I turned in time to counter it "IT WAS THE GIRLS FAULT" his hands had found my shoulders. I stood my ground the best I could, he was powerful, I thrust my hands to his throat only managing a loose choke hold. It caught him unaware bringing a tear to his eye "she made the horse rear up and lash out AT MY WIFE, my wife, My Violet. My true one..." as quickly as he had raised his voice, it broke, trembling, loosening the grip on my shoulders. Grabbing fistfuls of my shirt, then I felt it loosen as he let go.

I backed off, half sympathising with the man that stood before me, half seeing him for what he really was, a murderer, a cold blooded murderer. "Is that how you justified what you were doing? It was just an accident. Nothing but an unfortunate accident. Can't you... Couldn't you see that?"

"She killed my wife!"

"She didn't do it on purpose" I started to defend the innocent girl like a father might.

"You do not understand. You were not there. You did not hold her in your arms and watch the life drain out her" kneeling down on the ground he replayed the actions in front of me like a scene from a play "I felt so helpless, there was nothing I could do, I loved her so much. I held my Violet so tight in my arms. Never wanted to let her go. They made me let her go. They took her away. I watched as they took her away" his voice broken by quiet sobs " I couldn't stand it. My heart just wanted to stop. The pain did not go away." He paused, I felt so sorry for him, I didn't know what to say.

He stood up continuing with new found passion, voice stronger, anger in his eyes, raw emotion. "I wanted to make someone suffer the way I was suffering. Feel the pain I was feeling. I saw the little girl" his face contorted, and sarcastically, sadistically "SHE was crying. As though she was the one in pain. But what did she know. She did not know what it felt like. She had no idea what it was going to be like without the one she loved! There she was 'crying', being hugged and comforted. Poor little girl" He stopped and stepped away from me, then, turned to face me again "I knew what I had to do. I would make her suffer" He laughed heartily.

I had heard enough, I went for the knife. He beat me to it. He'd anticipated my next move.

"Were you going to try and be the hero?" he held the knife towards me there was about three feet between us.

"No, I don't want to be a hero, Just put things right."

"Right. You have no idea what is right."

We paced round in circles, facing each other off, my injured leg a distant memory.

"And do you know? They never knew it was me. Yes I started to drink more. I still turned up for work, played the dutiful little worker. We discussed the murders openly, the stories in the paper. Trying to work out who the murderer was. They did not have a clue. That was the best part and they provided me with the means to get around this town without being seen, these tunnels. He was an eccentric, rich, old fool, but you have got to love it. Part of me wanted to tell them."

"So what happened?"

He lowered the knife, putting the point of it on the middle finger of his left hand and twisting it with his right.

"What happened! The Police were hopeless they did not have a clue. The Froxidians, they knew. They were clever, they set up a trap, good it was too. You have to admire them, they used one of their own daughters, merciless lot really. What is sicker? Using your own daughter to catch a murderer. They were watching and I was drunker than usual. It was so stupid. They were watching. As I went to grab her."

"They jumped you?"

"Yes. They jumped me, kicking and punching, they had no mercy, they had there own brand of punishment, which I was about to experience."

"So, How did you escape?"

"I sobered up quickly not surprising when I was being kicked and punched. I managed to keep a cool head. I waited for the right time. It did not take long. They sent in one of the younger members to collect me, they must have thought I was too drunk to try anything, but I landed him one, out like a light. I put his gown on and even had the audacity to go and stand amongst them during one of their ceremonies."

My dream came back to me "They saw you, didn't they?"

"Yes" he said surprised by my statement.

"They pinned you to the floor."

Perplexed he carried on "I thought they were going to thrust the staff straight through my head and then, would you believe it, the police of all people burst in. I could not believe my luck. In the pandemonium that followed I ran. Not before taking a hold of one of their books. I headed straight to the only safe place I knew. These tunnels."

He was lost in his own world at this point. I lunged at him, caught him off guard wrestling him to the ground. We struggled neither seeming to get the advantage. Henry regained his footing, hauling me to my knees then pinned me to the wall. The knife at my stomach and his forearm across my throat, my leg began to hurt again. I must have caught it in the struggle. I looked around for anything I could use as leverage. Anything to aid me in my fight. There was nothing. With my free hand I took a handful of dust from the floor and rubbed it in his face. He released his grip and I was behind him swinging my arm round his throat in a choke hold, using my weight to get him face down on the ground. I cut out the pain issuing from my leg and reached to his right hand where I thought the knife was. It wasn't. Lost in the fight. Looking round I couldn't see it.

He let out a strangled laugh due to my tight grip and continued "What you going to do now?"

I had no weapon. No means to restrain him. I knew as soon as I let go he would be on me again faster than I could get to my feet, my leg was letting me know how much I had just abused it.

"Even if you kill me, it won't matter, as I had done all the killing in your guise. All the evidence points straight at you. So go ahead kill me. It does not matter anymore."

He was right. No matter what I did I was still a murderer in the eyes of the world. Only five people knew the truth. It was not a truth that anyone was going to believe easily, if at all. To put this right I needed him. As much as I hated that, it was the truth.

26

After a few brief moments I released my grip and rolled over on the ground sitting upright on the floor. My mind was a haze of thoughts darting round like little insects searching for food.

I looked over at Henry, he was getting to his feet rubbing his neck.

"You just have to hate life sometimes."

I didn't answer. I didn't want to speak to him anymore. A silent question came forth. Did I need him?

Truth was, I wasn't sure. I hadn't given Ann-Marie or Aunt Rose a chance to tell me about the solution. So caught up in being a hero, trying to protect the next victim when I should have been looking at the overall picture.

Now!

Now I was here, no communication with my comrades. Only the one I'd allowed myself to get consumed by.

I remembered the fact that the police were looking for two people now, not just one. I smiled and in the dim light Henry noticed.

"What are you smiling for? I can walk out of here a free man. Back from the dead, finish the rest of my life. No retribution for my crimes."

I smiled even harder, content at the disillusion. The evidence was here in this chamber to help convict him, although confirming his identity might be a problem, they'd know they had the right man. If I went down so would Henry.

"Go on then. Why don't you?" I said confidently.

"Because you made it obvious that I have a few loose ends to tie up first" with that he smiled and stared into my eyes.

It dawned on me, I hadn't even thought about the consequences for Ann-Marie. Did he know of her? Was he bluffing? I needed to know how much he knew. Was she one of those loose ends?

I held my leg, it still hurt. "So did you know that I could see the events through my... your eyes?" I corrected myself

"Really" he said not totally surprised, he carried on brushing the dust from his clothes "Well, looks like we both got more than we bargained for. What was it like watching but not being able to do anything about it?" he sounded deranged.

"What! Seeing what a evil person you really are?"

"I used to think that at first" He came in close to me "I have justified my actions. After a while you do not really think about it anymore. Drink numbs the pain. Then you can justify anything" he walked around the chamber, my eyes followed him

"So what was it like coming back? Back into the world after so long?"

"Like a blink of an eye. Last thing I remember is dragging myself from the bottom of the ladder in the theatre. I had lost my footing" he looked upwards "Yes" he pondered "I had just written the incantation on the wall" pacing like a man on a stroll he continued "Tied in the relevant ends, as your supposed to do, then bam" he clapped his hands together "I fell 30 feet or so" he paused "I remember being in a lot of pain...my leg. I thought I had broken it. Anyway, I crawled away the best I could into a chamber just to the right of the ladder and tried to get comfortable. The pain suddenly went and I felt nothing, no lights, or anything like they tell you" he reflected "the next thing I knew I was back in the corridor. I did not know what had happened at first. The entrance to the ladder was gone, bricked up. I could not find it. I felt around. It was dark. I bolted for the door. There were people on the stairs I did not recognise. I ran down the stairs, everything looked different from how I remembered it. People were calling 'Daniel'. I ran out the front door into the street. I was not lost exactly, yet nothing looked the same" He stopped and looked at me questioningly.

I felt uneasy.

"I ran along the street for a while until I slowed to a walking pace. I found myself in a familiar place, Waterwell Gardens, it had changed, do not get me wrong, yet it was familiar. I sat down. I remember sitting there a long time.

"I remember getting cold. I got up to go and I knew where, but I did not know why at first."

"Then I saw this girl, walking on her own, I felt the familiar stirrings. The anger. The pain. I felt compelled to act." Once again he smiled curtly.

"You just had to!" I tried to get up using the wall a few feet behind as support, the pain stung like a million bee stings.

"The urge. The anger. Came flooding back. Felt right. Felt so good killing her. Seemed like ages since I had done anything like that, yet only yesterday in my head. As I walked back to 'YOUR' flat my head became full of information, things that should have been unfamiliar to me, yet I know, were not. It was your life, every single experience you have ever had, every private thought."

I wanted to hit him, shut him up. I lunged but pained issued from the throbbing wound and I buckled falling back to the ground. He was using my life against me. He had access all areas.

"It was a strange feeling walking back to the flat, everything familiar, but everything new. I had blood on my clothes. It was dark though, I managed to avoid being seen at close quarters. Once I had found the correct keys and went inside, I found a mirror and studied the reflection that came back at me. You have no idea what it is like to see a different face staring back at you from the one you know" He came in close to me, face to face where I was on the ground "I stared at it for ages, pulling it this way and that. I did not know what to make of it."

I pulled away from him as much as I could, I was uncomfortable being this close and I was in no condition to move. "Why didn't you just get on with your life, you had my body, my life. Surely it would have been easy just to carry on, start again, a free man?"

Reaching full height again and putting his hands in his pockets he turned and walked away from me retrieving the knife from the floor.

"Well there's the thing, I could have done just that. Leave my life behind me. I was already going to do that before I died. I had only really gone back to the tunnels to gather my possessions as I had decided it was time to leave, decided it was a little uncomfortable here. People knew too much. I felt I needed a back up plan, just in case. However I did not expect to die at my own clumsiness. Some might say 'Poetic Justice"

"Once here though something nagged in the back of my 'new' mind, it was me again. I felt safe now. And I had a score to settle" an evil grin spread across his face, eyes of a demented madman.

"One child causes an accident that unfortunately kills your wife and suddenly it's everyone's fault. Then you get the chance to put all that behind you and you throw it away, you're insane."

"Yes. Maybe I am. Everyone has there own way of dealing with life this is mine" he said with a dignified shrug of the shoulders.

"Most people manage to deal with it, without harming others in the process"

What was I doing?! I was trying to reason with a man who didn't see reason. Despite my own anger at the situation I couldn't kill him. I couldn't let myself lower my standards to his. I didn't know what was planned by Ann-Marie I just prayed that it would put everything right again. I was powerless to stop

Henry from doing any more killing unless I could restrain him somehow, and now. Henry was strong compared to me and in my weakened state he could easily overpower me.

He had the advantage of being able to wander off into the daylight without fear of being arrested. I didn't have that luxury, and again the question of how I was going to contact Ann-Marie echoed round my head.

"You have not heard a word I have said. I wanted revenge. I lost everything I had that day. Everything! Nothing meant anything anymore" he came at me grabbing me by the shoulders forcing them back against the wall, a forceful yet controlled rage.

"And it means a whole lot more now" I managed to get out, the breath knocked out of me by the sheer magnitude of the strength Henry possessed, he crouched before me.

Loosening his grip "No you are right. I have finally said goodbye to her, I am ready to move on. All thanks to you." Despite this confidence there was distant tone in his voice, a sadness. "You have given me the opportunity. No one knows me anymore, I can start to live again, a clean sheet, as you might say. Whereas you, I am afraid, can pick up from where I left off" I could hear the contentment "See how cruel life can be" with that he laughed, loud, reverberating round the chamber, drilling home the hardship that I faced. If Aunt Rose and Heather didn't come through for me... they just had to!

The laughing ceased "It has been nice finally meeting you. I must dash. I have a life to lead. Thank you" with that he picked up one of the lanterns off the floor and strolled confidently towards the exit of the chamber "I will leave you the other one, do not get too comfortable though you never know who might find you here" he laughed in the distance as he disappeared.

I tried to get up quickly but the pain of my leg shot straight to my brain like electricity, and I reeled over onto the bed.

"AAARRRRGGGGHHH!! Damn you, YOU, YOU!" I shouted

voice trailing off. It was no use, nothing I said was going to change the situation and my words resounded off the walls until they faded. In a few days I had gone from average Joe on the street, to a murderer.

"He's going to tell the police where to find me" I said out loud, as if I needed clarification. My once secret, secure dwelling wasn't going to be that much longer. I had to move out post haste. But where?

I didn't know what the time was or exactly how long I had been down there, what I believed to be a short period could have been hours, and now it could be daylight outside. My heart sank. Once again I was thinking the worst case scenarios.

I eased myself to my feet and with the remaining lantern in hand I navigated my way through the tunnels back to the entrance I'd used, trying to avoid putting too much weight on my leg. I didn't pay any attention to the walls this time, I just wanted to make my escape as soon as possible.

Upon reaching the entrance, I could see lamplight flicker in the dark rainy sky outside through a crack at the edge of the door. I breathed a sigh of relief as it was still dark.

I pushed the door with my shoulder knowing it wouldn't be easy. It didn't budge. With gritted teeth I pushed harder, nothing. Still the door would not move.

Studying carefully through the slight crack I could just make out the shape of something heavy against the door. There was no way I was getting out this way.

"Shit, shit, shit, shit" I turned and looked back the way I'd come. I thought of all the possible ways I could get out. All those bricked up exits that would have once been so useful, now closed off permanently. No way I was going to clear any of them in the few hours I had left. Even if I did, I didn't know if there was anything the other side of them that would allow me to escape.

"The theatre" I said with a resounding air of clarification "I can get out through the theatre, no one will be there at this time. I can get out through a fire exit."

I was talking to myself as if expecting an answer that would confirm it as a good idea, rather than the only possibility.

Once again I headed into the darkness, proceeding along this now well trodden path. It occurred to me time was still passing. Although currently it was still dark outside I didn't know how much longer it would remain so or how long I'd have before the police would be notified of my whereabouts, if they were at all. Maybe he was bluffing.

My pace quickened, pain or no pain I had to get out of here quicker than I first thought, adrenalin kicked in. I'd underestimated Henry Highway, he was clever, calculating. Henry knew the theatre would be my only way out, would the police be waiting for me when I rose from the depths?

27

As I reached the steps that would lead me into 'that' corridor, where it had all begun, my body filled with trepidation, my heart sank to my feet. I was tired and scared. Scared of all that had happened, and all it could become.

My brain was too tired to register any pain in my leg. I tried to convince myself it would be ok, that the police were not waiting for me and that it would be an easy journey back to Ann-Marie's house.

With my hands on the metal ladder I took a deep breath and made my way up.

It was a slow ascent, the lantern in one hand making progress awkward. My energy level was dropping. I wanted to rest but knew I couldn't, I didn't have the luxury of time. So slowly; one hand after the other, one foot after the other, the constant clanging of the lantern against the ladder reverberating round this cylindrical tube, I carried on. The dim light illuminated the shaft as I made my way up.

When I reached the top I thrust the lantern through the opening and onto the ground, I hadn't realised how heavy it was until that point, the relief running riot through my arm.

I hauled my weary body through the hole and collapsed on the floor for a few minutes. I knew I didn't have the luxury of time, but there was no one waiting for me, I consoled myself with that. I needed the rest. I was tired physically and mentally.

"Can't stay here all night" I said out loud trying to motivate myself as I reluctantly rose.

I thought I knew the theatre well enough now not have to worry about the lantern. I blew it out and hid it behind some boxes before exiting the corridor and making my way to the stage door. I was also aware that the light could have been seen through the few windows that were backstage.

The silence was eerie and sent shivers coursing through my weary body like ripples of water. I remembered hearing talk of the ghosts that were sometimes seen. Great stories I always thought. Now I was here late at night, on my own, I wasn't so sure. I hastened my pace.

At the stage door I felt relief at not having encountered any paranormal activity and to be leaving the building. I pushed against the bar that held the door closed. It wouldn't budge, I tried again. I had never noticed the chain that locked it tight. I knew of only one other exit that I could gain access to and that was in the auditorium, a fire exit.

I went through the door that led onto the stage, into the massive black void. No outside lights penetrated this space. I crossed the empty performance area, where I had danced many times. I inched my feet across the stage daring not to lift them in case I met an obstacle. I knew the stage well but the total darkness confused my sense of size and space. Progress was slow. I had to be even more careful when I thought I was coming to the front of the stage as there was a four foot drop. I found the steps down into the main auditorium after feeling around on my hands and knees.

I felt my way the best I could, following the front of the stage. I found the wall that led to the double doors which concealed the fire exit. I knew the layout but it seemed so different in the darkness. Luck was against me, the fire exit doors were also chained and padlocked.

I knew the doors to the auditorium would be chained so that way was useless. I had to think of another way out. I sat down on the floor, too weary to think on my feet, and I mentally worked through the layout of the whole theatre, trying to find any possibility. The pitch black auditorium my only company. My options were few and running out quickly.

Some areas of the theatre I didn't know so well: there was a basement that had been sealed off until recently, that was no good as the access to that was behind the kiosk in the foyer. There was access to the roof, although I wasn't sure where, as I'd never been up on it, never had a reason to.

All the windows had bars on them so they weren't any good either. Time was passing. I knew there were clocks in the auditorium but it was too dark to see.

The lighting booth, of course. I slapped my forehead with the palm of my hand. Why didn't I think of that before? There must be a set of keys somewhere in there for the fire exits. I made my way with renewed enthusiasm to the lighting booth, adrenalin returning to my aching limbs, bringing with it some of the pain I'd shut away. I used my hands to guide me past the rows of seats.

The door was never locked and I managed to feel my way inside. The blackness was complete, no matter what I tried, I couldn't see a thing.

I ran my hand over the surface of the wall to my left, locating the light switch, flicking it down. Flourescent tubes flickered on all over the box, I had to shade my eyes from the sudden glare. The booth was a bit of a mess to the untrained eye but Mark knew where everything was.

Surveying the box I looked for keys, I wasn't sure where to start. I didn't expect them to be obvious, Mark was very careful about security. I sat down in one of the chairs behind the lighting desk, and thought about the most suitable place close to hand, nothing seemed appropriate, there were no draws, the shelves were full of coils of wire, bulbs, and other replacement parts.

After some futile searching I knew I was just wasting

time, so I gave up and left the booth, switching off the light. I had to give my eyes time to adjust again to the blackness, closing them and counting to ten, whilst counting I could almost feel the theatre breathing, feel its life pulse through me, there was something relaxing and secure about it. Options were running out, I was left with the roof. I thought about this as I headed to the backstage area again using the wall as my aide until I reached the stage again. I remembered seeing a fire ladder running down the side of the building on the outside. I don't remember it ever coming close to the ground. This was my last hope I had to take my chances. All that was left was to find the roof door. I was sure I'd seen Mark coming out of one of the changing rooms once with some roof felt in his hands. I had to remember which one, I racked my brains, searching for that memory.

'Yes' the back dressing room, there's a door to another area.

Back up the side of the stage I returned along the corridor.

Quite suddenly it turned very cold, every hair on my body was standing on end. I turned slowly, though I didn't know why.

In front of me was one of the ghosts that I'd heard about, running towards me at break neck speed. I froze in terror. The lad, 12 or 13 years old, ran straight through me and turned right, into the wall where a door used to be that lead to a walkway suspended 60 feet above the stage to steps down the other side.

Story has it that the lad was a runner for the back stage crew; usually the runner was a young lad who wanted to work in theatre, this is how he earned his stripes. They never got paid unless they were actually used and then it was at the discretion of the crew or actors. He'd take any notes or props to the other side of the stage if required, which was not very often. This particular night the boy was carrying a prop to an actor who had forgotten to set it on the OP side of the stage. The actor had signalled to one of the crew, asking the runner to bring it across, which he did.

Unfortunately for him one the boards on the walkway was loose and as he trod on it, it gave way and he fell to the stage landing awkwardly on a piece of set and narrowly missing one the actors. The boy died instantly. Now from time to time he could be seen, repeating that fateful journey always disappearing into the wall, which had been bricked up almost immediately. The runners then had to go out the backdoor of the theatre along the street and in through the fire exit.

Once I'd recomposed myself I carried on. I wasn't sure exactly where the roof access was, but had a reasonable idea.

There was a room which housed most of the electricity boards, outside of this there was a door which I presumed must hide the stairs to the roof. Again I was in pitch black until I found a light switch.

I was right.

The door onto the roof whilst being securely fastened with bolts on the inside, was not padlocked, or locked in any other way. Out onto the roof I went.

The view was incredible, but I became aware of the impending dawn as the night sky was starting to lighten and the dawn chorus was starting to chatter.

I walked round the perimeter of the building until I found the escape ladder fixed to the east side of the theatre, it seemed to run down to an obscure little roof about five feet lower.

Great! More jumping. I was concerned for my leg. Whilst I was aware I was limping I had not felt any pain for a while, I wanted to keep it that way, jumping, or rather landing was not going to help that.

I sat down on the ledge of the building lowering myself as much as I could towards the lower roof level, then gently let myself go, landing as softly as possible on my good leg.

"The next bit should be easy."

Climbing down the ladder I felt a few spots of rain. It didn't bother me that much as it was the least of my worries.

At the bottom of the ladder I realised why I wasn't quite sure where it had been, it was 15 feet short of the ground, in a recess hidden from the street.

I couldn't believe my luck 'Was nothing going to be easy?' I hung there contemplating my next move. With a sigh I eased my right foot off the bottom rung, planting it as firmly as I could against the wall. I then released each hand carefully in turn, replacing it on the rung below, feeling my body weight shift. I repeated this, leaving my left foot on the bottom rung as late as I could, poking my backside out into the night air. Then I took my left foot from the ladder, I hung there briefly, both feet about a foot beneath the ladder, both hands on the second rung up.

My right foot slipped, my balance shifted and I went crashing against the wall, my face making contact "shit" aware of the noise I was making.

I hung there like laundry out to dry. The rain was getting heavier and my hands, already tired, began to lose their grip. I braced myself for a shock of pain as down I went with a thud.

With gritted teeth I swore to myself, not knowing which part of my body to grab first.

The important thing was I was out of the theatre, on the ground and no police in sight.

Getting up I felt the pain in my left leg shoot at me like a nuclear missile making it barely possible to put my weight on it. I took a few deep breaths to gain control over the pain. I was cold and tired and just wanted to scream releasing all my pent up frustration. I had to keep telling myself it was going to work out ok in the end.

I made my way up Claret Street to the High Street, again putting the hood up on my coat, concealing my identity. There were a few people about and I scrutinised everyone from beneath the hood, wary of anyone approaching me.

I headed towards the town hall, where I would then proceed along Queen Avenue.

The only thing that slowed my progress was the limping. I'd landed heavily on my bad leg, spraining my left ankle as well. On reflection I had to laugh at myself, or I would go crazy the way my luck was going.

It was sometime before I got to Ann-Marie's house and the streets were starting to bustle with people leaving for their Sunday jobs, it occured to me that Ann-Marie's mother always seemed to be working.

I had to lay low for a while, at least until her mother had gone to work. More time in the cold and wet. I wanted to feel warm, have a nice hot drink to thaw me out, I was not having any of it. I retreated to the alley a little way from her house on the opposite side. Far enough down it to be out of sight, close enough to view the comings and goings of her house, there I waited.

It was cold and raining and it was not long before I started to shiver. I waited for what seemed an eternity, every extremity getting colder and colder until I couldn't feel them.

Her mother finally left and when she was out of sight. I made my way to the house and rang the doorbell.

Ann-Marie opened the door "It's flipping freezing out here" I said my teeth doing their best not to chatter.

"Come in" she said urgently, smiling.

I went in, immediately feeling the warmth of the house infiltrate me, making me shake as life came back into my fingers and toes.

"I've seen him in the flesh. He is nothing like I expected. So normal" my jaw chattering, making the words hard to understand.

"I'm glad you're alright. Do you want a cup of tea?"

"That would be great. Do you want me to do it? It's bloody freezing out there" I said rubbing my hands and stamping my feet trying to get some feeling into them.

"No, it's ok, I'll do it. You haven't been out there all night have you? It's just that Aunt Rose said you could have stayed round there. If you'd come back I was to send you round".

'Great' I thought.

We made our way into the kitchen, I took off the coat leaving it hanging over the banisters. The warmth of the house was soothing. I could feel my cheeks burning as the heat returned to them. My jeans were soaked so I stood by the radiator.

"I think that would have been preferable. But I spoke to him" I said urgently "He's wants to start again, a new life. Now! He doesn't regret anything. He doesn't think he has done wrong. In his head what he did was justified. He made me sick. He enjoyed what he did."

"Aunt Rose has found a way, or rather Heather has. It's powerful magic, it's going to take the power of the heads of all the local coverns, all seven of them. They normally wouldn't but Heather says under the circumstances they want to put things right, you're quite lucky. Crimes against children they don't tolerate."

"What do we have to do?"

"Heather says they need something personal of yours, it's got to be something you hold dear to your heart, something that represents all the good in you. And..."

Ann-Marie broke off. She put two mugs on the work-surface, then feeling round for the teabag jar, put one teabag in each mug and poured the hot water.

"And what?"

"And they need him there too."

"Henry!"

"He needs to be present so they can send him back."

"But how? I mean I can't just invite him over." I couldn't believe it, more obstacles. Everytime I was getting closer, the end would get further away. I pulled out a chair and sat down.

"Extrume Derm Har is what they have to perform."

"What?"

"That's the name of the enchantment."

"Right. Any particular place?"

"There is a small clearing by the old scout hut in Hockley woods, that's where."

"The WOOD!" I exclaimed.

How were we going to get him to Hockley woods? We couldn't just ask him to come for a walk. Could we? This went from the sublime to the ridiculous. I sank deeper into the chair, hoping that inspiration would attack me.

"There is one more thing."

"What?!" I was almost afraid of what was coming next.

"It still has to be done before the eight days are up."

"But I thought..."

"Aunt Rose says the eight days still stand because we didn't put things right before and things are still not as they should be."

"This is hopeless. Not only do I have to get him to the woods but I cannot fail."

"You'll do it, I know you will." I felt Ann-Marie's hand on my shoulder for reassurance.

I sighed, I didn't know what I was going to do now.

"When will they be there?

"They said it will have to be Monday night, they can't take the risk of doing anything during the day, they'll be there for nine o clock."

28

The doorbell rang out like an alarm clock inside my head. Ann-Marie was already halfway to the door. I must have not heard it first of all.

I rose from my seat to see who was calling, in the vein hope that it was Heather or Aunt Rose.

I stood in the kitchen doorway, the front door was just visible. Through the glass panelled front door I could make out a figure standing there in dark clothes, wearing a hat. The shape made me think it was male, and the glass being frosted didn't offer a clearer view.

Ann-Marie was at the front door, Mojo at her side, Mojo was barking, this was unusual for him, but then I had only ever been present when there were friends at the door.

My imagination came to life, an electric shock bringing every nerve of my body to life, I wanted to shout out, tell her to come away from the door. Pretend we were not there and that the house was empty. My hand reached forward as if by some miracle it would be able to reach her, pulling her back into the safe retreat of the kitchen.

Too late. I heard her call out.

"Who is it?"

My heart sank down to my feet. I looked around, searching for a weapon, believing it to be Henry, I wanted to defend myself and Ann-Marie.

There was nothing, no knives on display. Hastily I moved to the kitchen draws, pulling each one open in turn, in hope of finding exactly what I was looking for, which I would know as soon as I found it.

A rolling pin. No. A knife sharpener, that was heavy and solid. Yes that would do. I brightened and then thought again. I couldn't kill him no matter what he'd done I couldn't become a murderer as well, I couldn't, my strange sense of morality, I believed in an eye for an eye. I held the knife sharpener tight. I could render him unconscious or at least give myself an opportunity to secure him in some way. I wanted to avoid killing him.

I made my way back to the kitchen doorway, weapon in hand.

The front door was opening, Mojo now quiet. In my haste I had not heard the ongoing dialogue. Whoever it was had gained Ann-Marie's trust and was now crossing the threshold.

I stealed myself for the march to the front door, I tightened my grip around the weapon.

I stopped in my tracks, and ducked back as quickly as I could as I saw a uniformed police officer, standing in the hallway, notepad out.

Breathing deeply. Just in time remembering to keep grip of the weapon in my hand as I had felt it start to slip from my grasp.

My heart began pumping blood round my body so fast I thought I might pass out.

'Get a grip' I told myself. I leaned in to listen to the ensuing conversation.

"...days ago" said Ann-Marie innocently.

"And you haven't seen him since, that's right?" the police officer said matter-of-factly, while scribbling down in his note book.

There was a glass fronted picture on the wall opposite about halfway along the hall and carefully I tried to use it as a mirror and view the two reflections by the front door. I watched the real life situation unfold in front of my eyes. The police officer was aware that the question answerer was blind and was taking furtive steps, this way and that, trying to gain any sight into each room that he could, distrusting the answers he was getting, also aware that he was not in his rights to search the premises without the owner's permission.

He glanced in my direction. I pulled back even further, a knee jerk reaction. I knew he couldn't see me physically. Maybe he caught a glimpse of my outline in the picture. I held my breath.

He was staring intently in this direction, I could feel a pearl of sweat start to make it's way down my forehead, onto my nose, just hanging at the tip for the briefest of moments before falling to the floor.

"Is there anything else I can help you with, officer?" Ann-Marie's voice broke the deadlock.

"No. No thank you. If you do see your friend, it's important you contact us. I probably don't need to tell you how much trouble you'll be in if you don't" he said menacingly.

"I will."

"Thank you again" he glanced once more down the hall in my direction, then turned and went to the front door. He opened it halfway and just before stepping over the threshold "Remember these are serious charges he is facing, he needs to be stopped before someone else gets hurt."

"I understand" She was so convincing, her innocence rang out, a church bell breaking the morning silence.

Finally the door closed and he was gone.

I relaxed with a sigh of relief as the steel sharpener fell from my hand and crashed to the floor. The sound reverberated round the kitchen, but I felt safe again now, the threat abated.

Ann-Marie came down the hall towards me reaching the doorway "That was close, I didn't think he was ever going to go."

"Me too. Do you think he believed you?"

She walked over to the kettle, checked it for water by lifting it up, then switched it on.

"I don't think he did, but he had no proof anyway. How did he know about me though?"

"I think when me and Henry were sort of one, we knew things about the other. You must have been one of the things in me he picked up on. I'm sorry I didn't mean to, if I'd realized he was going to incriminate you, I wouldn't have come here. I stupidly thought I'd be safe."

"It's ok. Anyway I haven't" she emphasized that word "'seen' you in the last few days."

"What?" she puzzled me.

"I'm blind remember. I can't see anything so I didn't lie exactly."

I smiled, there was irony in her statement that I couldn't resist and to me it reflected exactly how Ann-Marie viewed life: simple, and everything is surmountable, whatever it is.

We stayed in the kitchen for a while and talked, normal talk, something we hadn't ever had the chance to do, but in the midst of all the chaos, knowing what we had to achieve, it seemed natural.

After lunch the mood changed slightly as reality came oozing back.

"How am I going to get him to the woods Ann-Marie?" I tried hard to hide the emptiness in my voice.

"I don't know."

We sat there pondering the question.

"I'd better get going, he can't be too far. Hopefully! Where and when do we have to be in the woods?"

"Aunt Rose said nine o clock in Hockley woods by the secret sunken garden, it's about... I think she said about 200 yards behind the old scout hut, to the North of the wood. The trees are really tall and thick so it can't be seen that easily from above. At the bottom there's a clearing and a stream runs alongside it. They'll be there about nine o clock tomorrow night, they'll wait."

"Tomorrow night. Nine o clock" That punctuated in my head, like a large neon exclamation mark. "Ok" I felt like a soldier on a mission for my country, except this was for my life, my freedom. I rose from the chair and headed to the front door. Deep down I knew I should wait for nightfall but I had wasted enough time already and I didn't know where I was to find Henry, I didn't even know where to start looking.

"Wait" shouted Ann-Marie from the kitchen and she made her way towards me, "take my phone with you at least we'll be able to keep in contact this time. I'll get you a torch as well, you'll need it tonight.

"Thank you, you think of everything don't you?" I took the phone from her putting it in my pocket and waiting while she got the torch. I put on the borrowed coat of hers again "See you later.....hopefully" I swallowed.

"Course you will, you have to be positive."

I smiled "Yes" I sounded daunted "By the way this personal item, does Heather need it now? Do you know?"

"I don't. She didn't say" Ann-Marie replied.

There was an awkward silence for a second whilst I thought then reluctantly I took off the silver plectrum that hung round my neck "Here you had better take this, just in case."

"What is it?"

"It's a silver plectrum, a gift from my parents on my 16th birthday". Suddenly I felt naked and vulnerable without it. I watched Ann-Marie as she turned it over with her fingers.

"What's engraved on it?" her question took me a little by surprise.

"It just says 'to the best son, happy 16th birthday love mum and dad'."

After a pause Ann-Marie closed her hand tightly round the plectrum and chain that it hung on "I'll look after it" then she smiled "if you promise you'll play something for me when this is all over."

"Ok you're on" I said before opening the door, it was still raining, I threw the hood up over my head, one thing about the rain, it made it easier to conceal my face without looking out of place.

I looked back at Ann-Marie. "Thank you"

"Go quickly" she said urging me out the door and closing it behind me.

I felt like a lost soul again, standing in the wilderness between life and death, not knowing which direction to go, what to be looking for. I couldn't stand here for the rest of the day.

At the end of the footpath, I looked both ways, debating which direction to take, I turned left and started briskly walking, all the time regurgitating the past events over and over in my head. Hunting for a clue and indication of how I was to locate Henry. Needle in a haystack sprang to mind.

All the while a picture seemed to be forming in my head. An idea although a part of me doubted it, it might possibly work. It relied heavily on past events and that there was still some sort of connection.

During our time as one, we had glimpsed and taken in information about each others lives, Henry seemingly learning more about me than I had about him, maybe that was because I had shut myself down, not allowing myself to be part of what I didn't want to be part of. Maybe I needed to explore that, open my mind and allow his part of me to wash over and consume me.

I didn't know how to start, then I realised that maybe Aunt Rose would. I convinced myself that she'd be able to help.

With a spring in my step I changed direction and headed to her house, I knew what road it was in, even if I didn't know the number, I was sure I'd recognise the house when I saw it.

As I crossed more and more roads I became aware of the

police cars passing. Each time I saw one I dipped my head even further down to conceal my face.

One slowed, drawing to a halt a hundred yards up the road. My steps slowed and my heart beat faster. I would have to walk past it, tension filling my shoulders. I subtly glanced round for other ways to go, avoiding the inevitable, nothing.

I drew closer. I couldn't turn and go back it might attract attention. My perception was that the world was focussed on me, all eyes staring right at me.

'Just keep walking, it'll be fine' I muttered under my breath. As I drew level, the police car drove off. Relief, I moved onwards as fast as my injuries would allow.

Walking down Aunt Rose's road, I was scanning the houses for a green and yellow door and it wasn't long before I saw it. I knocked and within a minute Aunt Rose answered.

"Come in dear, I've been expecting you."

I was surprised "You have?"

"Yes dear. Now take a seat and I'll put the kettle on" with that she closed the door behind me and went to the kitchen leaving me there in the hallway. Taking my coat off and placing it on the coat stand, I went into the lounge and took a seat.

"There we go. Just give it the right amount of time" said Aunt Rose placing a tray on the table a few minutes later. She took a seat in an armchair opposite me, organising the cups on their saucers. She lifted the lid on the teapot and stirred, the aroma sweeping upward "Yes I think that is ready now" she poured the tea. All the time I just watched lost for words. She'd caught me unaware when she had answered the door, always one step ahead.

"Drink your tea dear, it's a special herb tea. A yarrow root infusion that will help concentrate the mind and help improve the psychic connection. So just relax and drink."

I did as instructed, too amazed to say anything.

Putting the cup to my lips, the aroma flowed up my nose, a

pleasant lemon scent with a hint of something else that I wasn't sure of. As it touched my tongue it was sharp to taste, making me want to repel this liquid, but I swallowed. It went down my throat, filling my whole body with a warm glow. I could sense every muscle relaxing instantaneously. This was good stuff.

Then she spoke to me in her soft warm tones, easing me into assurance, encouraging me to recall every detail I could about Henry, slowly my mind drifted, focussing on Henry. I began to feel his presence, sense his torrid mind.

I felt the cup being taken from me. The rest was a blur of images.

The carriage. His wife. The shop in which he worked. The tunnels. His Mother and Father. The theatre. The first time he met Violet. My flat. My face in a mirror.

The pictures flashed back and forth faster and faster

"Ugh" I was bolt upright, breathing heavily, facing Aunt Rose.

29

"It's ok Daniel, just relax, let it do its job."

Pearls of sweat had formed on my forehead, I could feel the back of my t-shirt was damp. Shuddering I looked at Aunt Rose, she wore a rye smile, I was warmed by that. I felt safe again.

"Relax and let your mind wander. It will slowly start to become clear, you will have a better understanding of Henry."

I felt a bit foolish as I slumped back into the chair. Gradually a strange tingling formed in my head. My body felt relaxed and lifeless, my sight grappled with clarity and haziness. I saw it. I could see everything, it was all clear now, I felt Henry's presence again but in different way. I was not in control but knew what he was thinking and more importantly where he was.

I could make out shapes, images and I knew where it was somehow, familiarity. I'd been there before. The task at hand now seemed plausible.

Then it hit me, Southend-On-Sea train station, Platform one, it must be! This was the last stop on the line. He was going to head into London. From there he could go anywhere. I had to stop him and now I knew how.

"Thanks Aunt Rose. Have you got a telephone directory I can borrow?" my body still felt weary from whatever Aunt Rose had given me. However, the buzzing of adrenalin was countering it and I was engulfed by energy.

"I think I have somewhere. Let me think. Oh yes I know where it is."

I started drumming my finger on the arm of the chair, the adrenalin flowing, I had a sort of plan and was eager to implement it. I smiled to myself. He believed he was going to get away with this, he was wrong. I was going to take back my life.

I still felt a little light headed as I thumbed through the pages of the telephone directory that Aunt Rose passed to me, looking for East West Railways. I found their customer service number and dialled. It was early Sunday afternoon so I hoped there would be someone there to answer the phone.

"Do you mind if I borrow your phone?" I said apologetically as I waited for the call to be answered.

"No dear it's fine."

"Thanks."

It rang for ages, until "East West Railways, good morn... afternoon" came the dulcit tones of a Lancashire woman.

"Hello. I was wandering if you could contact one of your stations. It's just my brother hasn't got his mobile on him and we need to get hold of him urgently, he was due to get a train about now from Southend station going to London. There's been a family emergency and we need him home as soon as possible."

"I'm sorry sir you'll need to contact the station."

"Can't you transfer me."

"I'm sorry no."

"Well do you have the number?" I said impatiently.

"Just hold on one moment."

"Thank you" there was a brief silence " Have you got a pen and paper I can borrow please?" I called to Aunt Rose.

"Of course dear" Aunt Rose brought them out to me in the hall.

"Thanks."

There was a clicking sound on the line " Hello."

"Hi."

"The number you want..." I wrote quickly.

I hung up and immediately dialled the new number.

Again it took a long time to be answered.

"Southend station" the voice was abrupt but polite.

I explained the situation as I had done previously. The man on the end of the line was reluctant and took quite a bit of convincing, I was desperate. My scenario became a lot more detailed, my efforts of persuasion made a more authentic line of story that even the hardest of people would have had to concede to.

I was put on hold. In the background I heard the call repeated three times over the station tannoy.

A couple of minutes passed. I waited and listened to the background noise. Questions started floating round my head, Was he there? Had I got it all wrong? Did I just want to believe! Make myself feel better?

"Just transferring you" then I could hear the ringing tone of another phone.

A hesitant voice answered "Hello."

"Hello Henry. Didn't think you'd hear from me again did you?"

"I thought the police would have arrested you by now" came the cocky reply.

"I'm learning. From you" I was trying to give the impression that I had the upper hand.

He laughed "I really would like to chat, but I have got a train to catch."

"You might want to think twice about that. See if I'm going down I'm going to take you with me, and did I not tell you the police are looking for two people not just one? See they've been to my flat and they found your belongings and that last murder you did will tie up nicely with the others, your fingerprints will see to that. Then there's always your DNA, see things have moved on a lot since you were last around. You see there really is no way you are going to get away."

There was silence. I could only hear breathing and a little

background noise.

"You still there Henry?"

A very faint "Yes" came back. He had regained his composure "Well they still have to catch me. They are hardly going to believe your story, a killer back from the dead after 80 years. They will lock you up in an asylum."

"I haven't got to tell that side of things, just that I had an accomplice, that will be enough, I think I can give a pretty good description of you, it won't take long to pick you up and my stash of money that you're using won't keep you going for long" I heard a train pull into the station. I could hear the unease in his voice. He thought he could walk away. I had just turned all that around. I wasn't sure what his next move would be.

"I'll take my chances, must dash, got a train to catch".

Before he could put the receiver down I quickly added "Remember this, how do you think I knew where to get hold of you?" this was my last rebuff.

I didn't know how long I was going to have this power. If the connection severed permanently, he would be lost, just another face in the crowd.

The phone went dead. He'd hung up.

"Damn."

"What is it dear?"

"He hung up" I slammed down the receiver.

I didn't know what outcome I expected, but this wasn't it. I paced the room. Thoughts, ideas rushing round my head like rush hour traffic.

If I couldn't lure him to Hockley woods by deception I would have to use force, I knew where he was and that was where I was heading.

"I'm sorry to ask but do you have a car I could borrow? I'm going to have to take him to Hockley woods forcibly but I need a way of getting him there."

"No dear I've never driven."

"Damn! Well I've got to go and get him anyway before he gets too far away."

"Heather has a car dear, I can give her a ring and see if she can meet you somewhere."

"Yes. Thank you. I'll leave you this number so you can get hold of me" I took the mobile out of my pocket and dialled Aunt Rose's main phone, then did 1471 to get the number, writing it down on the paper she had given me. "Thank you for everything" I said before leaving the house to head towards the station.

I had the length of the journey to work out how I was going to hold him captive, if he was still in that vicinity. He was powerful.

It was getting dark again, rain clouds making it appear like night, it wasn't actually raining but it would be before long.

My pace was quick, the pain in my leg seemed muted, as if I'd become used to it. Every step I was getting a little faster, even though I appeared to have a slight limp. My breathing was heavy. In my mind I felt that Henry had not boarded the train. There were a few ways that Henry could go from the station. I believed he would hide in the tunnels. This was his only safe haven, he didn't know anyone else so he had nowhere he could go.

I double checked the station, he was gone.

Quite suddenly a strange uneasy feeling engulfed me.

"Oh shit" I realised exactly where he was going, the only other place he knew about, Ann-Marie's house.

Adrenalin fused every nerve in my body into action and I started to run, pain smarted in my leg, I shut it out, I had no time for it. He might already be there and this scared me, I'd put Ann-Marie's life at risk. She'd helped me more than she had to and this was how I might repay her.

As I ran I became hot, I pulled off the hood of the coat and undid it, an automatic reaction, I was not concerned with the consequences only getting to Ann-Marie's before Henry. I was oblivious to everything else going on around me, focussed on the mission at hand.

Road after road I crossed. Her house wasn't that far from the station, just a little further than the town hall, it felt like miles now, my breathing laboured.

When I turned into her road, there was no sign of Henry although I could feel his presence. I slowed to a walk as I thought out my next move and gave myself a chance to get my breath back. Should I go to the front door or straight to the back door?

The back door seemed the obvious choice. If he was inside already I needed to surprise him. If he wasn't then I didn't want to alert him to my presence. I ducked down the alley, following the course of it to Ann-Marie's garden, I could see the back door, the glass broken and the door slightly ajar, my heart sank.

I wasn't sure whether to enter, or call the police, I wanted the best solution for Ann-Marie, but also I didn't want to risk not getting Henry to the required place tomorrow night and if I called the police that might be the result. I was in a dilemma. I had to put Ann-Marie first.

Climbing over the fence was awkward with my bad leg, the adrenalin made it easier. I made my way to the back door cautious in case I was being watched.

A slight knowledge of the location of the rooms and doorways gave me an advantage, but not a great one.

I looked into the kitchen, my back against the wall, just outside the back door, observing, looking for Henry, searching for a weapon, something I could use to defend or attack with. There was nothing.

I knew where the knife sharpener was and went and retrieved it. Inching my way forward, back still against the wall, I reached out and pushed the door open. It moved silently.

Glancing into the kitchen I couldn't make out anyone inside, I entered. Hearing the crunch of glass under foot, I hesitated before proceeding any further, I knew Henry would be expecting me, there was no need to make it any easier for him, also I had Ann-Marie's life to consider.

I looked up the hallway, no sign of any movement. I edged my way along, glancing up the stairs in case he was waiting there for me. There was a strange eerie silence in the house, I thought I should at least hear some movement from Mojo, especially if Ann-Marie was in trouble. Unless. No I could even contemplate that scenario.

Each step I made didn't enlighten me, I glanced up the stairs, still no one. I was outside the lounge door. I stole myself for a swift entry counting to myself one, two, and three, I rushed in.

Nothing.

I started to relax, confident that there wasn't anyone in the house. I left the lounge and went upstairs, still cautious and observing, but at ease. At the top I looked into the bedroom at the back and the bathroom to my left. This just left two doors, Ann-Marie's room and the spare room. I stepped easier but still wary. Pushing the spare room door open it eased back fluently and stopped against the wall, I had a clear view inside, the room was empty.

Finally, Ann-Marie's room, I hesitated. Stretching out my hand, I placed it on the door I pushed gently against it. It inched open slowly, gradually showing the room.

Again it was empty. I didn't understand, I could sense he was close.

Bam. I was on the floor. My whole body felt heavy, I tried to push myself up off the ground. My head hurt. Then I felt another blow to the back of my head.

My eyes closed and I slumped on the floor.

30

When I came to I was in Ann-Marie's room. I couldn't move my hands or feet, I was laying on my right side, there was a pair of feet in front of me.

"So, did you really think you could sneak up on me?"

Disorientated I tried to remember how I got there and what had happened. It all slowly came back.

"Henry" I said attempting to sit up, only just managing to prop myself up against the wall that the bed was against.

"I was all ready to leave and then you had to spoil everything, I just wanted to get on with my life, the best I could. Start again, put my past firmly on your shoulders and walk away. You had to spoil that!" he was calm.

"Yeah, well I want my life back. You had your chance" I said wearily.

"Everyone is allowed to make mistakes. Forgive and forget." I detected sarcasm in his voice.

"What? Providing someone else takes the fall, is that it?" hate and anger finding it's voice.

"Sometimes situations arise and you just have to make the most of them." Henry sat down on the bed "Now, I have two problems." Deliberately pausing, he got up and kneeled before me about three feet away "You, whom I can easily eradicate with a simple phone call. After all, the police are not going to believe your story but they might be tempted to follow up your description, if, as you say they believe two people are involved. So I should really finish you off. However, the other problem is the girl I do not know how much she knows."

I was about to speak but he pre-empted my question.

"The girl, Ann-Marie, she is safe... well at the moment, unfortunately she was not here when I brok... arrived here shall we say. Which is lucky for you."

"Lucky for me. How do you make that out?" I was struggling with my bindings.

"Well as long as she is still alive" he drew in closer to me "then I need you to help me find her."

I lurched forward in a feeble attempt to attack, knowing full well it would be futile. Henry just jerked his head back and got up turning his back on me.

"You don't think I'm going to help you do you? Anyway how should I know where she is? Last time I saw her was this morning. She could be anywhere now."

"Yes I am sure that is what you want me to think" he turned and faced me again wearing a smug smile.

I felt uneasy, obviously he had a trump card that I didn't know about. The question was, what was it?

There was silence as he just stared at me intently, with that smile on his face. If only I could get free I would wipe it from him. Struggling as much as I could, I couldn't loosen the bonds that restrained my hands.

"Have you met Ann-Marie's mother?" he said.

Full realisation of the game he was playing hit me like a steam train, I stopped struggling with my bonds and stared speechlessly at him. I glanced around the room expecting to see a body lying somewhere, that I just hadn't spotted, nothing.

"Oh you will not find her in here."

"What have you done with her?" of course he hadn't done anything with her, if he had, he knew there was a strong possibility I might not go along with his plan. Also he might not have her at all. I couldn't see the clock on Ann-Marie's bedside table from here so I had no idea what the time was. It was dark outside, that I did know, but it could still be about

3pm, in which case it would be a couple of hours before she came home. Then again it could be the middle of the night.

"I have not done anything to her."

Good. That meant it was late afternoon and she hadn't got home yet, there was still time for me to try and resolve this stand off before she arrived.

"But I might, it really depends on how helpful you are going to be" he walked over to me, grabbed my shirt and pulled me to my feet. He was powerful. Even standing I was helpless, feet and hands restrained.

"Come with me."

My eyes widened with fright as he turned, walking away from me, but dragging me behind him, using a bit of rope tied to my belt to pull me along, I hopped precariously on both feet. He led me out of Ann-Marie's room, down the hallway to the back bedroom.

Pushing the door open, I saw her, gagged and bound to the bed. She was awake. She turned and saw us. Her eyes scared, she looked somewhat untidy as though she had been struggling with her bonds. Henry waved in a rather sick way. I thrust my weight against him as if it was going to make a difference, he lost his balance briefly but stayed upright, whilst I hit the door frame and fell to the floor.

I heard a crack. I screamed in pain, pearls of sweet formed on my forehead I felt nausea sweep over me, like a blanket, tears filled my eyes.

"That was not very clever was it?" Henry said looking down at me on the floor

I went numb then the pain ricocheted through every muscle in my body. The pain instantaneous, unbearable, my eyes started to close, the adrenalin kicked in killing the pain but trying to render me unconscious.

Henry slapped my face, I wearily opened my eyes.

"Now, now, get up, we can not have you falling asleep

just there."

He grabbed me and pulled me up by both arms, my face contorted with the pain, I felt too sick to make any sound except a wimper. I caught Ann-Marie's mother's terror.

Henry dragged me back to the front bedroom. My legs weak, I was shaking. A cold sweat took over my body, I shivered. I could feel the bonds getting tighter around my wrists, my damaged arm was swelling up, an automatic reaction to the injury.

He sat me down on the bed. He looked at and felt my arm.

"Now look what you've gone and done. Now are you going to help?" he stared at me satisfied he had the upper hand, convinced I would do his bidding. He was right, I didn't feel I had a choice anymore, I could risk losing my life but not Ann-Marie's mother.

I grimaced. "OK."

"Good. Now where is Ann-Marie?"

The pain was starting to find it's way to the nerve centre of my body, I wanted to curl up and cry.

"Come on, where is she?... We can stay here all night if we have to, I am sure that arm will become unbearable sooner or later... and I could always aggravate it a little" he said smugly, flexing his hand.

I didn't want to tell. The pain was torture in itself and caused by stupidly trying to be a hero. I couldn't see a way to avoid telling him what he wanted to know, I wasn't strong enough.

Then in the midst of all the fogginess, clarity formed.

If her mother was home, then this must be evening, possibly night time. Then why wasn't Ann-Marie home? She said she was always in when her mum came home otherwise she worried. She must be with Aunt Rose.

Aunt Rose must have pre-warned Ann-Marie about this situation, she always seemed one step ahead, unfortunately not far enough to stop Ann-Marie's mother from coming home. The first thing Ann-Marie would want to do would be to come home or call the police. Why hadn't she? I presumed she hadn't, not knowing if I was right or wrong.

They could end her mum's suffering here and now if they called the police, Why hadn't they? Maybe they didn't know the full extent of the danger except that it wasn't safe for her to come home just yet.

My thoughts formed a plan, a plan that hopefully, maybe, they wanted me to think of. It was one way to get exactly what we all wanted, but without Henry realising that we were playing him, instead of the other way round.

"I don't know where she is at this precise moment" as the adrenalin slowed so the pain started to course back and I started to phase in and out of consciousness.

I felt a slap to the face.

"Wake up, this is no time for sleep, Where is she?"

"I don't know..."

"Don't play games, you are playing with her mother's life" he had me by the scruff of my neck shaking me violently to keep me awake.

"Let me sleep... I'm tired."

"Not until you tell me where she is... Come on... Daniel."

I was finding it harder and harder to stay conscious. The pain seemed miles away, now I felt tired, maybe it was the shock kicking in. I wanted to sleep.

"Daniel. Where is she?"

"I told you I don't know" my words barely audible.

Finally losing patience with me, he let me fall onto my side on the bed.

"It's a shame Daniel, she seemed like a nice lady too. Oh well, if you are not going to tell me, I have no choice. He walked towards the door. As he reached it I mustered up every last bit of strength I could.

"Wait" I said deliriously.

He stopped, turned and faced me.

"I am waiting."

"I don't know where she is now" he about turned and started to walk out of the room again "But I do know where she'll be tomorrow night about 9ish" I quickly added.

He walked back into the room and leaned over me.

"And where will that be?"

I took a breath. I was slowly losing the battle to stay awake.

"The woods, Hockley woods."

"Where? It's a big place" he said gruffly.

I felt as if I had been out on the drink for the last twenty four hours, I was having problems saying my words.

"Behind the scout hut, the sunken garden."

"The what? Where?"

"North of Hockley woods, scout hut, sunken garden."

"Why would she be there at that time of night?"

"I can't remember... spirits... gatheri... spii..."

"What do you mean?"

I felt another slap to the face before blackness washed over me.

31

The daylight broke through the window, hitting my face, I stirred slowly taking in my surroundings. Drowsy and confused for a split second, unable to fathom why I couldn't move my arms and legs freely. I remembered the night before, the pain, the predicament I was in.

Looking round the room there was no sign of Henry. I listened carefully, the whole house was quiet. I still felt a little sick and as I rolled about trying to make my way to the edge of the bed. The pain in my arm checked itself with my brain, any pain in my leg gone although it felt stiff, I struggled to sit up and after a few attempts stopped trying as the injury to my arm made me feel sick when I moved. My thoughts passed to Ann-Marie's mother, I had to see how she was.

Taking deep breaths I gritted my teeth and tried to get closer to the edge of the bed something tugged at my feet, I looked round best I could.

I grimaced as the pain struck another chord. There was a thin rope of what looked like washing line, tying my feet to the bedpost. I wanted and needed to get free. A cold sweat covered my body, the twisting and turning exacerbating the pain in my right arm.

The front door slammed shut. I looked towards the bedroom door, expecting a visitor. I laid still. Nothing.

I returned my focus to my bindings, I had to get free no matter how much pain it would cause. How? I was never a boy scout so didn't carry around a handy little pocket knife, I didn't smoke, so no lighter either, sometimes I was my own worst enemy.

My attention was drawn to my trouser pocket, the mobile phone that Ann-Marie had given me was now vibrating, it had been set to discreet. Desperately trying to manoeuvre my body in the hope that I could pull it from my pocket, there seemed no hope, the more I tried, the more my arm hurt. The phone stopped.

I heard footfalls on the stairs. I ceased moving and settled, as comfortably as I could.

"Afternoon. Glad you could join us" Henry said cheerfully walking into the room.

I realised how hungry and thirsty I was as I saw Henry carrying a cup of tea.

"Don't suppose you've got one for me, have you?" I said rhetorically trying to disguise how rough I felt.

"You suppose right. What, do you think I want you to keep your strength up? I do not think so, but do not worry it will all be over soon". He walked over to the window and looked out. "Lovely day out there. Sun is shining, a little cold yet otherwise a very nice day. So how about you explain a little more clearly where I can find Ann-Marie" he sat in the wicker chair.

"Why should I? As you say I haven't got long, so I'v..." Ann-Marie's mother came back to my mind.

"Have you forgotten about our guest in the back bedroom?"

I kept my mouth shut, not sure what I had told him last night. It was a blur.

He walked back over to the bed and stood in front of me.

"Now I could make things a little nicer for you, if you promise to help that is. I will even make you a cup of tea, maybe even a bite to eat. Dry bread anyway, would not want you passing out on me now. The deal though is this. If I give you food and drink you have to show me on a map where in the woods you are meeting Ann-Marie tonight, and..." he paused "explain a little more clearly why."

I felt weak. I needed sustenance and in some respects agreeing was going to get me exactly what I wanted, Henry into Hockley woods and then straight back to hell, so I agreed with the proviso of food and drink first.

Ten minutes later he returned with bread, tea and a map of the local area. Placing them on the floor, he then sat me up on the bed to untie my hands whilst keeping a firm grip. I was weak so it didn't take much. He pulled my arms to the front. The blood flowed freely again, my muscles ached and I could see my right arm was swollen and badly bruised. My bindings had cut into my wrists and for what seemed a few minutes pins and needles tingled in my fingers. With my hands tied together in front it was awkward to eat. Part of me didn't want to eat, the effects of shock, but I knew I had to keep my strength up. I ate slowly, I must feed myself, however uncomfortable. As this deal was going to get me what I wanted I wasn't about to struggle and make my life harder still.

"There you go. Enjoy" He sat in the wicker chair drinking his tea, watching me all the time.

After eating and drinking I laid back down on the bed resting my head on the pillows, feeling refreshed and more coherent but still slightly nauseous.

I took stock of the situation, taking time to study my arm. I pinpointed the pain as the wrist, fractured or broken I couldn't tell, it hurt, I was sure of that.

Henry got up. He'd sat there all this time as if it were just a lazy Sunday morning between two friends sharing breakfast. He came over, bent down and picked up the map, opening it and placing it front of me, resting it across my legs which were still tied to the bedpost.

"Where is this scout hut you speak of? I know... knew the woods quite well Violet and I used to go there for walks" he looked thoughtful, loving, caring. "...but I don't remember any hut or sunken gardens."

"The scout hut was only put there about 45 years ago. It was only by accident that the secret garden was found. One of the scouts was out exploring one day when he fe..."

"I don't want a history lesson just the details."

"Do you want me to tell you or not?"

"Do you want Ann-Marie's mother to suffer?" he pointed in the direction of the back bedroom.

"No."

"Well, then get on."

I looked at the map. It was an ordinance survey map showing the wood in great detail. I had never looked at the wood on a map. It seemed a little strange and disorientating at first until I got my bearings.

I found the car park and the trail that led north-east near to the sunken garden and the stream that flowed by it, then I put my finger where I believed the gardens to be.

Henry picked up the map, folding it so it showed only the immediate area, placing his finger where mine had been, he walked out of the room.

I flexed my back and shoulders easing life back into the muscles after they'd been still for so long. I caught sight of something trailing out of Ann-Marie's wardrobe. It looked like the tie from the canvas bag that we had taken from the flat days before.

If that were the case I knew there was a knife inside it. I began to pray that he hadn't noticed it or even snooped around. I still had to get to it though. That was not going to be easy.

Henry was gone for ages. I lay on the bed wanting to attempt to undo my bindings now they were in front of me. I didn't know how long I had before he would return. If he returned and saw me fiddling with them he would surely make them tighter and place my hands behind my back again. If I didn't try then he might forget, but I might not get another chance. I had to try regardless of the consequences.

I used my teeth to gnaw at the bindings. A tear trickled from my eye as once again the pain issued its presence. With perseverance I managed to untie the first knot, it was not easy with my injury rendering my right hand useless. I was beginning to sweat again, pressure from the injury and fear of getting caught. He was good at knots.

I felt the vibration in my pocket again. I was now in a position to answer it if I wanted to. I could easily reach into my pocket now but I also needed to get free. I continued with the rope finally loosening the second knot. It had taken too long, and although I thought he was going to catch me out any second, luck seemed to be on my side at last.

The rope fell away from my ankles.

My shirt was soaked with sweat, clinging to me, making me feel uncomfortable, that was the least of my worries.

My legs were stiff after so long. I made my way to the wardrobe I had to cross in front of the open door. As I checked the coast was clear, I could see a shadow moving in the back bedroom, that was obviously where he was. Silently I opened the wardrobe door.

Sure enough Henry's things were there. Rummaging through them I found the knife which had been wrapped up again in its rag. The only place I could possibly conceal it was in my sock, my jeans holding it in place, resting the tip carefully into my soul of my shoe beside my foot. I carefully placed everything else back in the wardrobe, closing the door quietly.

Once back on the bed, I re-tied the restraints the best I could, trying to make it look as though they had never been undone and then relaxed once more.

The phone rang again. This time I answered.

"Hello" I whispered, all the time listening for foot steps in the hall.

"It's me, Ann-Marie."

"I can't talk much."

"Where are you? Are you at my house."

"A-ha."

"Aunt Rose said I wasn't to go home there was danger there."

"A-ha" I wanted to say more, but the more I said the more I risked being caught by Henry.

"You can't talk, is that what your hinting at?"

"A-ha."

"Is my mum ok?"

I thought about this longer than the others, I didn't want to upset her.

"A-ha."

"Can you get Henry to the woods tonight?"

"A..." I heard foot steps in the hall. I quickly put the phone in my pocket, ending the call first.

Henry appeared in the doorway "Looks like we've got transport for tonight. So we just need to wait." He came closer "You might as well make yourself comfortable. It's going to be a long wait for you" he smiled smugly "Oh when I say we, I mean me and the mother." He left the room I didn't know what he meant.

A split second later he returned.

"Better make sure you are tied up nice and tight don't want you getting loose do we?"

"No of course not" I added sarcastically.

"And I think a gag is in order."

He untied my wrists, eyeing his work, questioning it then ignoring it. He re-tied them behind my back, I struggled initially, but he warned me not to, I realised the implications and acquiesced. Henry left the room.

A while later I heard a commotion going on in the back bedroom and could only surmise that Ann-Marie's mother was struggling, being scared, not knowing the full story.

The front door closed and the house fell silent.

I gave it a few minutes before cutting myself free with Henry's knife, which I could still reach and manoeuvre enough to cut the bindings.

It felt good to have full movement in my legs and arms.

I headed to the back bedroom, which now stood vacated. He'd taken her as collateral.

Downstairs I made myself something more to eat. I felt hungry now. I would need my strength later so this respite was important. I also found a bandage and wrapped my wrist tightly. The leg wound didn't seem to register at all and I found myself walking normally, if a little stiffly.

It gave me the opportunity to gather my thoughts and formulate some sort of plan. I needed to get to Hockley woods. How though? It was a few miles away, I couldn't use public transport for risk of being caught. I wonder.

While the second round of toast was browning itself nicely in the toaster, I checked the garden shed. Through the glass I could see a mountain bike, a man's one. I thought it was a bit strange, but it was what I needed. I searched the kitchen for the keys to the shed (eating my toast at the same time, dropping crumbs everywhere) I found them hanging just behind the back door.

It was a struggle to get the bike out, my wrist was useless. I knew it was going to be tricky cycling with only one good arm but I would have to try regardless. Breaking might be difficult but I had no choice, it was as simple as that.

An hour later I left via the back alleyway which was just wide enough for the handle bars. At the edge of the alley I checked that the coast was clear, pulled the phone from my pocket and checked the time; 3.57, it was later than I thought.

Hockley woods was about 10 miles away, normally I could cycle that easily in an hour or so, at full speed. I had five hours. Plenty of time. Then a thought occurred, I could go to Aunt Rose's then I could go with them, simple.

Exiting the alley, I got on the bike, turned left and started peddling. There was no wind about that day, which was good. I rested my hurt wrist in my lap. It was dark and I had no lights so I kept to the pavements.

All I had was the use of the back brake so I couldn't afford to go too fast because I wouldn't be able to stop. The bike had 21 gears. with only one hand I could use the first seven. That was enough. There was no-one at Aunt Rose's house. I didn't want to waste more time so I headed for the woods.

Progress was good. I started to relax a little bit enjoying the passing scenery, forgetting for the first time that I was a wanted man. My only mistake was to cycle past a police car oblivious it was there, hidden down a side street, I should have been looking for it.

I heard the rev of an engine, and saw the reflection of flashing lights in the windows of the houses to my left. Looking over my shoulder I saw it hurtle towards me, past and then it braked sharply in front of me blocking my progress.

With my bad hand I didn't have time to stop and I careered into it, sprawling headlong over the bonnet, the bike rearing up underneath me. Before I knew where I was I felt handcuffs being placed on me, I cried out loud at the pain in my wrist. In the daze I heard my rights being read to me. It happened so quickly I didn't have time to react.

32

A few minutes of thoughtlessness had caused me to get caught. It was over as far as I was concerned. I couldn't get to Hockley woods and I needed to be there, to complete whatever the plan was. What the outcome was going to be now, I didn't know. All I knew was that I was in the back of a police car and under arrest for some things I hadn't done, positive I was going to spend the rest of my life behind bars.

If only I'd taken more care, been more observant, stayed off of the beaten track. I knew so many back streets. I had time. It would have been easy for me.

How were they going to perform the ceremony without me? To put things right surely they needed both of us present. Was it all really now hopeless?

I was taken to Southend-On-Sea Police Station an old building with new offices added on to the side with no thought for the character of the facade. It had always been associated with the police in one form or another.

When it was first built, the local magistrate held it as his residence, a prestigious and formidable building having an impressive grand double oak doored entrance with an ornate stone archway and larger than life windows. In time it became the courthouse for the whole of the county, with the help of a lot of internal remodelling, the cellar forming the prison cells. Then it became staff quarters for the police training centre.

Now it was a police station and offices with new holding cells on the grounds along with a new training centre, and car depot.

We pulled up to the security gates, I saw hoards of photographers. I was surprised how quickly word had leaked out; they had their man and they wanted people to know that the streets of Southend were safe again.

I can't remember feeling much pain in my wrist, I knew it hurt, I was numb from the goings on, despair flooded over me. I was in a kind of trance, not really aware of anything anymore, just viewing it as if I were to play it back at some later date.

The car parked and the back door opened up, they pulled me out.

"Aaarghh" I cried in pain.

They had no sympathy for me. Why should they? I was accused of atrocious crimes, I could feel the distaste and hatred they had for me.

Leading me inside, I could still hear the clicking of cameras going off, trying to take every last picture they could, before I was hidden from view.

My poor parents, the next day they would see the headlines on the papers, hear the headlines on the news, How could they face their friends again? Everyone soon to know that their son was a killer, a murderer of innocent young girls. They'd be forced to move, vacate the home they had made; all those years of memories, good memories savaged by recent events. They'd have to leave everyone and everything behind, all because of me.

Inside I was told to sit, I did so and they handcuffed me to a rail fixed to the wall, there was just me in the empty waiting room.

"Daniel Stephens?" a man said.

"Yes."

"Custody Sergeant Harris" he said as he reached behind me and undid the handcuffs "Not going to give me any trouble are you?"

"No. Aargh."

"What happened to that?" He observed my swollen wrist.

"I fell" I wanted to tell the whole story, I was innocent, the real killer was still out there, loose and about to kill again later that night, How many times had they heard that? I didn't know what to say, I really believed that they wouldn't listen to me, they'd have me committed. I had to try something, but I couldn't, if they arrest Henry before the ceremony then nothing will have been achieved (at least this way he won't go free) but if I'm not there the ceremony won't take place. I didn't know what to do.

"After we've booked you in we'll get the doctor in to look at it" he took various details, question after question, fingerprints, belongings, belt, shoelaces. Then I was shown into a cell and behind me the door was shut and the bolt driven home, the sound reverberating round the hard, cold cell walls.

There was a bed in one corner, a metal bucket in the other, the plain white walls. I felt cold and lonely. I sat huddled up on the bed. Scared, I started to cry, I could understand how the toughest could fall to pieces in here.

A little while later the bolt was slid across and the door opened.

"This is Doctor Fingle, he's come to look at your wrist."

In walked a middle aged man in a tweed jacket carrying an old fashioned doctor's bag. The officer stood guard at the door, truncheon ready in case of trouble. He wasn't going to get any, I knew that but he didn't. He had probably experienced a few rough customers in the past and was ready for anything now.

The doctor put down his bag on the floor and sat on the end of the bed.

"Can I see your wrist please?" he was polite but curt. Probably only doing his job because he had to, not because he wanted to. Wanting to help a killer made no sense, as far as he was concerned I deserved everything I got.

He felt around my wrist, moved it this way and that, asking

me if this hurt, then if that hurt.

After a minute or so "I don't believe it's broken, just fractured, I'll bandage it up for now, there is not a lot else I can do. I'll give you some pain killers. Just rest it" his voice cold and emotionless.

"Thank you" I said meekly "But I need to tell you something, there's someone else."

"Save it for the interview room" Sergeant Harris commanded.

"But it's important."

"Shut it I said."

I couldn't stop the tears forming in my eyes, my cause was lost now, no one was interested in what I had to say.

The doctor spoke to the custody sergeant about the medication I was allowed, I only half listened, I didn't care anymore.

He shot a glance at me as if to say I was the scum of the earth. I felt ashamed, but I hadn't done anything wrong.

The door slammed closed again, bolt shifting into place. I was alone, except for the noise of other prisoners coming and going from time to time, it was like time had been suspended and meant nothing anymore.

The trap door in the main door slid open, the custody sergeant stood there, he placed a cup of water on the tiny shelf, next to it was a tablet.

"Take this."

"What is it?"

"Just take it and shut up."

I stood up gingerly, took what was offered and did as I was told. Then he was gone again. This time I paced the cell, only a few feet across and not much more in length, they certainly didn't want you to get too much exercise in here.

All I could do was wait.

A meal was served to me at some point. It didn't look very appetizing. I wasn't hungry I picked at it. I lay down afterwards and drifted into an uneasy sleep occasionally woken by the noises outside my cell.

There was a circle of witches standing round wearing ceremonial gowns, the only light visible was from large candles standing on the ground in front of them, a strange stillness hovered in the vicinity. I could see the dark shadows of the trees in the dim moonlight and could hear the wind winding it's way through them, yet not even the slightest draft hit this sheltered spot. The flames from each of the candles burned brightly and rose to an extraordinary height, each seemed to glow a different colour, blue, green, red, an unusually bright yellow, mauve, orange and white.

The witches were standing behind the candles, chanting, large pendants were visible round their necks, each one reflecting the colour of their candle's flame. I couldn't understand what they were chanting. They all seemed to be saying different things.

A shape had been drawn out on the ground, from the angle I was at it looked like a seven pointed star, each witch, with her candle at a point.

In the septagon that marked out the centre of the star, a figure lay still on the ground, bedraggled and rather worse for wear. Then it stirred as the chanting grew louder. Gradually shoulders lifted off the ground, followed by the head, it was a man. He took a second to look round the circle of women, who all now had their arms about chest height outstretched to the sides.

Each witch seemed to have a separate purpose in this task, their own part to perform in this ceremony. The volume of their voices grew. Their actions took on different forms. A couple held their pendants out from their chests, another hovered hers above the candle in front of her, four different coloured flames seemed to escape from them in bursts of light, shooting three feet into the air then back in to the pendant. Then they emitted a immense beam of multicoloured light into the centre of the septagon.

The figure in the centre attained full height. It was Henry, I could see him clearly. He looked directly into my eyes, anger in them, alive for all to see. He went to move from the centre but was thrown back by this light, he fell to the ground. Then he got back up, this time not trying to move from the septagon that held him like a prisoner. He shouted something that wasn't audible.

The candles erupted into a blaze of light as if fuel had been poured over them. Seven columns of light shot high into the air, joining in one mass, like the tip of a pyramid. The tails of these columns joined, a split second later they hovered in the air for a few seconds more. The chanting grew to a crescendo. The flames elongated from the tips of the candles towards the centre of the septagon, all meeting at the same point, within Henry. Pierced by the burning lights Henry screamed in pain, arms reaching upward towards the sky. Then I saw a hand to my right throw something towards Henry. It was my hand! The object glinted as it twisted in the air. For a brief second it became clear what it was, my silver plectrum and chain. As it collided with Henry a ball of flame shot up into the air high above him.

The chanting started again this time in unison 'CASKIMOTAR' they were saying, quietly, effortlessly, picking up speed and rhythm as it grew into a thunderous sound that echoed around the woods. The witches pointed at Henry, palms face down, fingers following the flow of the arms. The flaming ball then hovered above him changing its form to an arrow shape and shooting towards the ground to meet the rest of the flames, somewhere within Henry.

Henry screamed louder, so loud I thought he was going to burst my ear drums. He looked at me, pity in his eyes, I began to feel guilt. I looked deep into his eyes.

I wasn't sure if I was dreaming. I looked round breaking off the stare. Everything seemed real, every noise, every colour, the intoxicating smell. To my right Mojo was sitting on the ground, leaning against my leg, Aunt Rose was to my left, she appeared taller than *before. I couldn't see Ann-Marie.*

A mild panic swept in and I scoured the area hoping to catch her sitting under a tree somewhere.

"AAARRRRGGGGGGGHHHHHHHH" I screamed. Shooting pain elicited from my heart. Toes and fingers burning intensely, heat drifted along my body, cramps contorting me into a ball where I lay. I tried to reach out to the door of my cell, attract attention. I screamed again, my insides on fire with pain.

The door of my cell opened in walked a different policeman. He stood there looking at me, doing nothing.

The pain was immense, gritting my teeth, closing my eyes, clasping my hands tightly into fists, trying to shut it out. None of which helped.

Once more I reached out for help from the officer, eyes felt swollen in pain, tears streaming down my cheeks, he just stood there.

My heart felt it was going to burst, pounding harder and harder against my rib cage. I felt myself being thrown against the wall, and I passed into unconsciousness.

When I came round I was in complete darkness, laying on my back on a hard concrete floor. I lifted myself up, numb from everything. It took me a while to register lack of pain in my left wrist. I grabbed it with the other hand, rubbing, it felt fine. My head hurt though, I could feel a bump on the back of it.

Standing up I put my hands out touching the walls that were close, barely an arm span apart. I inched my way forward, I kicked something, something stacked against the wall. As I was feeling my way around there was a light behind me.

"You ok Daniel, There's been a powercut" the voice was familiar.

"Mark?"

"Yeah, you OK?"

"Fine" I didn't know whether I was dreaming or it was reality.

"You OK?"

"I'm not sure. This may sound strange but where am I?"

"You're in the theatre, there was a power cut..."

"Is it Sunday?" I asked hopefully.

"Er Yes. Why?"

"Yes" I said out loud, pinching myself to make sure I was really here.

It was Sunday again, I was back in the side corridor. Whatever Heather had done it had worked. I made my way towards Mark and the open doorway. I grabbed the torch off of him and went back to where I had been.

"What you doing? You alright?"

"I'm fine" I smiled to myself.

I scoured the walls, glancing at the graffiti until I found what I was looking for. I placed my hand on it, whilst searching the floor for something hard, anything, I found a piece of an old chair then I rammed it into the plaster destroying the incantation. I watched as with every strike another piece of plaster crumbled and fell from the wall.

"What you doing? Some of that graffiti is years old" He came towards me, but I'd stopped before he made contact.

"I know" I was done.

"What you smiling for?" Mark did not look happy.

"Nothing, absolutely nothing."

"The others are down in the foyer" Mark looked at the mess I'd made, displeased.

I walked down the stairs, I could hear talking. I was definitely back. My head was still brimming with all the events of the last eight days. I couldn't control my relief that it was all over.

"What happened to you Daniel?" Susan, one of the girls, asked.

"What?"

"You look as though you won the lottery."

"Nothing so small" I said sarcastically. If only they knew.

It was no good I couldn't stay there any longer I had to leave, there were things I wanted, needed to do that couldn't wait.

I asked if I could go but before they answered I had healed off into the darkness of the auditorium, found my way back stage, picked up my jacket and was out the stage door.

I ran faster than I had ever done before. Breathless and exhausted I was outside Ann-Marie's house within 30 minutes. I stood on the other side of the road trying to get my breath back and looked, it was raining and I was getting soaked but I didn't care, the curtains weren't drawn and I could see both Ann-Marie and her mother sitting down talking in the living room. I was so relieved.

Did she know about the past weeks events? I wanted to say thank you, but was too afraid to knock. What would I say?

Aunt Rose. She must remember, either way I wouldn't feel so much of a fool if I went round there and introduced myself and she didn't know, I don't know why I thought that, I just did.

Half an hour later I was ringing the doorbell to Aunt Rose's house.

The door opened.

"Daniel, I was expecting you, come in, you're soaked."

I did as I was told. She took my jacket from me and hung it up, I left my wet shoes by the door and went and sat in the lounge as instructed.

Aunt Rose brought in a towel and a pot of tea. After pouring the tea she settled down in her armchair. I went to put the cup up to my lips and hesitated. She saw.

"It's ok dear this is normal tea."

I smiled "So you remember as well. How about Ann-Marie?"

"My dear boy she won't remember. As you can guess everything went well, Henry is back where he belongs, and time is back as it was. There is one thing though."

"What's that?"

"You must destroy the incantation before it causes anymore trouble."

"I've done that already."

"Good."

"One thing though. I saw it all happen but How? And I couldn't see Ann-Marie. I could see Mojo. Yourself , even if you seemed a little taller, you were both standing next to me. Where was she?"

"Aunt Rose smiled. "Dear, you were viewing it through Ann-Marie's eyes. She told me how she could see when you shared contact." I nodded agreement "Well it appears a little of that remained."

"But she's blind and then she saw through my eyes."

"Daniel she held what you hold most precious and that enabled her to see temporarily as if you were there, that is the power, strange as it may be sometimes."

We sat in silence, then I thought "But what about me being there?"

"That" she thought for a second "Talisman for want of a better word represented all the good in you and that is what gave you the connection to each other that night and Heather said that if you could not be there then the witches only needed something that represented the good and love in you, but it had to be true.

"But if I had been told that I could have just laid low for a while instead of taking risks", I was starting to feel agitated when I shouldn't, everything was right, as it should be.

"Daniel, if you didn't have anything that represented your true self then yes you would have had to have been there. Ann-Marie was told this but she was also told that she was not to ask for anything to be given to her you had to relinquish it because you wanted to, because you trusted her."

Inside I was a mix of feelings and emotions, Aunt Rose

patiently let it all soak in.

The doorbell chiming broke my thoughts.

"Do excuse me."

"Yeah sure" I reached to the tray and took another biscuit. I was about to take a second bite when I heard a familiar voice. I stood up to go into the hallway, but they were already coming into the lounge led by Aunt Rose.

"Daniel this is Ann-Marie and her guide dog Mojo."

"Pleased to meet you" she said in a friendly voice.

"This is her mother Karen."

"Pleased to meet you" I said.

We all sat down Karen, Ann-Marie and myself on the settee, while Aunt Rose went and made a fresh pot of tea.

"Have we met before?" Ann-Marie said, I didn't know how to answer this "Do you mind if I touch your face?"

"No I... I don't mind" with that she put her hands up to my face, feeling every feature, studying it with her fingers.

"You've got a nice smile."

"Thank you" I said blushing.